What the *Willows* Know

Claude Douglas Bryan

© 2014

Published in the United States by Nurturing Faith Inc., Macon GA, www.nurturingfaith.net.

Library of Congress Cataloging-in-Publication Data is available.

978-1-938514-44-9

DEDICATION

Dedicated to the Ora Maes, male and female, remembered and forgotten, who provided support, nurturance, and guidance in the shaping of our lives.

ACKNOWLEDGEMENTS AND APPRECIATIONS

What the Willows Know represents a new phase of life and career, a new extension of observation, reflection, personality, and creativity. Compelled by the magical allure in the simple words of look, see, work and play learned in first-grade, I continue to follow those early directives.

Words of appreciation and acknowledgement must proceed the telling of *What the Willows Know*. A number of patrons were those friends who provided the encouragement, the correction, the guidance that made *What the Willows Know* possible. These encouragers include

A high school teacher, Evelyn Burrell, who taught me the importance of sentence variations and transitions that I still treasure today;

Two university colleagues in my early teaching career, Evelyn Romig and Wallace Roark, who read early drafts of an immature manuscript and who still gave the encouragement to write and not to abandon writing for the pursuit of water colors;

More recent university colleagues, Nancy Bottoms and Joseph Webb, who continued to provide encouragement not to give up the life-long dream of writing a published novel;

An author friend, Phyllis Tickle, whose unwavering encouragement kept me persistent throughout the complex pathways of the publishing world;

Two deeply loved sons, Matthew and Stephen, who have been the primary audience for my modeling the love of learning and the art of creativity; and most importantly,

My devoted and beloved wife and best friend of over thirty years, Julie, who has always supported my career and interests and who offered always whatever fashions of encouragement needed along the way.

To these I pledge my continuing appreciation for their encouragement with my adventure with words and my ongoing commitment to encouraging others to create new worlds with words.

— Claude Douglas Bryan

CONTENTS

CHAPTER ONE

Grow, O little willow, grow!
Listen, leaves for great and small;
Guard the secrets that you know
Till their time is right to call.

Grow, O little willow, grow!
Shade from sun and pain we see;
Keep our roots and ghosts below
Till our past no longer flee.

The workmen favored arriving no later than seven-thirty in the morning to begin excavation—anything to escape, even a few precious hours, the heat of an August day. Soon the Carolina sun would produce eyebrows drenched and underarms soaked with sweat, appropriate offerings for those who labored under her power. Preliminary evaluations had already been made. Yesterday the foreman announced the septic tank at 217 Orchard Street had to be replaced.

The workmen in tight jeans, cut-offs, and faded tank tops were priming themselves for another eight-to-ten-hour day, gulping steaming coffee from convenience store refillable mugs, lighting new cigarettes from faintly glowing ones, and moaning about their previous night's sexual adventures. Only one, Harvey Mullins, stood aside and did not join in the morning banter and rituals. He stood out like the lone Virginia pine did in the yard full of willows. No imagination was needed to know what the college student was thinking. Harvey had said it often enough on lunch breaks. He was only working this job to earn money. With no intention of staying, he was moving on and everyone knew it. Today was his last day. In a few days, Harvey would return, with a much more ample and much needed bank account balance and a new workman's vocabulary, to his familiar world.

A fading red-flame pick-up pulled up in the front yard. The sound of its engine announced in advance that Tommy was running late again. Slowly a lean figure emerged and walked to the backyard where the other men were gathered.

"Hey, there, Tommy. You're walking funny, boy. All stove up from a night with Sally?"

"You, you . . . you . . . know . . . it," *stuttered Tommy, a twenty-five-year-old whose waist size barely exceeded his age. Tommy gave a confident grin, showing his upper two front teeth separated from each other by a quarter of an inch, a minor flaw in a family of occasional second-cousin marriages. A cigarette hung between Tommy's front teeth framed with his dirty blonde handlebar mustache. The crew and the neighborhood children liked it when Tommy entertained them by telling jokes with a lit cigarette wedged between his two front teeth.*

"What about you, Harvey? Did you get any last night?" a nearby work-man growled.

The eyes of the men focused on the young college student, waiting for his response. Harvey clenched his lips, glancing to the side where his eyes meet Jake's stare. Harvey said nothing.

"Now, boys," Jake said, accustomed to interrupting the banter that had traditionally centered on Tommy and now on Harvey. "Let's get to work. This woman's gonna want her toilet running soon enough." Jake, the crew's foreman, prided himself on his understanding of both septic tanks and human nature. He knew how to unclog both and keep things flowing smoothly. Harvey, a cousin on his wife's side of the family, had religion. Jake had religion, too, but not enough religion to prohibit enjoying an earthy joke.

Minutes later it was obvious that the septic tank had indeed collapsed. It had been a hard half-hour's sweat if the number of cigarette butts were any indication. The crew's dog, Cooner, a mongrel pup that joined the crew one morning from behind an oil drum trash can, was faithfully walking back and forth around the spot like any good supervisor, getting both his pats and curses from the men who labored.

"Willow trees," Jake said. Why in God's name would anyone plant willows near a septic tank? They're just asking for trouble. We're going to cut 'em down." Jake glanced at Harvey. Immediately, from Harvey's grimace, Jake realized that he had uttered a forbidden profanity. "Sorry, Harvey."

Harvey nodded.

Cooner started barking that morning around eight-thirty. The dog's eyes were fixed onto the widening hole. Suddenly Cooner began digging frantically as though trying to get in the hole.

"I wish you guys would work as hard as ole Cooner," Jake said. "What is it, boy?" Jake bent down, rubbed Cooner's head and leaned over the hole, expos-ing the band of his silk underwear. "Found a bone did you, boy? Tommy, get that bone there for Cooner!"

Tommy jumped into the excavation. "Here, Coo . . . Coo . . . Cooner," Tommy said, placing a dirty long bone on the edge of the hole. "They're some mo . . . mo . . . more down here, I'll ge . . . ge . . . get 'em."

Jake grinned at Cooner, always liking it when Cooner got a little something extra that cost Jake nothing. Jake's eyes, like Cooner's, were now fixed on the bone that the dog was sniffing and licking.

"Ur . . . Ur . . . Ur," growled Cooner. Jake smacked Cooner's face away from the bone, knocking him away from the hole. Cooner's growls, mixed with loud high-pitched moans, did not detract Jake's careful reexamination of the bone. Jake handed it to Harvey for his inspection.

"What is it?" Tommy asked.

"A humerus, I think," Harvey said.

"What's funny about it?" Tommy asked.

Before Harvey could respond, Jake took the lead. "Tommy, get the hell out of that hole. Somebody call the Sheriff's office. That's a arm bone—a human arm bone."

"What a time to go back to school," Harvey muttered. "I'll have a lot to share with the prayer group."

One Year Later . . .

The commuter airport was crowded when I disembarked from the jumper flight from Atlanta. Only a few steps outside the plane confirmed what the pilot had announced—highs in the 90s. Hot summers, like unquenched human passions, make us vulnerable. Although I did not recognize it then, I was both hot and vulnerable. Two familiar faces were in the airport terminal—my daughter Caroline, and my secretary and Caroline's aunt, Morriah.

"Daddy, Daddy," my nearly thirteen-year-old shouted. "Over here, over here." Her waving arms, full of energy, reminded me of how excited she was years ago when I picked her up for her first time at day care.

The familiar warmth of the sun invigorated my bones, and familiar sounds of Carolina voices renewed my lonely spirit. Already it felt good to be home after a nine-month sabbatical leave from my employment at Hunter-Harwell University.

"Caroline," I said, with my voice cracking at the sight of my daughter after months of separation.

In the midst of our hugs and my kisses, I heard her say,

"What did you bring me, Daddy?"

"Nothing, but me," I replied.

"Now, Daddy. Aunt Morriah said you would bring me back lots of presents to make up for being away so along."

"In a minute. Let me first speak to Morriah." I turned to Morriah who stood a few feet away and asked, "How are you, Morriah?"

"Fine enough, Adrian," Morriah said. Indeed, she was fine looking for a woman in her mid-sixties. Her thick gray blonde hair was shaped into what I jokingly called her Pentecostal coiffeur—cascades of sprayed hair, twisted and turned around the top of her head. Her hairstyle was the only indication of her Pentecostal background. Morriah had long ago left the holiness tradition for what she herself called "a more matter-of-fact approach." Morriah, who was both endearing and exasperating to me, had been my secretary for about ten years. She had continued in the position part-time for the last few years.

"Good to see you," I said. "You're looking well. I see that you're still providing commentary on my actions."

"I always do. Looks like you've put on an extra weight. Ten pounds or so, I'd guess."

Morriah's eyes and smile gave her traditional examination, looking me over from head to toe. I struggled against my natural instinct to check my zipper every time Morriah stared at me without speaking. I suspected that Morriah's stare made most men check their zippers at least twice.

"No more comments about physical changes," I said.

"Well, give the girl her presents. She's waited long enough."

Waited long enough, I thought. Caroline had stayed with Morriah for almost nine months with only a three-week reunion with me at Christmas. Morriah's frequent letters and phone calls, bordering on diatribes, reminded me weekly of her conviction that I had abandoned Caroline for the sake of my career.

"Yes, Daddy," Caroline said. "Show me."

"Okay. This carry-on is all for you." She snatched the bag, rummaging through the contents, like she was looking for the toy in a sack meal from her favorite drive through restaurant.

Morriah and I walked to the waiting crowd gathered around the nearby baggage claim area.

"Any problems at home or office?" I asked.

"What do you want first?" Morriah asked. I had always suspected that she relished playing her role of a female Hermes.

"Just tell me," I said. My eyes were looking for my three canvas bags.

"Adrian." Morriah paused, "The renters left the house in shambles! Looks like something from Tobacco Road."

"Why did you let that happen?"

"Let it happen? You're the one who decided to let that exchange faculty couple stay in your house. If it had been me, I would have required a security deposit."

"Morriah . . ."

She interrupted me. "No, not you. You're so naive about people. Just because the man and his wife both had an education didn't mean they knew how to use a vacuum cleaner or clean around a toilet seat."

"Morriah, I did have a security deposit. How bad is it?"

"Well, I hope it's enough to cover the damages. I've already made arrangements for the cleaners to come tomorrow. We'll then need to talk about the painters."

"That bad?" I asked. I stretched to pick up the canvas suitcase with the nametag clearly marked Adrian Stockwood. As I reached back for the second suitcase, Morriah pulled the first one to the side.

"Pretty bad," Morriah said.

"What about the office?" I asked, still searching for the third suitcase.

"It's not in too bad a shape. I do have some news for you about Harper Adams."

"Did Adams get the job?"

"No, he did not," Morriah said.

"I thought it was a sure bet."

"No, at the last minute they didn't want him. My sources say it came down to two candidates and the trustees went with a younger man. Of course, to hear Adams tell it, he withdrew his name from consideration. He says he had too much love to leave Hunter-Harwell."

"Too much love to leave it?" I said.

"Too much to leave it, my ass," Morriah said.

"Mine, too," I laughed. "So, I'll be under his academic leadership for another year."

"Maybe or maybe not," Morriah said. Her eyes grew wide and her lips tightened, luring me to ask for more information.

"What do you mean?"

"A letter came a few days ago . . . from Duke," Morriah said.

"Why didn't you tell me?"

"I couldn't reach you."

No need to argue. "Did you bring it?"

"Yes, but don't you want to get your luggage?" Morriah asked. Her index finger casually pointed toward the conveyer belt. "It's already been twice around the conveyer."

"You get it," I said. "Give me the letter."

Like an official courier, Morriah withdrew the envelope from her straw purse, placing it soundly in my outstretched hand. Out of the corner of my eye, I watched Morriah approach the attendant and direct him to my last bag.

My eyes quickly scanned the already opened letter. My heart raced until my eyes found the word in the first sentence. My heart paused. *Pleased.* They were *pleased* to offer me a one-year renewable teaching contract for this coming academic year.

"They've offered me the position. They offered me the position," I repeated. "You knew it several days ago."

"I know everything worth knowing. I had to sign for the letter and naturally I had to open it in case there were problems. Now get the luggage. I'm double-parked. I need to check on my girl and see what you brought her."

Caroline had the contents of the canvas bag spread out beside her on two chairs. "Daddy's become an angelphile," Caroline said.

"An angelphile?" Morriah asked.

"Yes, he just loves all this stuff from England."

"He's always had a fondness for stuff," Morriah said. "Just something more to dust if you ask me."

"The word is 'Anglophile'," I said.

"Oh, well. Thanks anyway," Caroline said. "This looks interesting." Ignoring my carefully chosen presents, Caroline examined the British supermarket tabloid in which I had carefully wrapped the china tea set with little red roses. The only two words I could discern on the page were sex and alien.

"A tea set?" Morriah said. Her head vibrated. "We need to talk."

Morriah reached down and examined the wool jumper with little lambs on the sleeves. "This pullover's too small."

"It's called a jumper, Morriah," I said, defending my expensive purchase.

"Whatever you call, it's still too small for Caroline. Just like a man, buying things too small for women." Her eyes quickly assessed my other purchases—some brass rubbings from Westminster Abbey and several books by Beatrix Potter. "Yes, sir, we must talk before you go shopping again."

Clutching the tote with her gifts, Caroline crawled in the back seat of Morriah's car. I was about to close the trunk when I turned to Morriah, who had her keys in hand. I had waited to ask the inevitable question.

"Do you think Adams will release me from my contract?" I asked.

Morriah dangled her keys close to her eyeglasses, searching for the ignition key as carefully as if she were selecting a fine piece of jewelry from a velvet display case. "Only if you or I put a gun to his head," Morriah said.

Harper Adams, the Provost and Chief Academic Officer of Hunter-Harwell University, was responsible for the day-by-day operations of the University. Morriah was correct. As much as he disliked me, Harper Adams would not easily release me from my teaching contract. I still remember his words, spoken only once to me, "It may not be today, or tomorrow, but one day you'll help pay the cost for my not being elected president of Hunter-Harwell."

Although Adams never mentioned his threatening words again, I knew those thoughts were hidden deep beneath his correct surface persona. Adams would not easily release me from my teaching contract. Teaching at a major university had long been my dream, but Adams held the power to make it a middle-age reality or a middle-age fantasy.

Hunter-Harwell University, located in Brunson where I taught and lived, was one of those small private Christian colleges and universities that adorned and protected the landscape and people of the Bible Belt. Founded after the American Civil War as a private preparatory academy, Hunter-Harwell was nurtured and sustained by a Southern tradition of reverence for the Bible, service to mankind, belief in God's created order, and the privilege of being at the top of that order. Supported by church and private contributions, Hunter-Harwell was now a coed school comprised largely of would-be teachers and would-be preachers. In fact, the university was comprised of would-be's. We would be better paid, we would be better students, and we would be more academically challenging. The would-be's ruled our lives. Like many of us who taught there, Hunter-Harwell lived with a solid financial instability and a clouded vision of the future.

The phone call came a few days after my return. Obviously the caller wasn't a Carolina native. Her voice had a Northeastern quality—deep, dark, suspicious, and alluring. Her name was Rachel Simmons.

"Dr. Stockwood, does the name Ora Mae Chapman mean anything to you?"

"Yes, I know Ora Mae," I said.

Ora Mae Chapman. I had not talked with her for some time. Although I had sent her occasional birthday cards and Christmas cards, I had failed to have more intimate contact. As I had moved forward, Ora Mae and my affection for her had been neglected, a casualty of trying to escape. Too busy, at least that was my excuse, to keep in close contact with her and Caruthers' Gap. Building a career and being a single parent took time and energy. At the end of each day, little time or energy was left after I had washed the dinner dishes, kissed my daughter good night and graded my papers.

Ora Mae Chapman. Ora Mae was the keeper of secrets, having kept my secrets and thus fulfilled her promises. While she possessed no academic degrees, having gone only through the fifth grade, she was the one to whom the lonely came with their problems, their hurts, their misfortunes and their joys. Her ebony hands, palms whitened and aged through washing clothes and picking cotton, were those of a healer. These hands held you when you cried, comforted your head when you vomited, touched your shoulder when you trembled, and rubbed your back when you needed encouragement. Quietly she had healed me and quietly she had let me go.

Ora Mae was in trouble. Rachel Simmons, the assigned social worker, spoke about Ora Mae's unwillingness to cooperate with her own defense. Accused of murder, Ora Mae was caught in a legal dispute in the town where she had spent her life, never having traveled more than fifty miles away. The death of a man long forgotten by the community had once again become the talk of housewives at the washateria and at the farmer's market, and the talk of retired men on the courthouse steps and in smoke-filled cafes. Ora Mae was accused of murder. Impossible, I thought, as I listened to the social worker's description. Not Ora Mae.

Rachel finished by saying, "Ora Mae asked that I remind you of your promise to come when she called. Dr. Stockwood, she's dying of cancer."

The word "cancer" jolted me. I had lost too many women to that disease. "I'll have to come," I said automatically. "I'll be there as soon as I can."

"Come when I call" were the words that I remembered Ora Mae's having said to me each time I departed from her. I knew I had to go.

Only later when I had hung up the phone did I reflect on what I had said instinctively. I looked outside my office window. I didn't want to go back to Caruthers' Gap, not even for a few days, but I had to see Ora Mae. Ora Mae was a part of what I had tried to forget. Still, I had made her a promise.

I continued to argue with myself, battling my heart and my head. Too many things to do. Always too many things to do. Adams had not yet heard my request for release of contract. I still had not been able to accept the offer from Duke.

No, I wanted to spend my summer here in my office and at the university, working on my manuscript. My sabbatical time had been spent daily in lonely libraries where the smell of old learning penetrated the tall ceilings. I had carefully held relics, drawn diagrams, taken pictures, and made notes on my laptop computer, all under the careful scrutiny of mildly cooperative curators. My natural Carolina accent, with its elongated syllables and over-emphasized vowels, set me apart from the proper enunciation of British intelligentsia. There I was a parvenu among those who were quick to notice my awkwardness, with their elevated intonations and raised eyebrows. My deceased father would have said it differently. "You can take the boy out of the country, but you can't take the country out of the boy," would have been his words.

Now, once home, like my own father after a long day at work, I did not want to leave. But more than that, I didn't want to go back to the small textile hometown.

"Are you making progress with your back mail?" Morriah said, entering my office and interrupting my gaze out the window.

When my wife Meredith died, Morriah stayed on to take care of Caroline, but I knew she was there to keep an additional watchful eye on me. Morriah had become successful enough in real estate transactions to divorce the husband she had tolerated for years. She had then turned her time and money to travel and do what Morriah wanted to do. Currently, Caroline and I were the focus of Morriah's attention.

"You should be doing this for me." I pointed toward the computer terminal, knowing it would irritate her.

"I told you ten years ago, when you first came to Hunter-Harwell University, that I don't do windows."

"I know. And you," I began. She now joined me in saying, "don't do computers." Morriah had a fear of computers. "I received a phone call from a social worker in Caruthers' Gap. Ora Mae Chapman, the woman who kept me as a child, is waiting trial for murder. She's also dying of cancer."

"I'm sorry. If I'd kept you as a child, I'd probably commit murder, too." Morriah had a natural way of conveying sympathy along with editorial comments.

"When I need your commentary, I'll ask for it. Ora Mae wants to see me. I don't have time to go back now. I've got all this work to get ready for the second session of summer school. I still must talk with Adams about my teaching contract."

"Don't make excuses. Is this the woman you've always used as illustrations in your class lectures about how she raised you and taught you about people?"

"Yes."

"Then you owe it to her. If half the stuff that Meredith told me about you when you were a child was true, you'd never have made it to puberty, if I had taken care of you."

"I know I owe it to her. I'll go."

"Good."

"I expect to be gone only a few days. Will you keep Caroline for me?"

"Don't I always?"

"Thank you. Would you call Corrine in the library to do some research on the death of Wayne Daniels in the summer of 1964?"

"Who's Wayne Daniels?"

"The man that Ora Mae supposedly killed." I leaned back in my chair.

"Oh. Have you talked to Corrine since you've been back?"

"No, I haven't had time."

"Haven't had the time? You should have made the time. Corrine was good for you and for Caroline. You have a hard time keeping your commitments, just like most men I know. That reminds me. Here are your new business cards. Corrine said your e-mail address has changed. The new one's printed on the card."

I opened the package and placed some of them in my coat pocket. "Thanks. Will you please call Corrine?"

"That I can do. I like working over the phone."

Rachel Simmons, a shapely woman, pushed back the red checked fabric that hung over the doorframe and walked into the kitchen. Against the massive porcelain single basin sink stood another woman facing the sink and staring through the window to the backyard.

"What's that odor?" Rachel Simmons asked, raising her nose, widening her eyes, and waving her hands back and forth.

Lola turned from the sink and faced Rachel. "I'm cooking collard greens. Miss Ora Mae said she'd like to taste my greens. I'm making them for her," Lola said.

"That odor is positively nauseating. It's permeating the entire house."

"That's collard greens. The smell of collard greens always made me sick to my stomach when I was pregnant. Are you pregnant?"

"No, I'm not pregnant."

"I suppose not," Lola said. Bubbles from the store brand detergent soap had created fluffy gloves over Lola's black hands. She turned her back to Rachel and resumed washing the mismatched plates and bowls.

"I made the phone call," Rachel said, sitting down at the Formica kitchen table.

"Good, Miss Ora Mae will be pleased." Her head nodded and Lola repeated herself, "Miss Ora Mae will be pleased."

"I know you were listening to me. I saw your reflection in the mirror over the phone stand. You were spying again on me. Don't you trust me?"

Lola turned toward her. "Not particularly."

"What more do you want from me? I told you that I'd phone him and I did. He's promised to come soon."

"Miss Ora Mae wanted him here a week ago. Her T-count was higher then. She was stronger then, had more life in her."

"T-count. That's all you talk about. T-count. Miss Ora Mae and her T-count."

"Miss Ora Mae is the reason we're both here, ain't it?" Lola said putting down the spatula. "The poor woman doesn't have much time left. I want her to live and to die in peace. I'll see to that. Let's both give her what we can." Lola went to the vintage one-door refrigerator that had as much frozen ice around its freezer compartment as it did food on the shelves. Pulling out the clear pitcher of iced tea, she held it up toward Rachel. Once again she offered Rachel a smile.

"No, thanks. I never understand how much you people drink tea. All that caffeine and sugar. You must spend half your life staying up all night and in the bathroom urinating, or should I say in the outhouse?"

Lola's sweet smile slowly turned tart. "That sure is true. We people do enjoy our tea and our urine. We may be full of urine, but at least we're not full of crap."

"Cute," Rachel said, getting up. "Isn't it time for Ora Mae's bath?"

"Yeah." Lola left and under her breath, she murmured, "uppity white Yankee bitch."

Rachel went into the living room, called the front parlor by Ora Mae and her generation, to make another phone call.

"Yes, I phoned Adrian a few minutes ago," Rachel said. "I delayed calling him as long as I could. If I had waited any longer, Lola would have phoned him. He's scheduled to come into town on Monday. Yes, I know. I'll keep him occupied. It can't be much longer. She should have died days ago. She says that she wants to live until her birthday. She'll never make it. I'll keep you posted." Rachel hung up the phone.

The older man who had been talking to Rachel replaced the receiver and looked at the woman seated in front of him. "He's coming. Don't worry. Wipe that frown from your face. We have plenty of diversions in mind. There's no way he's going to cause trouble and upset anyone. Trust me. I can guide him. I always could."

"I hope so," said the woman. "All this heat makes me thirsty. How about you?"

"Would you care for one?" he asked.

The woman nodded. From his lower right desk drawer, he pulled out a liquor bottle and began pouring its contents into two cut-glass tumblers. "Maybe this will calm your nerves, dear," he said, revealing deep lines when he smiled.

CHAPTER TWO

My appointment with Dr. Harper Adams was for three thirty, just thirty minutes before Hunter-Harwell's early closing on summer Friday afternoons. One year, in a spirit of appeasement, the administration offered employees time off in lieu of increased compensation. Whether pleasant or unpleasant, the meeting could only last thirty minutes, I thought. Adams was always punctual.

I tilted my head toward Adams' office door and asked, "Good mood?"

"Not bad," responded Phyllis Brown. At fifty, Phyllis knew as many university secrets as Morriah, but unlike Morriah she rarely confided any to me. "Would you like one?" she asked.

"You know I would."

Without breaking eye contact, Phyllis reached into the bottom left desk drawer and lifted out a small pressed green glass bowl filled with liquor-filled chocolate balls and placed it next to her desktop candy dish filled with butterscotch and peppermint. Her private bowl of chocolates was reserved for a select few. In a coming of age moment, I knew that I was accepted within a select inner circle when she shared her chocolates.

I reached for a piece. "Just like I remember," I said. "Thank you."

"We've missed you. Good to have you back from your sabbatical."

"I'm not sure that all of you have missed me," I said. My eyes moved to Adams' door.

"I'll tell Dr. Adams that you're here," Phyllis said with a tight smile. "Don't forget to put your foil in the trash can."

In just a few moments, Adams stood at his door. His massive frame would appear more comfortable in an agrarian setting, rather than an academic one. He looked none the part of the poor, overworked and under-nourished academician. A successful academic administrator, Adams wore three-piece suits, even on casual Fridays. His shoes alone cost more than any one of my suits. While Adams may have come to do "good" at Hunter-Harwell, he had, in fact, done quite well.

"Have a seat, Adrian," he said.

"Thank you for your time on Friday."

"Tell me about your sabbatical leave."

"It was rewarding. I made genuine progress on my next book." As soon as I said it, I knew my academic faux pas, considering that this administrator had never written his first.

"I see, Dr. Stockwood," Adams said.

Once more I was Dr. Stockwood, his having noticed the word "next."

"I have been offered a teaching position for the upcoming academic year at Duke University."

"At Duke. Well, very impressive. Very impressive, indeed."

"I wish to be released from my contract with the university."

"I see," Adams said, leaning back in his Corinthian leather chair with brass tacks embedded around its arms. Pausing for what seemed like several minutes, he began, "It is rather late in the year to make a request for release of contract, especially considering that you're returning from a sabbatical."

"I recognize that," I said. "I believe that you could easily redistribute my fall course load to others in the department and to our usual adjuncts. In fact, I even have a revised schedule with me."

"Well, it would be a loss for the university for you to leave, but we want to be fair to you, too, Dr. Stockwood, just as you want to be fair to us."

The phrase "fair to us" reverberated.

"Of course," I said.

"I will discuss your verbal request with the Executive Council and inform you in a few days."

"I hope that you will look favorably upon my request, Dr. Adams," I said.

"I can't make any promises on behalf of the University, but we will give it the consideration it merits." He glanced at his watch. "Look at the time," he said, standing up and walking me to the door.

"Good afternoon." I closed the door behind me. Glancing at my watch, I saw that it was fifteen minutes to four. Phyllis was watering the plants in her windowsill. On her desk was her private bowl of chocolates.

I looked into Phyllis' gray eyes. "I know Morriah talked with you. You know what goes on here as much as anyone else. Will he grant my request?"

"I think you've got as much chance as my chocolate balls do on the summer pavement. Here, take another. She held out the bowl. "Be careful where you put the foil," Phyllis said, once more not breaking eye contact.

On Saturday afternoon I stopped by the Hunter-Harwell Library to visit Corrine and to collect the information she had researched on the murder of Wayne Daniels. Except for a brief conversation that morning, we had not talked since I had returned from England. Strange, several years ago we were inseparable.

Corrine was at her desk on the main floor of the library. With only sporadic handfuls of students present, Corrine had always said she liked summers best because it was a chance to catch up on her work and her new passion—exploring the Internet.

"Good to see you back," she said. When we were dating, Corrine always had stood when I approached her desk. This time she did not stand. At first glance, only her hair seemed different, shorter.

"Good to see you, too," I said. In those few moments I had detected more than just shorter hair. There was a new distance between us.

"Well, how was it?" she asked.

"England was wonderful," I said, repeating the rehearsed speech I was now giving to colleagues—the months of research, the side trips, and the one major excursion to the Continent. My comments were clean, concise and controlled. Like us, I thought.

Corrine still had not risen. She swiveled in her chair toward her printer where a folder of material was stacked. "Here is the search that Morriah requested."

Instinctively I touched her hand to take the material. She pulled away, and then carefully handed the folder back to me. "I do appreciate it," I said.

"Naturally. Look through it. If there is more detail that you want let me know. Based on what you need, I can either widen or narrow the search. I might even try a different search engine. You may wish to redefine the parameters."

Her speech was changing. Computer jargon and high tech language replaced the literary images, metaphors, and similes. Quickly, Corrine concluded our conversation by saying, "I must be going. I have a dinner date."

I stood there watching her go through the double glass doors. She was still pleasingly well proportioned for her five foot seven inch frame, I thought. She was dressed differently. A long slit in her skirt. Her tanned legs and the strategically placed slit worked well together. That's what it was— Corrine now had a new slit and a new attitude.

Someone met her on the other side of the glass door. I didn't know his name.

"Excuse me," I asked one of the student workers. "Is that Dr. James?" I knew it wasn't Dr. James.

"No, that's Mr. Lewis, the new professor in computer science. Don't you remember me, Dr. Stockwood? I'm Harvey Mullins. I was in your intro class last year."

"Yes, of course, Harvey. How are you?"

"Fine. I'm working here this summer. Best summer job yet. Sure beats working on septic tanks," Harvey said, grinning.

"Good for you," I mumbled. My thoughts returned to Corrine and Lewis. Judging from how close they were walking, her right hip pressed against his left, Corrine was exploring more than the Internet these days.

Caroline and Morriah had gone to Brunson's version of a mall—a dozen specialty shops only half occupied—to buy Caroline summer clothes on sale. I wasn't sure why Caroline suddenly wanted to go shopping until Morriah whispered to me, "Caroline's embarrassed by her developing body." Caroline no longer wanted me to help her select her clothes as I had done since her mother's death. Fortunately, Morriah's fascination for fashion coincided with Caroline's needs.

In their absence, I was becoming reacquainted with my house. I carried a tall glass of sweetened ice tea and a bowl of popcorn as I headed to the storage room, which held my private memories and mementos—photographs, special books and trinkets from around the world. In the corner, I sat down in my oak rocker. Every room in a house should have a rocker, my grandmother used to say. Grandmother was a big woman who enjoyed getting off her feet, "rocking and recollecting." The best "recollecting," she said, was done when "rocking."

This windowless room, with my sequestered memories, always attracted me when I was feeling low and alone. My deceased wife, Meredith, said I always got my perspective back when I looked through my memories and mementos. Looking back helped me see where I was going.

Between sips of tea and the swaying in my rocking chair, I pondered what I had to do. Thoughts of going back to Caruthers' Gap still left me uneasy, even after twenty plus years. Southerners are at best ambivalent about their origins. Being root-bound in Caruthers' Gap was how I felt when I first left. Leaving Caruthers' Gap behind me, I had moved on to other soils more fertile than the one that had birthed me.

Education, I had thought, would insulate me, fuel me and fulfill me. If I learned enough and traveled enough, I might be somebody. Although I had ventured far, the birth of my daughter shaded my ideas and lured me back. When the right opportunity came, Meredith and I returned to the Carolinas. While I remained distant from the immediacy of Caruthers' Gap, I was still near enough to breathe her air and walk through her soil.

Footsteps through the house, one set running up the stairs and the other walking steadily down the hall, broke into my thoughts. Morriah, with her head shaking, appeared at the door.

"Next time I go shopping with that girl, we're going to Atlanta. I'm tired of spending my time in these rinky-dink stores where you come out looking like everybody else. I like to see myself in the mirror, not to meet myself on the street."

"Did Caroline enjoy herself?"

"Yes, she did. She's upstairs now, packing for Caruthers' Gap."

"Packing? She's not going. You agreed for her to stay with you?"

Morriah stood firm, not entering the storage room. "I changed my mind. Besides, Caroline needs to go to Caruthers' Gap as much as you do."

"How did you reach that conclusion?" My voice grew more defensive with Morriah's nudging me toward my hometown.

"Simple. You spent a year in England researching your book and 'getting in touch' with your British heritage. You spent a year trying to resurrect a two-hundred-year-old past, but you won't spend a few days going back and visiting your family. That's damn stupid in my book."

"Morriah, you're still angry that I went away from Caroline on my sabbatical leave, aren't you?" I stared at her, feeling the shakiness in my voice.

"You're right about my feelings. It wasn't good for the girl to be without you."

"You know that I offered for her to come with me," I said.

"You don't offer a child, you just take 'em," Morriah said.

"Caroline didn't want to leave her friends, and you were quick to offer to keep with you."

"I know," she said.

"I had to get away. I felt like I was dying. I had the opportunity. My career needed it. I needed it. I wanted Caroline to be with me, but I would be in the library every day. You said it was better for you to watch her in familiar surroundings."

"I know I said it, but maybe I was wrong. Maybe, I needed to be with her, too. Now, it's Caroline's spirit that I'm concerned with. She needs to go to Caruthers' Gap with you."

"Morriah, you've been back there. You know why I've tried to put my past behind me."

"I understand that. However, Caroline deserves a chance to know some of her father's people. She can make her own decision about what influence they will have on her life. You're giving that girl only half a root system. Half a root system can't take in enough nourishment. People grow from both the pleasant, as well as the unpleasant."

Morriah's words stung me. She knew exactly how to penetrate my defenses—mentioning Caroline and her well-being. The thought of raising Caroline alone was the most frightening experience of my life. What if I made a mistake? Morriah had secured my attention.

"Your people aren't devils, Adrian. Ignorant, maybe, but they're not the monsters you imagine them to be. You're like a child who never confronted the night monsters who lived under his bed."

Painful as any bee sting, her words stung, again at deeper levels, jabbing at old pains, seeable at the surface but difficult to remove. "You're right," I admitted.

"Of course I am." There was no inflection in her voice that indicated anything other than conviction and strength. "Look at yourself. Meredith told me that when you get in one of your brooding moods, you return to these old boxes of memories and discarded dreams. The past draws you back, something there that you haven't made peace with."

"I don't know what to say or do," was all I could say.

"Don't say anything. Just get out of that damn rocker and take your daughter to your hometown. Give her a chance to meet some of your people. You owe it to her and to yourself. Adrian, Caroline's had a hard year in school. She's been having nightmares. You need to talk to her. She's afraid of going on to seventh grade. Caroline's entering a hard time—puberty without a mother. You better learn to communicate with her now or you'll lose her for a long time. I know what I'm talking about."

"I'll never get used to your coming on like a Sherman tank in a tailored suit."

"I say what I say because I care. Otherwise, I'd say the hell with it all and walk away."

Morriah did care. She turned and walked away, leaving me to ponder.

The room was filled with midday shadows provided from the remaining trees outside Ora Mae Chapman's bedroom window. Lola had already taken away Ora Mae's dinner dishes. Estelle Cameron walked through the bedroom door as she had done every Sunday after morning church since Ora Mae's confinement.

Ora Mae turned to the familiar figure and said, "I knew that you'd be here soon. I just listened to the gospel singing and the preacher on the TV and had my Sunday dinner."

"Did you eat much?" Estelle asked. Estelle moved to the faded toile upholstered chair near the metal bed.

"Not much. Not much appetite. All this medicine. Can't taste anything."

"You need to keep up your strength as best you can," Estelle said, as she shifted her weight and cushions in the chair.

"I got good news," Ora Mae said.

"News from the doctor?"

"There's no news from the doctor. But my boy's coming to see me soon. Adrian's coming."

"Well, good. He should come to see you," Estelle said. "You always took such great pride in him."

"Sure do. He's coming to see me real soon."

"I hope you'll let him help you. You won't let me."

"We done been down that road too many times before. I keep my word," Ora Mae said, her shaking head kept a steady beat to her words. "I'll go to my grave. It's just that I don't want folks, especially him, thinking I just killed a man when they don't know the whole story."

"I think you're putting too much hope in Adrian. I don't think he's got what it takes to help you. Too fickle for me. He's still running away. I've seen it before in others."

"If he runs long and hard enough, he'll catch himself," Ora Mae said. "And he just might help me. Might just help me."

"I hope so," Estelle said. Estelle picked up the magazine section of the Sunday paper and began reading to Ora Mae.

Later that Sunday evening I made my plans to take Caroline to visit Caruthers' Gap and my family. Several years had passed since my last phone conversation with Maggie, my sister. Maggie's voice was cordial enough and yet restrained. The longer we talked, the friendlier her voice became. Awkwardness gave way to friendliness. She said she was looking forward to seeing Caroline and having Caroline spend some days with her daughters.

Out of courtesy more than practical availability, my sister encouraged me to spend a few days at her house. Maggie mentioned proudly that she had a new striped sofa sleeper for me. I declined the offer of the sofa sleeper in favor of a motel. Still, I assured her that Caroline could spend some time visiting her cousins while I visited with Ora Mae.

That night Caroline's excitement erupted in endless questions. "What are my cousins' names? How old are they? Do they like boys? Will there be boys around? What should I wear? Will they like me?" She kept rehearsing with me the names of the family that she might meet. I went over names, ages and relationships. For the first time, I saw the hunger in her eyes and her need to be related to someone other than Morriah and me.

Caroline was in bed when I went in to say goodnight. Once more she told me that it was good to be back in our own home again. While she enjoyed staying with Morriah, she was pleased to return to familiar surroundings.

"It's good to be home with you," I said.

"I'm glad you're back," Caroline said. "I missed you."

"And I missed you. How was the end of sixth grade?"

"Sixth grade, I'm glad that it's over."

"Why?"

"Some of the girls were mean to me," Caroline said. Caroline played with her hair as she spoke.

"Morriah says that you've been having some nightmares."

"Yes."

"Do you want to tell me about them?"

"No," Caroline said.

"Do you know why you've been having them?"

"Morriah says that I'm afraid to go to seventh grade?"

"Are you?"

"Maybe. It's going to be new buildings, new teachers and new kids. Sixth grade was hard. Seventh grade might be worse."

"I see," I said, moving closer to her on the bed. "Well, Caroline, I can't promise that seventh grade will be better. But I can make you another promise."

"What's that?"

"Seventh grade won't be good unless you give it a fair chance."

"What does that mean?"

"Well, you'll never have to go through sixth grade again. That's behind you now. Over and done," I said.

"Seventh grade. That's the big question," Caroline said.

"Seventh grade is the unknown. You've got to put your sixth grade hurts and disappointments behind you. If you don't put them behind you, it will make seventh grade harder. Does that make sense to you?"

"I'm not sure," Caroline said. She yawned, obviously exhausted from a busy day. "I'm tired now."

"Okay, we can talk later," I said. I kissed her cheek and turned out her bedroom light. Father-daughter talks always made me uneasy, never sure if I were communicating with Caroline. I missed Meredith's guidance. Communicating was always easier in the college classroom.

When I went to my room, I noticed the message on my answering machine. I pressed the play button and collapsed on the bed. "Adrian, this is Davis Morgan," the voice said. "Your sister tells me that you're coming to Caruthers' Gap. I want to see you, boy. It's been too long. I'll find out where you'll be staying. Don't worry, I'll find you. I can find anybody in Caruthers' Gap. See you soon."

I had not seen or heard from Davis Morgan in several years. Obviously it didn't take Maggie long to start spreading the word about her brother's return home. Davis had been like a surrogate father to me, helping me through the adolescent and the college years. It would be good to see him. Maggie said he was quite the man about town, having prospered in the years since I left Caruthers' Gap. Lots of money and always being kind to people, Maggie said. I owed much to him. Like my obligations to Ora Mae, I had additional obligations to Davis Morgan.

Sitting up in bed, I reviewed the folder that Corrine had given me. I read the familiar names in the articles, many of them friends, teachers, and neighbors. These printed names evoked forgotten memories of childhood— building forts in the woods, spending time in detention for talking, and hanging out clothes in the backyard.

Ora Mae was charged with the murder of Wayne Daniels, the father of my childhood friend. His remains had been found beneath the septic tank in Ora Mae's back yard. A murder weapon, a rusty butcher knife, was found near the body. Aging witnesses recalled that Ora Mae had threatened to kill Wayne Daniels.

Victim, motive, and weapon—all three neatly packaged and pointing toward Ora Mae. It seemed too convenient and almost contrived. Too cut and dry. Life in the South was neither that simple nor that cleanly connected. The dots may be present, but what picture did they portray when correctly connected?

CHAPTER THREE

After breakfast at the university cafeteria and a stop at a floral shop, Caroline and I left Brunson mid-morning for Caruthers' Gap. Caroline and I had packed enough clothing for a week's stay in Caruthers' Gap, about three and half hours away from Brunson. The old two-lane highway that I remembered had become a four-lane highway, allowing people twice the opportunity for leaving as before.

Caroline put the well-worn mystery paperback novel down on her lap. "Daddy, what's our itinerary for today?" she asked as if we were still on a sightseeing tour.

"Well, we'll stop by the cemetery as we go in," I said.

"Daddy, is it just like in Europe? Do we have to do more rubbings on headstones?"

"No. We'll put some flowers on my parents'—your grandparents'—grave." Two floral arrangements were carefully secured in the backseat.

"Seems like a waste of money to me. They'll never see them." Caroline had obviously inherited her mother's practical nature.

"You're right." Putting the flowers on the grave was more of a sense of obligation to my sister and her expectations. After the "oohs" and "ahs" of how good it was to see me, the first question Maggie always had for me was, did you visit mama's and daddy's grave? Her second question was, did you put flowers on the grave? On more than one occasion, my answers were disappointing. Consequently, I often scrambled late at night creating full bouquets of cut flowers from smaller ones sold at the neighborhood store.

"Who gets the other flowers?"

"Your Aunt Maggie."

"Oh." Caroline picked her book and returned to her reading, leaving me to my thoughts on Caruthers' Gap.

Caruthers' Gap had prospered as a textile community since the early 1920s. As a child of the 60s, I watched the textile industry provide the greatest number of jobs for the men and women in Caruthers' Gap. Four separate mills were the primary employers of the community. Each mill, owned by members of the same extended family, influenced the various facets of

employees' lives such as housing, shopping opportunities, church attendance, recreational activities, and voting habits.

The traditional housing areas of the town, apart from the larger,
though sometimes decaying, homes around the Courthouse Square, were
the villages surrounding the mills. In my early years, I never imagined that
people could live in something other than a mill village or the plant as it
was called. Because of new high tech industry, new housing tracts with such
romantic and tranquil sounding names as Chautauqua Hills, Cherokee Acres
and the Highlands had been developed for more affluent and newly relocated
residents.

As we approached, I pointed out the large cemetery on our right. The
original cemetery, like the separated public water fountains in times past,
had two divisions—one for blacks and one for whites. I turned onto the
cemetery's property. Instinctively, my hands guided the steering wheel in the
curves leading to my parents' graves. A familiar tree, a park bench and a fountain had been etched in my memory like trail markers to their graves. Those
turns in the cemetery road reminded me of what I had lost.

"We're here," I said. We walked toward my parents' graves and
Caroline carried the flowers.

"What do I do with them?" she asked.

"Take out the urn in the center of the marker. Place the urn in the
holder, turn the urn clockwise, and put the flowers in. Add the water." Maggie
would say that I had neglected my girl's education on cemetery protocol and
family responsibility.

"Looks nice," I said as she pushed the cut flowers into the bronze vase
and added the water from the small jar.

"How did he die?" Caroline pointed toward my father's grave.

"While in his forties, your grandfather died of a heart attack."

Her eyes looked up to me. "You're in your forties."

"Yes."

"How did your mother die?" she asked pointing toward my mother's
name.

"Mama died of breast cancer."

Caroline's eyes once again looked up to me, acknowledging that she
knew little of her father's family, and she stared. "Just like my mother." Both
her eyebrows and forehead were raised, and she looked to me for answers.

"Yes." I glanced away from her, taking a deep breath and pretending to
look at graves. When I turned back, I saw Caroline's downcast eyes and her
hands' touching the outlines of her developing breasts.

I put my arms around her shoulders and hugged her. Our eyes were both wet. What I felt was no longer merely about my parents, her grandparents, or my wife, her mother. It was about Caroline and her future. What should develop into sources of pleasure and nurturance might become in later years sources of pain and death for her, my young daughter.

"Daddy, let's go walking," Caroline said, taking my hand.

We walked through the memorial gardens, looking and commenting on the types of markers there, some bronze nameplates and other upright granite headstones. The modern nameplates had little variation—all neat, orderly and predictable. The older graves had headstones of various designs and proportions—angels, birds, and crosses and an occasional Confederate insignia.

"They really knew how to make death special, didn't they?" Caroline said. Her hands traced the outline of a dove carved into a granite monument.

The gardens were well maintained—grass not too high, trees pruned for uniform shade and shrubs trimmed for symmetrical appeal. Benches and fountains were scattered through the park, marking it a quiet and appealing place. Caroline said, "It's sad that these people have in death what some people could not have in life—a beautiful place of rest."

We came to another section of the park that was also well maintained although the grave markers were not as elaborate. "This section feels different. Why is that, Daddy?"

"Originally this section was for blacks only."

"Why? A dead body is a dead body. It's not like they're in the same coffin."

"I'm glad that you think that way. Not all people thought that way years ago. White people didn't want their family members near black people."

"The cemetery was zoned?"

"In a matter of speaking, yes. All of our lives were zoned. I was a part of the final generation to see the last public marks of segregation—separate restroom facilities, separate hospitals, separate schools, separate churches, and separate eating facilities. Everything was to be separate but equal."

Caroline asked, "How can something be equal if it's separate?"

"It can't be. But people tried to make it so."

"You told me that death makes us all equal. This cemetery kept people separate. Doesn't make sense to me!"

"I know," I said as we walked back to the car. My arms were once more around Caroline's shoulders.

The retired, seventy-plus-year-old schoolteacher, Estelle Cameron, never trusted elevators. Only one major accident convinced her that climbing one or two flights of stairs was not too arduous a task to avoid the potential embarrassment of being trapped in an elevator. People with bladder control problems, she often said, should never allow themselves to be at the mercy of enclosed machinery. Deliberately, she walked the two flights of stairs to the District Attorney's office, pausing at the landing to gain both breath and composure.

Ruby, the fifty-year-old secretary/receptionist, looked up from her crossword puzzle when Estelle walked through the door.

"What's a nine letter word that means dark and gloomy? It starts with the letter 'T.' Got any ideas?" Ruby asked.

"I wish to speak with Barrister Morgan," said Estelle.

Ruby put down her newspaper folded to the crossword puzzle section and let her glasses drop on the chain around her neck. "Do you have an appointment?"

"No, I do not."

"I'm sorry, Mr. Morgan has left instructions that he is not to be disturbed. I'll be glad to set you up with an appointment later in the week." Ruby took out her pen and began turning pages in her desktop calendar.

"No, thank you, I don't need to be 'set up.' Is Mr. Morgan the district attorney of this county?" Estelle asked.

"Yes."

"Mr. Morgan is an paid servant of the community, is he not?"

"Well, yes, I guess he is," Ruby said. Ruby put on her jewel-framed glasses to stare at the woman.

"I am a tax-paying member of this community and wish to speak to the paid community servant."

"Like I told you, I'm sorry, but Mr. Morgan left word that he is not to be disturbed."

"Nonsense. Tell him that Estelle Cameron wishes to speak with him. Please convey that information now."

"Well, I never," Ruby said. Getting up from her desk, Ruby arched her shoulders back to Estelle as she walked down the narrow hall.

A few minutes later, Ruby returned. "Mr. Morgan has said for you to come into his office. Come this way."

"I know the way. I've known at least half a dozen district attorneys in my lifetime. Many of them I personally taught, including the current one. I know the way."

J.D. Morgan heard the heavy footsteps and immediately opened the door to greet his former social studies teacher. "Miss Cameron, please sit down," he said.

"Thank you, J.D.," Estelle said.

"What brings you to this part of the legal world?" he asked.

"I'll be concise. I want you to drop these trumped up charges against Ora Mae Chapman."

"Now, Miss Cameron, you know I can't do that. In fact, I cannot discuss the case with you at all. The grand jury has indicted Ms. Chapman. That's part of the public record. My office will seek to pursue justice, as well as mercy."

"The woman is dying. Let her die in peace."

"I know, Miss Cameron. If Ms. Chapman is indeed in the terminal phase of her life, my office will not pursue the case. We will allow her the merciful act of dying with dignity in her own home."

"Dying with dignity? Half the town has already convicted her. She'll die, but everyone else will live, without knowing the truth."

"What truth is that?" J.D. asked.

"The truth of who actually killed Wayne Daniels."

"We believe that we have the murderer, Miss Cameron."

"What you have is only circumstantial evidence. I know what you're doing, J.D. You're waiting for her to die and you'll close the case. The real killer will go free."

"How do you know there is a 'real killer,' other than Ora Mae Chapman?"

"Simple enough. I know Ora Mae Chapman. She's no murderer."

"There's no point in us debating this issue any longer. I'm sure that you've got other activities planned for the day. I know I have." J.D. stood up from his swivel chair.

"I'll be back, J.D. I won't let this matter rest until she has been exonerated of all charges."

"No doubt, you will be back." J.D. flashed her his public servant smile, one that had been identified clearly in his junior high and high school elections.

J.D. and Estelle walked back through the long corridor to his waiting area. Before he turned away from her he said, "You will consider me when it comes election time, I hope."

"Yes, I will consider you, but not for very long."

"Why not?"

"I do not consider people who do not take seriously their assignments or obligations."

"I take issue with you, Miss Cameron. I take my work very seriously."

"You did not in the seventh grade," Estelle said. *"You never turned in your five-page paper on the 'Values of a Free and Democratic Society.'"*

"Didn't I?"

"No, you did not. J.D., I do not like contractions. I recommended failing you. But your father talked with the superintendent and my recommendation was overruled."

"Obviously the superintendent did not feel that your recommendation was appropriate for my oversight."

"Your daddy gave the superintendent a hundred dollars. Always remember this, J.D.; men brag and secretaries listen." Estelle looked at the secretary who was half-involved in her crossword puzzle and half-involved in Estelle's conversation.

"What could I do to make amends for my wayward youth's lack of academic integrity?"

"Write the paper. Turn it in to me."

"I shall. I shall. You have a good day now," J.D. said.

"Tenebrous," Estelle said.

"Beg your pardon?" J.D. asked.

"Tenebrous, a nine letter word meaning dark and gloomy, that starts with a 'T.'"

Ruby looked up and picked her pen. *"Thanks. Now how do you spell 'tenebrous'?"*

"Look it up," Estelle said. Estelle Cameron headed for the stairs. When she was out of eyesight, J.D. turned to Ruby.

"Ruby, how old is that granddaughter of yours?"

"She's thirteen."

"Good. Would she like to make some extra spending money?"

"I'm sure she would," Ruby said.

"Here's a twenty. Have her write a five-page paper on the 'Values of a Free and Democratic Society.' Handwritten of course. Make sure the handwriting's not too feminine."

"Sure thing, J.D.," Ruby said putting the twenty in her purse. When J.D. left Ruby's office, Ruby muttered the word 'tenebrous' and reached for her dictionary.

The blinds were partially drawn, permitting only a hint of late afternoon sun to penetrate her private room at the nursing home. A few keepsakes—a home-made afghan of baby yarn, a pillow made of antique quilt scraps and artificial flowers arranged in a brass basket—gave the room warmth in contrast to the otherwise sterile surroundings. She had carefully chosen a few pieces of furniture, an oak rocker in which she had cradled her only baby and a small sewing chest that contained her half-finished needlepoint that she could no longer see. From her bed she could see the gold-framed mirror that her mother had given her on the day of her wedding. Carefully she had arranged family pictures in clear protective covers throughout the room so she might see family from whatever location she might be, no matter how lonely. On some days she remembered her possessions and where she was; on other days she had no recollections of her location, possessions, or persons.

Two women, one lying in bed and the other seated beside the bed, were in the room. "I know you can't hear me. That's why I can talk to you," Laurel Morgan said. Laurel took her mother's hand in her own. "You still have such pretty hair. I can never talk to you when you're awake any more. I'm so afraid that I will upset you. Mother, why did you marry him? We were much better off before you married him. I know it was hard financially, but we were much better off without him. I hoped you loved him, because it was a terrible price for love." Laurel Morgan put her head on the white blanket and wept.

Later Laurel heard a soft knock at the door. "Come in," she said. Carrying a small bouquet, an older man entered the room and smiled at her.

"She's sleeping now," Laurel said. "The room's so quiet."

"The nurse told me that she had a bad afternoon," the older man said. Pulling up a chair, he sat near the seated Laurel. Both looked at the sleeping woman, who breathed slowly and serenely.

"All afternoon," she said. "Ranting, raving, saying things that didn't make sense."

"What happened?"

"Mother overheard one of the orderlies talking to a nurse about Ora Mae Chapman. Mother became irrational."

"What did she say?"

"Who can make sense of what she says when she's like this?"

He reached out his hand and held the hand of Winnie Daniels, Laurel's mother. "What did she say?"

"She talked about Dad, about all the years living without him, and how she didn't want him to die."

"I'm sorry, Laurel," he said.

"Davis, what am I going to do? I can't stand to see her agitated. It happens over and over since Dad's body was found. The papers and the people are gossiping about what happened decades ago. This nightmare has got to be laid to rest. My nerves and my marriage can't take this pressure, Davis."

"I know, Laurel. I'm going to take care of it. She can't live much longer and then it will all be put behind us. You and J.D. can move forward with your life."

"What about Mother?" Laurel diverted her eyes from Davis and back to the sleeping figure.

"I'll always be here to care for your mother." Laurel's eyes looked into Davis' steel-grey eyes and found that her tears match his own.

"You're so good to all of us, Davis. You really do care."

CHAPTER FOUR

That afternoon Caroline and I arrived at the local university where I was to meet Rachel Simmons, the social worker who had called about Ora Mae. The state-supported school was a sharp contrast to the private school where I taught. The buildings were newer, the landscaping was fuller, and the library was more technological. I left Caroline in the library while I went to Rachel Simmons' office in the Department of Social Work. Earlier that day, Rachel had explained that she was an adjunct teacher, in addition to her responsibility as a member of Hospice.

When I knocked on her door, a deep voice said, "Come in."

As I entered her office, I was struck by her azure blue eyes. The room centered on her eyes. Afterward I could not recall any of the contents of her office—the number of bookshelves, the clutter of the desk, the type of chair or the computer. Those were items that I always scanned in a colleague's office. What I remembered after leaving her were her eyes—her azure blue eyes.

"I'm glad you were able to come," Rachel said. She did not take a seat until I did.

"I'm glad that you called about Ora Mae. I've just returned from a year's sabbatical in England. I had no idea about Ora Mae. It's inconceivable to me that she could be accused of murder."

"I understand," Rachel said, repeating that phrase several times and demonstrating her reflective listening skills.

I talked freely about my relationship and memories of Ora Mae, my helping her work on projects and her helping me with bullies. Rachel listened, making periodic reflective statements that began with the phrases, "You're feeling," and "I see" as a way of establishing rapport. Her "oohs" and "ahs," like her fleshly curves, were spaced in the appropriate places. Rachel could build rapport and she was built for rapport. Half an hour passed before I realized that I had been sharing all the information. It must have been those azure blue eyes.

"Tell me what you know," I said.

"Ora Mae has given me permission to talk with you. She's signed a release statement." She held up a paper for me to review, which I did. Ethics was obviously important to her. "Ora Mae is terminally ill." Rachel unclenched her hands and laid them flat on the desk that separated us.

"Dying," I said. Saying the word "dying" helped me to focus more clearly on the reality of Ora Mae's plight than the more clinical and clean word "terminal."

"Ora Mae has been diagnosed with lung cancer. She's undergone the traditional forms of chemotherapy and radiation. Currently she's engaged in prayer and meditation to relieve pain. Physicians advise that she's in the final stages. Hospice is involved."

"All those years I warned her about her smoking. I remember reading the report of the Surgeon General to her years ago. She wouldn't listen."

"She still has a strong volition."

"I bet," I said nodding.

"Ora Mae is trying to achieve a sense of ego integrity through life review. Dr. Stockwood, with your training, you're aware of the questions that she's having about her life. In her life review, you're playing a very significant role. She has a great deal of pride in you. You represent a part of the generativity resolution."

I smiled at her, thinking about her psychological and social work jargon, using it like a student intern. "I haven't been as close to her as I should have been for a long time."

"She mentions that fact from time to time." Rachel smiled and moved back in her blue leather swivel chair.

"I bet she does."

"She trusts you."

"Trusts me?"

"Ora Mae has been hesitant to trust me. I sense resistance."

"You're not from here, are you?"

"No."

"Blacks of Ora Mae's generation have trouble trusting whites, and education, and especially educated white women."

Rachel said nothing, responding only with a murmur and a nod of her blonde head. Had I insulted her? Listening to her talk about Ora Mae was like listening to a case study. She talked not unlike one of my better students.

Given her professional background, she should have been familiar with issues of trust in cross-racial counseling. Rachel looked hurt like one of my students when corrected. That's no way to impress a woman, I thought. I was amazed that I had instinctively responded to her as a student.

"What can I do to help?"

"I'm hoping that she will talk with you. She wants peace at the end of her life. She wants closure. Her primary concern is what people remember about her."

"Sounds like you've spent considerable time with her."

"I have spent many hours in dialogue and observation.

Will you help her?" Her question was more of a plea—like a student's needing help to finish a project.

"Of course, I will. I'm here to visit Ora Mae and do whatever I can."

"Good. It would help me if you spent some time discussing your relationship with Ora Mae. It might help me, as her social worker, to work more effectively with her. I hope that it wouldn't be an imposition?"

"Not at all."

"When do we start?"

"We could have dinner, tonight, if you don't have other plans?"

"I wish that I could, but we will be spending the evening with my sister."

"I hope you and Mrs. Stockwood have an enjoyable time."

"I'm a widower." In her presence, the word "widower" was less hurtful to speak. I watched for any change in her eyes.

"I'm sorry. Perhaps another evening, when we can both plan ahead."

"I look forward to it. What about Ora Mae? When may I see her?"

"That would not be advisable today. Mornings are usually best for Ora Mae. She only has a few hours each day when she's more lucid. Shall we meet tomorrow at her house at ten o'clock?"

"Okay. I'll see you tomorrow." I pulled out one of my new business cards from my jacket pocket. Taking a pen from her desk, I wrote the name "Morris Court," where we would be staying, on the back of the card. "Just in case you need to reach me," I said.

That afternoon Caroline and I settled into the local motel, Morris Court. Their only available two-room suite overlooked the rear parking lot. Picturesque no, but the on-duty manager promised it would be quiet. Caroline and I spent the afternoon settling in and rehearsing the names of extended family members and fragments of family history and relationships. I informed Caroline of family conversation topics to avoid—church and denominational politics, political parties, and who made the best banana crème pie. Once more, I rehearsed with my daughter the names of relatives who did not talk to one another but only talked about one another.

That evening Caroline and I were in my sister's home, which had changed little in the four years since I was last there. A three-bedroom brick ranch style house, their home was furnished with television sets and enormously stuffed couches and recliners. The house was accented with collections in each room—football memorabilia and new prints of Jesus. A stately, lighted-mirror curio cabinet, made of a fine cherry wood, stood in the living room. Inside were unopened soft drink bottles imprinted with names of regional colleges. When I admired the contents of the cabinets, Maggie's commentary was, "Tom says some day they're going to be worth something."

Over the sofa hung a cutout of a pig in oak stained pine with a clock mounted in the center. The pig's snout was located at the three; a teat at the six; and the tail at the nine. When we looked at the pig clock, Caroline whispered to me, "Where did they get that?"

Quietly, I responded, "Don't ask." Should we demonstrate any interest at all, I feared that we might find a proudly wrapped pig clock as a Christmas present under our tree.

Later I felt oozing air when I sat on their bathroom commode seat, a foam seat proudly emblazoned with the name of the nearby state football championship university, which no one in the family had ever attended. While seated in the bathroom, I noticed that an embroidered picture hung on the wall with the words "What Would Jesus Do?" While some decorated their homes in contemporary, country or modern, Maggie and Tom's home was "evangelical football."

The smell of fresh paint permeated the house. "Have you recently repainted?" I asked. The color seemed the same from what I remembered from my previous visit.

"I like to have the house repainted each summer," Maggie said.

"Same color?" I asked.

"Of course, pure white. It goes with everything. I never go with shades of white like antique white. I start out with the basic pure white. With time, white always darkens. Start out as white as you can, I always say," Maggie said with a smile.

Although five years older than I was, Maggie always seemed younger. Her voice had its own particular sweetness, an unassuming and innocent quality. She still maintained her teenage body proportions—small waist and full breasts.

Immediately following high school graduation, Maggie married Tom Crowder. A full-term baby followed in less than nine months following the wedding ceremony. Soon came the birth of another daughter. Now in their mid-twenties, these two girls had their own families living in Caruthers' Gap. The two girls had been approaching their teen years when Maggie's new babies were born.

Maggie and Tom's second family consisted of twin fourteen-year-old girls, Jennifer and Jocelyn. When I saw Caroline smiling, her eyes glowing, and her soft giggling with Jennifer and Jocelyn, I knew Morriah's assertions were correct. Caroline craved more family contact.

Tom led the family in a protracted blessing at dinner in the narrow dining room off the kitchen. Tom's prayer took on its own honest shape that included concerns for the lost in all parts of the world, for being a better witness in everyday life and for a deeper understanding of the Bible. Caroline and I were accustomed to more succinct mealtime prayers. Initially suspicious, I thought the prayer might be an attempt to impress me, but looking at the naturalness with which the four prayed and the reactions when they opened their eyes, I knew the sincerity of their ritual.

Tom Crowder had been, in my father's words, a dishonest hell-raiser. Seven years older than me, Tom had accomplished little more in high school than on Friday night football and Saturday night dates. No matter what was achieved, celebrated or debauched on Friday and Saturday nights, Tom was in church on Sunday morning.

To his friends, Tom was a good old Carolina boy. He focused on what he and his friends called the three "Fs" of Carolina living—football, fishing, and fornicating. Unlike my own, his future plans appeared never more than forty-eight hours away. Tom lived in the present and I lived in the future.

After everyone had plates filled and first bites taken, Maggie asked, "Did you visit Mama's and Daddy's graves?"

"Yes, Caroline and I took flowers there this morning."

"Just like the ones that we brought you, Aunt Maggie," Caroline said.

"That's wonderful. Mama would be so pleased. Daddy, too," Maggie said. "Adrian, how do you like counseling people? I bet it must be exciting listening to all of their problems and then giving them the answers." Her head shook as she asked the question and made her own commentary.

I shifted my eyes briefly to Maggie. "I don't counsel anymore," I said.

"Don't counsel anymore?" Maggie asked.

"No, I don't. These green beans are really good," I said. The limp green beans were draped over my fork as I brought their taste to my mouth.

"Secret's in the bacon drippings and cooking them all day long," Maggie said. "After all that education, I can't imagine not counseling. We never thought you would get out of school." Maggie turned to Caroline and said, "Your daddy went to school forever."

"I just wasn't smart enough to stop, I guess," I said, taking another forkful of green beans.

"Adrian, now you don't counsel anymore? I can't imagine," Maggie said.

"I'm sure Adrian's got his reasons," Tom said.

"Well, I just think it would be exciting to know all those secrets about people—their hurts and heartbreaks." Maggie was beginning to sound like a country western song. "And of course, to be able to help them, too. People sure need help today with life's problems. The other day I was listening to the Christian radio station. I like to listen to it in the mornings when I'm doing my housework. Well, there's this man doctor who comes on. Well, people phone in their problems to him and he solves them right there for them on the air. I bet he makes a lot of money and gets to meet some interesting people. Tom, you know what?"

Tom was in the middle of a mouthful of fried chicken when Maggie posed her question. "What, hon?"

"Adrian could do that. He could have his own call-in talk show right here in Caruthers' Gap. He's got a good voice, sounds real educated. I bet he would be as popular as ... now, what's that man's name? What's his name? Do you remember, Tom?"

"No, hon, I don't." This time Maggie's question reached Tom before the chicken wing met his mouth.

"What do you think, Adrian? Would you like to have your own call-in show? I could talk with Reverend Cobb. He's got connections at the Christian radio station. I bet he could get you on down there. Then you could move back to Caruthers' Gap and we could be one big happy family. What do you think of that?"

"That sounds real nice, Maggie, but remember, I no longer counsel," I said.

"I guess that would make it kinda hard, wouldn't it?"

"Aunt Maggie, could I have some more of your banana pudding? I've never tasted anything so good," Caroline said.

"Sure thing, darling," Maggie said. "I bet you don't get much chance for home cooking." Maggie smiled and looked directly at me. I felt her message. "Get this girl a mother who can cook good," Maggie added.

After we had finished dinner and while Maggie and the girls cleared the table and washed the dishes, Tom and I sat on their porch. The air was still warm at eight o'clock.

"You don't get here often enough," Tom said.

"We all stay busy," I said.

"How long will you be staying?"

"A few days, at least. I need some time with Ora Mae, helping her."

"Adrian, you and I ain't been close. After I gave my life to Christ, I thought we could become friends if not brothers in Christ. It ain't worked out."

"Tom, we've just not had time together."

"Maybe so," Tom said.

Pretty and polite words, I thought. The night was silent to the unspoken truth. In spite of Tom's effort at being family, I had politely rejected both him and his offer.

"Listen to what I say," Tom said. "Be careful when you start visiting Ora Mae. This town and certain people have deep feelings about Wayne Daniels and the woman accused of murdering him. No telling what might happen if you start digging up people's skeletons. It could get ugly."

Later, inside their home, Caroline informed me that she and her cousins had plans for a trip to the nearby lake under Aunt Maggie's supervision. I agreed to bring her to Maggie's house after breakfast. We said goodnight and returned to our motel.

While Caroline slept, I worked on my laptop. I thought about Tom's words about wanting to be a brother and the warning not to cause trouble. I thought about that pig clock. I made myself a drink with cola from the vending machine and a dash of bourbon hidden in my suitcase.

I opened my e-mail, finding my first message at the new e-mail address. I leaned forward to read the note. Putting the bourbon and cola down, I reread the message. "Be careful. Possible danger for all if you delve too deeply into Wayne Daniels' death. A friend." I looked at the sender's address, which was unknown to me.

I opened the door between our rooms and watched a sleeping Caroline and rechecked the outside doors and windows. I kept Caroline's door open to my room. As I finally drifted off to sleep, I kept rehearsing the e-mail's message—"Be careful. Possible danger for all if you delve too deeply into Wayne Daniels' death. A friend."

CHAPTER FIVE

The phone awakened me from my on-again, off-again night's sleep and I heard a familiar voice. "I knew you would want to know as soon as we received the letter," Morriah said. "Yes, I have it in my hand. Just like Adams. He had it sent to your campus mail. If I hadn't been in the student center early this morning after my walk and if Mrs. Lancaster had not said, 'there's an letter for Dr. Stockwood,' I don't know when we would have received it."

"Please, just open it," I said.

Three full days had passed since I had visited Adams who said he would bring my request for contractual release before the Executive Council at Hunter-Harwell.

"I'm opening it now," Morriah said.

"What does it say?"

"Hold your horses. I never took an Evelyn Woods speed reading course."

"What's the bottom line, Morriah?" I asked.

"I'll read it to you. 'We regret to deny your request for release from your contractual obligations agreements with the University. The lateness of your request, which would produce undue hardship upon both faculty and students, makes it impossible to honor it. Additionally, your receiving a sabbatical leave was contingent upon your return of a two-year service to the University following the leave. We hope your disappointment will not be too great. We look forward to another two years per your contract. Sincerely, Harper Adams, Ph.D.'"

"Adams strikes again," I said.

"I'm sorry, but I told you so." Morriah said. "What are you going to do?"

"Appeal, of course."

"Good. We'll appeal. You'll probably need a lawyer."

"I know, but I'll need my papers. Will you go to the office and bring all the material regarding my request for sabbatical leave and contractual agreements?"

"What about the Hunter-Harwell Policy and Procedures Manual?"

"I'll need that information, too. When do you think you can get here?"

"Day after tomorrow," Morriah said.

"Could you come sooner?" I asked.

"That anxious to leave?" Morriah asked.

"There's another reason. I received a message on my computer last night, advising me not to pursue any investigation into Ora Mae's case. The message said could be danger for all. What do you think?"

"I don't think. I act. I'll be there by night."

"Good. I'll inform the motel that you'll be staying with Caroline. I'll have them reserve a key for you at the desk."

"Do you have any idea who sent the message?"

"Not a clue. I'm not sure how to go about finding out?"

"Try Corrine."

"Corrine?"

"Yes, Corrine. She knows a lot about computers. If she doesn't know, she knows how to find out."

"Do you think she could help?"

"She'll help, but she shouldn't, not the way you ignored her, but she cares about Caroline."

"Caroline?"

"Yes, she and Caroline have become closer."

"I didn't know."

"There's a lot you don't know. Get your head out of your books and smell the coffee," Morriah said.

"I'll see you tonight."

Like the older sections of Caruthers' Gap, Ora Mae's neighborhood was neglected—invading tree roots shattered the sidewalks, grass grew in the cracks, abandoned tireless automobiles stood on the lawns, and old upholstered furniture stood unashamedly on the front porches. The smell of dandelions, cut grass and cooking pinto beans were summer companions. Children's voices and women's voices, sometimes playful and sometimes corrective, but always robust, filled the air.

The trees, with their massive rough trunks and outstretched skinny limbs, guarded the neighborhood. The skirts of the trees barely missed touching each other, much like ladies in full gowns crowded in the hallways trying not to touch each other. Their roots, occasionally breaking through the ground, ran and intertwined underneath the broken sidewalks and driveways. Those trees, never having received the nourishment of fertilizer, thrived at their own pace.

Rachel was on the front porch. "I'm glad you're here," she said.

"Good to see you," I responded, glancing down at my none-too-small waist.

Rachel knocked. Slowly a woman opened the door and observed us through the screen. Rachel introduced me to Lola, the nursing attendant from Hospice.

Lola's eyes grew wider and her body began to quiver as she motioned me forward with her hands and arms. "Dr. Stockwood, Miss Ora Mae's been asking and asking for you. She made me promise that I would phone you." The attendant's eyes darted from me to Rachel. "Miss Simmons insisted that she'd call you. I'd have called sooner if I'd had my way." The nurse's eyes darted again quickly to Rachel and then back to me. "The most important thing is that you're here. Come on, get in this house."

Shaking her head, Rachel turned from Lola. "Adrian, you go ahead. I'll give you some private time with Ora Mae."

Lola led me through the living room and into the small square hall that connected to Ora Mae's bedroom. Lola murmured, "She'll give you some private time. Who does she think she is? Only God gives time and we're running out of that."

The door to Ora Mae's bedroom was open. The sights, sounds, and smells were familiar. The walls were covered with peeling wallpaper, the air permeated by tobacco scents, and the floors creaked from our footsteps. Inside, the scratched bedroom furniture was covered with towels and embroidered scarves.

"Miss Ora Mae," Lola said, "Miss Ora Mae. You got company."

Ora Mae raised her head from her pillow on her iron bed. Her formerly coal-black hair had turned white. "Give me my glasses," Ora Mae said. Her hands reached out, moving from side to side.

"Here you are, honey." Lola took the glasses from the bedside table and placed them on Ora Mae's face. "Dr. Stockwood has come to visit you, just like you said he would."

No one spoke. It was a few moments before Ora Mae responded, as though she were focusing both her eyes and her words to the light. "Adrian, is that you?"

"It is I, Ora Mae."

"It's been a long time since I last seen you. I hardly know you. You putting on some weight. Good, you were always too small. Had the waist like a young girl. You use to stand sideways and I couldn't swat you, couldn't find you." Ora Mae's chuckle, deep and raspy, sounded like that of an old man suffering with smokers' cough. Greetings from Ora Mae often involved commentary on your weight, either you were gaining too much or had lost too much.

"You're sounding cheerful," I responded.

"Mornings are better."

"Miss Ora Mae has been looking forward to your coming," Lola said. Lola had remained in the bedroom straightening the room, placing a light shawl around Ora Mae's shoulders and tucking an extra pillow beneath her head.

"Leave us alone now. I want to talk with Adrian."

For the next half-hour, we talked about my daughter. I had learned long ago that in the South you were half-dressed if you didn't carry with you photographs of children and grandchildren. Proudly I shared my photos of Caroline. We talked about my deceased parents and the years when Ora Mae worked for our family. We rehearsed the same stories over and over, much like a choir preparing a familiar hymn for a morning worship service.

Lola reentered the room carrying a tray. "Here's your medicine," she said. "Miss Ora Mae will be drowsy in a little bit. She'll then take her nap. You've got about half an hour." I smiled at Lola and nodded.

"Ora Mae, why did you want to see me?" The words didn't sound right, but I knew no other way to focus on what she wanted from me.

"You know what they've been saying about me." Her chin quivered, showing her missing lower teeth. "They say I murdered Wayne Daniels."

"Did you?" I asked slowly, hoping the slowness would take away the sting of the words. I had to ask; I had to be able to say that I asked.

"When I meet my Maker there will be redeemed blood on my hands," Ora Mae said, holding up her hands.

"I know."

"You remember Wayne Daniels?" Ora Mae asked.

"Yes, he was Laurel's father and Miss Winnie's husband."

"Laurel's step-father. Mr. Wayne was Miss Winnie's second husband. Her first husband died in Korea. He's the one who sent me that kimono on the wall. When I was young and it was young, we looked good together. I was the style." Her hand pointed to the faded yellow garment. "I hated that man."

"Hated?"

"Yes, sir. I hated that man."

I was confused. "Who did you hate?" I asked.

Her head shook with rage. "Mr. Wayne. Mr. Wayne was the meanest and the lyingest man, black or white, I ever did see. And I've seen some mean ones."

Ora Mae was silent. No need to probe her with questions. This was her time to collect her thoughts.

"Those shadows get darker and darker each day. Sad to die that way— without your people saying goodbye to you." Ora Mae shook her head, saying, "Never wanted him to die without his people."

"What do you know about how he died?"

"Miss Winnie mourned Mr. Wayne. She never remarried. I told her she was too young, but she never would listen. She could have, too. She carries his memory with her."

"Do you still see Miss Winnie?"

"Use to visit her in the nursing home. She's not right in the head. Comes and goes, like my mammy did. Sometimes she's home and sometimes she's out. In for a couple of hours, out for a few days. Sad. She still a pretty woman. Crazy as a loon."

"A shame," I said.

"She worked so good with the children. She could get anybody to do anything she wanted. A good actress. She even fooled me sometimes, pretending to be mad at me cause Mr. Wayne said I needed to be corrected." Ora Mae's robust laughter and smile filled the room.

"Do you ever see Laurel?"

"Use to. Now that Miss Laurel, she's something else. She was always starting something and never finishing it. Miss Winnie use to get on to her so. Always starting with big ideas and never finished nothing."

"Really?" I asked.

"She was going to make her own clothes. Miss Winnie bought her a nice sewing machine with all the gadgets. Could make any kind of stitch you wanted. That girl didn't even finish cutting out the pattern. Miss Winnie and I had to finish the dress for her," Ora Mae said.

"Oh," I offered in response.

"Yes, sir. Never knew who was coming through the door when Laurel came home," Ora Mae said laughing. "Always kept me guessing. It was like a whodunit or mystery guest like on that TV show," she said.

"You don't see them much anymore?" I asked.

"Laurel use to bring Miss Winnie here to see me when I couldn't get out to see her. No more. Not since the papers said that I killed Wayne Daniels. I wanted to see this man dead. He was mean, the meanest man I ever saw." Ora Mae turned her head away from me.

Lola must have been standing in the hallway because she entered the room as if on cue. "Miss Ora Mae needs her rest."

I stood up, bent over and touched Ora Mae's hand. "See you later."

"Tomorrow," Ora Mae said faintly, turning toward me. "Adrian, you still remember our promise?" She held up the palm of her left hand.

The palm of my left hand burned with the memory. "I remember."

"You will keep your promise?"

"I will."

I left the room and walked away less confident about Ora Mae. All I had learned was that she hated Wayne Daniels. Never before had I heard Ora Mae use the word "hate" with such venom. Had she killed Wayne Daniels? At best, her responses left me confused.

Rachel was in the living room, reading a journal, and waiting. We left the house silently. On the steps, she turned to me, "Well, how did it go?"

I summarized what had happened for Rachel, sharing everything but the promise.

"I received an e-mail message last night, warning me that it could be dangerous to investigate Wayne Daniels' death."

"Are you afraid?"

"Concerned, especially for Caroline." I suspected my eyes and voice showed that I was more than merely concerned. "Caroline's the only person that I have left."

"I'm sure that everything will be fine for both of you," Rachel said.

Rachel pressed me for more details about Ora Mae until I responded, "Next time you need to be in the room. I can't remember enough details for you. You should have come in."

"Lola wouldn't let me in," Rachel said. "Tomorrow she won't keep me out. I know her immediate supervisor."

I believed Rachel.

I decided to follow Morriah's suggestion about phoning Corrine to help decipher the senders of the e-mail message. After several unsuccessful attempts, I made the phone connection. "Corrine, I need your help," I said.

"What do you need, Adrian?"

"I've received a computer message and I need to know the sender," I said.

"Okay."

"Can you help me?"

"I'll try. Give me the information that you have about the sender's address," Corrine said.

I repeated the words and the punctuation marks, hoping it meant more to her than it did to me.

"It may take a few days, but I will let you know just as soon as I know anything," Corrine said.

"Thanks. How are you doing, Corrine?"

"I'm fine, Adrian. Why do you ask?"

"I want to know. I do care, Corrine."

"Yes, I will try to get more information for you. Adrian, I have someone at the desk. I will be in touch. Bye."

"Bye and thanks, Corrine," I said.

That afternoon I went downtown to visit J.D. Morgan, the District Attorney. His office was located on the second floor of the courthouse, a red brick building over a hundred years old, firmly situated on the town square. When I was a young child, its columns, massive steps, and three stories seemed as large to me as the great pyramids of Egypt. I had always felt if you were in trouble, you could go to the courthouse. There justice prevailed.

J.D.'s secretary was reluctant to let me see him without an appointment. She was a large-framed woman with equally large-framed glasses and big dangling golden earrings. She proudly wore a large nametag that said "Ruby Jackson, CPS," which I knew to mean a certified public secretary. Everything about her was large, commanding, and public.

After the customary greetings and my explanation of family ties in Caruthers' Gap and friendship with J.D., I persuaded her to let him know I was there. I assured her if he did not have time to see me, I would make an appointment.

Although J.D. and I had been friends since grammar school, we had not kept in touch. We had met as bully and victim—J.D. was the bully and I the victim. That marked the beginning of our relationship until the afternoon that I chose to fight him back. J.D. pushed me, pulling my shirt and tearing my shirt loop, a common practice among my generation of classmates. I pushed him back, yanking and tearing his shirt. I still remember my words to him, "You might win but I'll put up a damn good fight." J.D. laughed. Thinking back, it must have been funny. I was shorter than J.D. and at least twenty pounds lighter. After that, though, we were friends. J.D. said he had to become my friend. Otherwise, he would have died laughing as he beat the hell out of me.

Though we had not maintained regular communication since college graduation, almost twenty years ago, I knew he had gone on to the state law school and now worked in the District Attorney's office. He and Laurel, Wayne Daniel's stepdaughter, had married about fifteen years ago. At one time, the three of us had been good friends not only to each other but also to Ora Mae.

When J.D. came through the door, I saw that his hair was still dark brown, almost black, thinning at the top. He was well dressed and thin in his tan suit. He had a familiar open smile that showed a small space between his two front teeth.

"Adrian, good to see you," he said. "Mrs. Jackson, hold my calls. Come on in here, buddy."

J.D.'s greeting was as warm and as familiar as if we had only been separated for a weekend and not twenty years. It was like the old days when he and I worked on the school newspaper along with Laurel.

"Man, it's good to see you." J.D. repeated himself. He sat on the edge of his desk while I sat in his guest chair.

"It's been a long time. Almost ten years, I think."

"It was at your mother's funeral, I believe," stated J. D. as he lit himself a cigarette. He held the cigarette between his thumb and his index finger.

"When did you start smoking?" I asked.

"You can't stay in this line of work and not engage in some deadly habits," he said. "Besides, it helps relax me." Looking at the cigarette butts in the otherwise immaculate office, I thought J.D. must be one of the most relaxed men in Caruthers' Gap.

When he flicked his ashes in the ashtray, I remembered. Ora Mae had held her cigarette that way. She had taught the three of us how to smoke that summer after she caught us smoking in her backyard. Ora Mae gathered the three of us around her back steps and said, "If you're going to smoke, don't be a sissy about it. Do it like a man!"

Ora Mae held her cigarette with her index finger curled around the cigarette pressed against her thumb. Ora Mae took a deep drag of tobacco, and then cupped her hand to hide the cigarette. She had the three of us smoking until our eyes watered and we coughed till we vomited. Her plan had worked on me but apparently not on J.D.

"Buddy, what brings you to these parts?"

"I'm here visiting my sister and Ora Mae Chapman."

"I see." J.D. turned from me and went around to his desk where he sat in his massive oak chair.

"What can you tell me about her case, J.D.?"

"Not much. It's pretty simple. You may already know if you read the papers. We have an airtight case against Ora Mae. We have the motive, we have the weapon, and we have the body. It fits together like a neat little package."

"What about the motive?"

"We have documented accounts of Ora Mae's having had loud altercations with Wayne before his death. We even have a police report of her being verbally abusive to him."

"Certainly couldn't have a black woman arguing with a white man in the 1960s." I teased him to see his response.

"Buddy, now don't try that civil rights stuff with me. You and I both lived through that mess. Besides, we have Wayne Daniels' body and a weapon."

"What weapon?"

"A butcher knife with the initials 'O.M.C' carved in the handle."

"That could be coincidental."

"Sure," he said sarcastically. "The knife was found buried with the body under Ora Mae Chapman's septic tank. Hardly coincidental. Bodies and engraved butcher knives are not standard equipment when putting in septic tanks, not even in the backwoods of the Carolinas."

It sounded funny, but I could not laugh. Instead, I said, "I think your package is too neat. It's too simple."

"What do you mean?"

"Examine your own facts, J.D. Ora Mae's not stupid. She wouldn't kill anyone with her own knife and then bury the knife with the victim in her own backyard."

J.D. was silent, gazing at me as if he were in a trance.

"J.D., you can't believe she did that. You, Laurel and I, we were her friends. She took care of us that summer that Wayne Daniels died."

"In my profession, I deal strictly with the facts, and not feelings, unlike your profession. The facts point to Ora Mae. I have a responsibility to the citizens of Caruthers' Gap. I'm simply carrying out my sworn responsibility."

"How does Laurel feel about all of this?"

"Laurel wants to put that part of life to rest. We all thought Wayne had drowned in a fishing accident. Now we discover that he was murdered. And the murderer has been living among us."

"What's going to happen to Ora Mae now?"

"If you're asking if she'll be brought to trial, the answer is probably not. I understand that she's in the last stages of cancer. She wouldn't live to stand trial. Besides, if she did go to trial, she wouldn't live longer than the appeal process. She'll not serve any time in jail. She can die in her own home."

"Die with everyone believing she killed a man."

"The facts say she did," J.D. insisted.

"What if she didn't?"

"If not her, then who?"

"That's what I need to find out."

"We can't help you. All the facts that I have indicate Ora Mae's guilty. Believe me, Adrian, I have looked at this case objectively. So have my colleagues. I've asked for peer review on this one."

"I'll keep on trying," I said. "Someone sent me an e-mail message about digging into Wayne Daniels' murder. They said it could be dangerous."

"Interesting. Any ideas who sent it?"

"No," I said. "I didn't think e-mail was used much here."

"Adrian, come on. We're not that country. Everybody has access to computers or knows someone who does. Sounds like a prank. Lots of people want this murder case over. Let me know if you receive any more messages."

"Okay."

"Will you come out to the house and visit with Laurel and me? She'd love to see you."

"Would she?"

"Of course, buddy. You're one of her best friends. You knew her before I did."

"Okay." I wrote my motel name and room number on the back of my business card for J.D. "Here you go," I said.

"Thanks. I wish we had more time, but now I do have an appointment across town."

"Thanks for the time, J.D. We'll talk later."

I left him at the doorway to his office. I was still unwilling to believe that Ora Mae was guilty. I did know that what I must discover would be on my own. J.D. and his office would not knowingly help me. Their records and, more importantly, their opinions were fixed.

Upon arriving back at my motel, I discovered the cellophane wrapped basket containing fruits, crackers, canned meats, and cheeses. The card simply said, "Thanks for your help, Rachel."

The phone rang, awakening me from my pleasant speculations. Laurel called asking if I would like to meet her and J.D. at the country club for dinner. Like a proper little Southern matron, she apologized for not giving more advance notice. She said that she generally frowned upon same day invitations.

I accepted on one condition, that I could arrange for Caroline to have dinner with my sister. At the end of the conversation, Laurel said, "If you'd like to bring a dinner companion, that would be marvelous." I simply responded, "We'll see." Up to now my "we'll sees" had meant probably not. Tonight it meant I hope so.

Immediately I phoned Maggie, hoping they had already arrived back from the day picnic at the lake. When she answered, I explained that I had a dinner invitation with Laurel and J.D. Morgan. Having dinner with the local district attorney and his wife was described by Maggie as "traveling in high cotton."

"I wouldn't call it that," I responded.

"Will you be going alone?" Maggie's voice lifted.

"Is that a leading question?"

"Don't know about that. But will you be taking Rachel?"

Taking Rachel, I thought. I suspected that Rachel was not one who was "taken" anywhere. "Where did you hear about Rachel?"

"Caroline. Girls love to talk, especially about their eligible bachelor daddies. Besides you've 'bached' it too long."

"Well, it's possible that Rachel may go to the country club with me."

"Country club! Hum. Only time I was ever at the country club was that summer when I worked in the kitchen. You didn't know that you had family with country club connections, did you?" Maggie laughed.

I found her comment funny. "So my older sister has been before me to the Caruthers' Gap Country Club."

"Yeah. Except we're on different sides of the double doors leading from the dining room into the kitchen."

"Caroline can have dinner with you tonight?" I asked.

"Of course, let her spend the night. My girls want to get to know their cousin."

"Not tonight. I've been away from her all day. I'll be back by nine or nine-thirty. No later."

"Let her stay tonight."

"Maybe another night," I said.

As I put down the receiver, I heard Maggie's parting comment, "Bring Rachel by for pie." I smiled. Rachel was not the type of girl one brought home for pie. It was the first time I recalled feeling unashamedly amused when talking with my family. Morriah may have been right. Maybe both Caroline and I needed the visit.

I was about to leave for dinner when there was a knock at the door. There stood Morriah with a purse and travel bag.

"Come in, Morriah,"

"Going out?"

"To dinner" I responded.

"You're a little too dressed up for a down home meal," Morriah said, eyeing me from my bow tie to my freshly polished shoes.

"Did you bring the papers?"

"They're in my luggage. Why don't you go and bring my bags? I'm parked next to you."

"Alright."

After the bags were placed in Caroline's room. I turned to Morriah and asked, "May I have the papers?"

"In a minute, first, where's Caroline?" Morriah demanded.

"She's with Maggie. I'll bring her home later this evening."

Apparently satisfied, Morriah pulled the papers from the travel bag that she had first carried into the room. Slowly, she handed them to me as she sat on Caroline's bed.

"I should have known," I said.

"Always carry the important things with me," Morriah said.

"Thanks," I said. I took the folder of papers. "I'll look at them when I return."

"This dinner must be important to you," Morriah said as she kicked off her high heel shoes.

"Are you going to be okay being alone?" I asked.

"I'm one of the few people I know who fully appreciates my own charm and company. Besides, I need to soak my feet. Takes a lot to wear high heels at my age. I'll get something to eat at that place across the street, if it's not too greasy. Now go on."

"Thanks," I said, leaving the folder on my lighted desk.

CHAPTER SIX

Rolling manicured lawns of St. Augustine grasses with islands of trees and dwarf shrubs surrounded the two-story homes in Chautauqua Hills, one of the most exclusive of the subdivisions in Caruthers' Gap. The J.D. Morgan home was similar to the other homes in the area with its rear-entry garage, brick mailbox, kidney-shaped pool, and curved brick entryways. It was a neighborhood of both written and unspoken covenants, equally binding, that guided and protected both properties and persons of Chautauqua Hills.

In their master suite, Laurel was sitting on the couch reading a magazine when J.D. emerged from the shower.

"What time are we meeting Adrian?" J.D. asked with a white towel wrapped about his waist.

"I asked him to meet us at the club at seven," Laurel said. "J.D., why are you wearing that old bath towel? I wish you would wear the monogrammed robe that I gave you for Christmas."

"It's a perfectly good bath towel," J.D. said. He shook his head and dripped water on Laurel.

"Towels are for drying, not parading around the bedroom."

"There was a time when you enjoyed my parading around the room in my bath towel."

"We lived in a three-room apartment. We couldn't afford a nice bathrobe. Now we can," Laurel retorted, putting down the magazine.

"We were closer when we were struggling financially," J.D. answered. "I wish we could go back."

"Not I. I much prefer this lifestyle."

"But we were happier then."

"That's a price you pay for success," Laurel added. "Life is full of compromises and accommodations. We're simply accommodating."

"Accommodating?"

Laurel was silent.

"I love you, Laurel," J.D. said quietly. "I need you."

"J.D., I've done everything you've asked. I came back to Caruthers' Gap. I've agreed to be supportive of you and your political aspirations, or should I say your father's political aspirations. What more do you want?"

"I want you," J.D. said. J.D. moved closer to her, putting his hands on Laurel's shoulders.

Laurel's body stiffened. "Not now," she said.

"It's always not now," J.D. said. He moved back from her. "What do you want from me? Do you want anything?"

"I've told you. I will, as the wife of Caesar, be supportive. Beyond that, J.D., it's difficult. I want your promise that you will protect my mother. She's very vulnerable. I don't want anyone bringing up my dad's death. Neither she nor I can handle the stress."

"I promised you that I would always protect you and your mother."

"You will keep your promise?" Laurel asked.

"Laurel, I love you. I'll protect you." J.D. moved closer to her.

Laurel smiled. "I'll keep my promises, all of them."

Laurel stood up and moved closer to J.D. She drew her face closer to his and kissed him full on the lips. She ran one hand through his wet hair and with another hand, she unwrapped his bath towel.

"Oh, Laurel," J.D. murmured. He led her by the hand to their poster bed and lifted her slight frame onto the bed.

"The shades," Laurel said. "Draw the shades."

J.D. nodded. Half an hour later, Laurel, still in bed, awakened a napping J.D. by pressing her body closer to his. Laurel whispered in J.D.'s ear, "Do you know who Adrian is bringing to the club?"

"No," J.D. said.

"Rachel Simmons," Laurel said.

J.D., his eyes widened and his eyebrows raised, lifted his head from the folded pillow, propped his head on his arm and asked, "Will that be hard for you?" J.D. asked.

"What about you?" Laurel responded.

"No," J.D. said.

"Neither for me," Laurel said.

J.D. nuzzled closer to Laurel's body. As she turned her resting body away from him, J.D.'s arm encircled her. Laurel's eyes were wide open as J.D. pressed his body still closer to hers. "Time for one more?" he asked. Laurel stared at the ticking clock on the bedside table.

Rachel had said yes to my dinner invitation with Laurel and J.D. Apparently, same-day invitations were not offensive to Rachel. Her directions led me to the apartment complex where university students resided.

When I arrived, only one couple was taking advantage of the apartment pool that hot June evening. The way they swam—chasing, capturing and embracing each other—left little doubt that they were more than casually acquainted. The open books, obviously college texts, red spiral notebooks, and soft drink cans indicated they were taking a study break.

At her apartment door, Rachel met me in a skin tight three-quarter length dress, the type of dress that commanded a second glance and then a longer lingering one. The deep cut in the front complemented and accented her natural endowments. Matinee length creamy white pearls were nested between those tanned breasts. Her blue eyes were illuminated and magnified by the indigo of the fabric. As Ora Mae and my mother would have said in unison, "She was dressed fit to kill." Rachel was definitely killing me.

"Come in," she said, "I'm almost ready." Before she had completed her greetings, I had assessed how ready she looked.

"We have plenty of time," I said.

"Good. Have a seat. I'll be back."

Sitting on the couch, I glanced about the room. It was graduate student housing—the furniture sparse, the books plentiful, and wall decorations limited. Her plants, unlike my own during similar years, were thriving, obviously well watered and well sunned.

When she returned from what I surmised was her bedroom, I stood. "Would you like something to drink?" she asked.

"No, thank you. Maybe at dinner." I was tempted to say yes in order to discover the contents of her beverage list.

"Good choice," Rachel said.

"Are you ready?"

"Yes, let's go."

After she locked the apartment door, Azure Eyes took my arm. Her manner had changed considerably since our first meeting. When she stood near me, I noticed that she appeared shorter than she did the first time I met her. I glanced down at the steps as we were leaving and noticed that she was not wearing heels.

On the drive to the country club, we talked mostly about her vocational plans. Rachel hoped to continue her doctoral studies and then obtain a teaching position. Her questions showed she still had much to learn about the realities of college teaching. Her thoughts and questions were refreshing, reminiscent of my first years of teaching. Rachel was still holding my arm when we went into the country club's dining room. Immediately, J.D. stood up and motioned for us to join him while uttering the words, "Over here, folks."

I began the introductions. "Laurel and J.D., I would like for you to meet . . . ," I said.

"Rachel," Laurel said, interrupting my carefully planned and triumphant introduction. "I didn't know that you knew Adrian."

"Good to see you, Rachel," J.D. said.

I helped Rachel with her seat. "You three have the advantage. Laurel, you didn't tell me that you knew Rachel."

Laurel did not answer my comment that I had intended to be a question, not a statement.

"Yes, we knew each other in Columbia when J.D. was teaching at the law school there," Rachel added.

"I only taught part-time," J.D. said. "Rachel was in one of my classes."

"Tell me, how did the two of you meet?" Laurel asked.

Turning my head toward Laurel, I said, "Rachel called me about Ora Mae. She's been working with Hospice and Ora Mae."

"I see." Laurel's stare was as icy as the water glass she held in her hand. I wondered if I were the only one who felt the chill as Laurel swallowed her ice water.

"How is your mother?" I asked.

"Why do you ask?" Laurel said, putting down her glass.

"Just out of respect and concern. She was my teacher."

"I'm sorry," Laurel said. "Mother's in a nursing home, Adrian."

"Nursing home," I said. "But she's so young."

"Early onset Alzheimer's Disease," J.D. said.

"I'm sorry," I said.

"She's become forgetful and confused. She even gets lost in the parking lot around the Winn Dixie. Columbia or Atlanta I could understand, but not the local Winn Dixie parking lot. Mother has good days, but her bad days, which are so unpredictable, are heart-breaking to watch."

"I'm surprised that she's in a nursing home. In the early stages of Alzheimer's, it's often possible to stay home," I said.

"We're doing our best. People don't understand her situation," Laurel said. "Mother was home alone and forgot she had food cooking. If a neighbor had not seen the smoke, I don't know what would have happened."

"I'm sorry, Laurel. I didn't mean to sound accusatory."

"Most people don't understand how difficult it is, Adrian," Laurel said, tightening her lips.

"Laurel visits her mother practically every day," J.D. added.

"I'm sure that it is hard," I said.

After our dinner orders were taken and while we waited for our dinner, Laurel asked Rachel if she would like to join her in the powder room. While Laurel and Rachel were away, J.D. and I were left alone at the table. "Buddy, you've done well, real well. Rachel's a knockout."

"She is beautiful. How did you get to know her?"

"Well, it's like Rachel said. Rachel took a class with me and she worked real hard to get an 'A.' We became acquainted outside of class."

"How long has she been in Caruthers' Gap?"

"About a year. Adrian, are you thinking seriously about her?"

"No," I said shaking my head. "We just met."

"That grin says something different. What gives, or rather who's been giving?"

"Nothing like that. Since Meredith died, I've been involved seriously only once, but it didn't work out.

"Be careful, Buddy. Rachel is a woman with ambition."

"Ambition?"

"Rachel's dedicated to what she wants. She'll do most anything. Just be careful."

"I will," I said. "Laurel looks wonderful."

"She can still hold her own with anyone." J.D. smiled. "Now. Tell me about your daughter."

"Caroline is almost thirteen years old."

"The adolescent years. That will put more gray around your temples."

"It already has. She does well in school. Really interested in music."

"How has she adjusted since her mother's death?"

"Seems okay. We've been to family counseling. It's hard not having a mother. Fortunately, Meredith's Aunt Morriah provides a lot of interest in and guidance for Caroline."

"Good."

"You and Laurel don't have children?"

"No, not that we haven't tried. Maybe for the best. Children might not fit into our lifestyle."

"You quickly learn that you fit into their lifestyle."

"Yeah."

"How have things been between you and Laurel?" I asked, using my best clinician's voice—calm, slightly warm and yet remotely and appropriately detached, avoiding all appearance of being inappropriately voyeuristic. I wondered if I were being too personal and intimate with my old friend. I was reasonably sure that I would not be candid if I were asked such a question, even if it were by a trusted friend.

"With women, you never know," he said quietly.

"What do you mean?" I asked, while staring down and rearranging my fork.

He looked at me straight in the eyes, glanced briefly down toward his plate and then once more looked straight into my eyes, and said, "Sometimes I just don't understand her."

Beneath his brief sentence, I sensed deeper emotions. "People, male or female, are always hard to understand," I said quickly, trying to put my old friend at ease.

"Yeah."

"Can we talk about Ora Mae?" I asked, knowing that we had spoken enough about Laurel. We needed to change subjects, and I needed to find out about Ora Mae.

"Not tonight. As you can see, Laurel is easily bothered, especially by old memories. Here they come."

Our meal was served and our conversation centered largely on safe childhood and adolescent memories. I was sure that Rachel must be bored. Instead, Rachel insisted that she was fascinated with friends' reminiscing about their school years.

At the conclusion of our meal, Rachel asked, "Would you like to come to my apartment for a nightcap? Adrian?"

"I'm sorry, but it's getting late. I promised to pick up Caroline. Maybe another time."

"Another time for us, too," J.D. insisted.

I intentionally took a longer route to her apartment, winding through the hills of Caruthers' Gap, blaming my choice on my confusion with directions and on my poor night vision. Rachel did not seem bothered. At her door she said, "Are you sure that you can't come in for our own private night cap?"

Her invitation was tempting. One phone call to my sister would free me for the night, the whole night. When she turned away to unlock the door, my hands wanted to reach out and touch her.

"No, I can't. Not tonight."

"You don't know what you're missing."

"Oh, I have a pretty good idea." We both laughed, feeling both the warmth of the night air and the warmth of our exchange.

"Your choice. See you tomorrow at Ora Mae's house."

I let Rachel close the door that night. I loosened my tie, unbuttoned my collar button, and thought that Azure Eyes could have been doing that for me.

Within minutes, Rachel was on the phone saying, "I called as soon as I could. Don't draw premature conclusions. I know men. Trust me."

Rachel took off her shoes as she listened. "Yes, I'm well aware of the deadlines. Everything is going as planned," she said. "I'll let you know when I make progress. I will. Good night."

"When will this business be over?" Rachel asked herself. She reached for her glasses, glanced at the clock, and headed for her computer.

Caroline ran to the car when I pulled up in front of Maggie's house. I waved to Maggie on the porch as we drove away. "Did you have a good time?" I asked.

"Yes," Caroline said.

"I'm glad."

"There was one thing that happened, Daddy," Caroline said.

"What's that?"

"Aunt Maggie kept asking me why you don't counsel any more. She kept asking and asking."

"She did?"

"What am I supposed to say when she or anybody else asks me?"

"What did you say?" I asked.

"I just said you were too busy to counsel. You were too busy writing books. Was that the right thing to say? I wish people wouldn't ask."

"I know. You gave a better answer than I could have given."

Caroline smiled and said, "Good."

"That will be our answer from now on," I said.

"Okay."

/‹‹‹≈

"Calm down, honey," he said.

"Calm down?" Laurel exclaimed, pacing the bedroom floor. "We're talking about my mother."

"I know, I know," J.D. said. "You're just way over the line, sugar. No one's going to hurt her. I promise."

"You promise?" Laurel said, moving closer to him and slowly putting her hands about his waist.

"You always know how to get what you want," J.D. said with a growing smile and pulling her body closer to him.

"Of course, as long as I give you what you like," she said, bowing and bending her head toward her husband.

/‹‹‹≈

The next morning the Reverend Samuel T. Cobb maneuvered out to his front-yard azalea bed as he did each morning. Aided by a walking cane, he carefully guided his two hundred and fifty pound frame down the sidewalk. Meticulously bending down, using his cane to prod the morning newspaper from under the bushes, Samuel T. held his breath, bent his knee, said a morning prayer and picked up the local newspaper.

Once inside his breakfast room, Samuel T. turned to the second page. Reading the morning obituaries was as much a routine for him as drinking his three cups of perked black coffee. As he sipped his coffee, Samuel T. smiled, remembering the argument with his wife Claire. Claire nagged him to switch to instant decaffeinated coffee. "Samuel T., the doctors say that the caffeinated coffee is bad for your heart," Claire had said.

To which, Samuel T. responded, "I'll have none of that. I won't defile the temple of the Holy Spirit by polluting it with some decaffeinated coffee, instant at that."

"Yes, Samuel T.," Claire had said dutifully.

Each morning before Samuel T. read the morning obituaries, Claire filled the old percolator given to her on her wedding day. Carefully she measured out the spoons of coffee from the clown ceramic jar. Once the container had been devoted to the homemade spiced apple cookies she had made for her children. The children, like those cookies, were now only present deep in her memories. She put the *lid back on the smiling clown face. "Only you and I know, Mr. Clown," Claire said. "Half caffeine and half decaffeinated coffee. It's our little secret from Samuel T.," Claire said, talking to the jar as though there was mutual understanding.*

"What's the news today?" Claire asked as she brought the morning coffee and toast for Samuel T.

"Not much. No one died that we know," Samuel T. said.

"Why is it that you start the day looking at death? Death's almost looking us in the face every day. Won't it come soon enough for all of us?" Claire asked.

Samuel T. was silent, still engrossed in the newspaper.

"It's just like your sermons. You begin with death and end with death," Claire said.

"What would you suggest, woman?" Samuel T. asked.

"The funnies would be a good start," Claire offered.

"The funnies?" Samuel T. asked. He shook his head and reached for his coffee cup after Claire had poured the coffee. "The Lord has given me charge over his flock. It's important that I keep track of the dying."

"Oh, Samuel T. There's more to life than death and avoiding hell."

"Death is more important than life because death brings us closer to God. Death is our friend, if we are true believers."

"Samuel T!"

"Here, take your funnies." He handed the paper to Claire who turned to her favorite comics.

"I talked with Maggie yesterday," she said.

"How are the plans coming for the July 4th celebration week-end?" Samuel T. asked.

"Fine. Maggie's a real hard worker. She needs a little more organizing."

"And you can provide that," Samuel T. said.

"Maggie told me that her brother Adrian is visiting for a few days."

"Adrian?" Samuel T. put down his coffee cup. "Imagine that. The scholar, the secularist, returns to Caruthers' Gap."

"Samuel T., it's time you forgave Adrian," Claire said, putting down her paper. "That was a long time ago."

"Seems like only yesterday."

"Adrian's life went a different direction, just like our boys'," Claire said.

"Don't bring the boys into this discussion," Samuel T. demanded.

"Yes, Samuel T. But Adrian is in town and I think it would be good for you to visit with him. He was one of our brightest young people."

"*He was the brightest. He was to come back and help me in the work. He was to help us start our own private Christian school. He betrayed me, Davis, and the congregation.*"

"*He didn't betray anyone, Samuel T. Adrian has a good mind. He was meant to do more than just run a private school in Caruthers' Gap.*"

"*Where you serve, woman, whether it is with the high and mighty or the low and poor, God is pleased. This place was good enough for me. It should have been good enough for Adrian,*" Samuel T. said.

"*Adrian chose a different path. I'm sure he's just trying to follow God's will for his own life.*"

"*I doubt that,*" Samuel T. said.

"*For a man of God, you can be too easily judgmental,*" Claire said.

"*You're not to be my judge,*" Samuel T. said.

"*You're not to be Adrian's judge.*"

"*What's he doing back here?*" Samuel T. asked.

"*Maggie said that he's visiting Ora Mae Chapman.*"

"*Ora Mae Chapman. Why's he visiting that murderess?*"

"*We don't know for sure that she murdered anyone.*"

"*She murdered our dear brother, Wayne Daniels. Don't you forget it!*"

"*Ora Mae helped raise Adrian. She's always been his special friend.*"

"*Nonsense. He should have been helping us—his friends—and now he is helping a murderess who killed a white Christian brother, a pillar of the church.*"

"*Samuel T. Samuel T.,*" said Claire, shaking her head and putting down the newspaper.

CHAPTER SEVEN

Twenty-four hours had passed with no more e-mail messages. Once again Caroline was to spend most of the day under the supervision of Maggie at her cousins' house. The excitement in her voice and the brightness in her eyes confirmed for me the rightness of our visit to Caruthers' Gap. When I talked with Maggie about the plans for Caroline to spend the night with her cousins, the giddiness in Maggie's voice showed me that she was as excited as Caroline was about the sleepover adventure.

Lola met me when I arrived at Ora Mae's house around eight-thirty. "Dr. Stockwood, I'm glad you're here. Miss Ora Mae's had a bad night."

"What do you mean?"

"She's been talking all night about her daughter."

"Daughter?"

"Her daughter, Ruth. Miss Ora Mae said she's been dead more than twenty-five years."

"It's been years since I've heard Ruth's name."

"It's bothering her now. She talks about Ruth all the time."

"Mother was like that in her last days, talking about my brother who had died."

Lola nodded and said, "I need your help today. Miss Ora Mae wants to visit Ruth's grave, talked about it all last night."

"Is it safe?"

"She wants to see the grave and talk to Ruth. She doesn't have much time left. Best to do it while we can."

"Let's do it."

Gently and patiently, Lola supported Ora Mae from her bed to a folding wheelchair. Just as we were about to leave, another car pulled up in front of the driveway, and Rachel emerged.

"I was hoping to get away before she came," Lola said.

Rachel walked up to me on the driver's side of the car. "What's going on?" Rachel asked, tilting her head toward me.

"Looks like we're going on a field trip," I said, turning and smiling at Ora Mae. "Ora Mae wants to visit her daughter's grave."

"Sure do," Ora Mae said. "Get the car on the road. Get the car on the road," she repeated.

Rachel looked at Lola and asked, "Is this advisable?"

"It's what Ora Mae wants," Lola said, getting in the back seat with her patient.

"You're taking a tremendous responsibility with your patient." Rachel put her hands on the back door on Lola's side of the car.

"Like I said, it's what Ora Mae wants," Lola said, locking her seat belt.

Lola forcefully and enthusiastically closed the car door. Rachel had good reflexes; otherwise, her hand and manicured nails would have been crushed.

"Would you like to go with us?" I asked.

"Yes, I would."

Rachel got in the front seat with me. Lola passed a thermos and two large blankets forward for Rachel to hold. "Thanks so much for the extra room," Lola said.

"No problem," Rachel said, placing the two blankets at her feet and the thermos on her lap.

We listened to Ora Mae's reminiscing about the places that we passed—abandoned stores where she once shopped, aging schools where she once walked children, and deteriorating houses where deceased friends once lived. I glanced over at Rachel and noticed her writing on a note pad.

Once parked inside the cemetery and out of the car, I went to Ora Mae. "I'll need directions," I said, gripping the handles of the wheel chair.

She pointed with outstretched arm and finger. "That way." We maneuvered up and down curbs to what at one time was the black section of the cemetery, where Caroline and I had come when we first came to Caruthers' Gap only days ago.

"There, near the fence," Ora Mae said. "Miss Winnie and I came here a lot."

Near the wrought iron fence, we found the grave. A simple marker had the words, "Ruth Chapman, May 18, 1944—May 26, 1962." Ora Mae's hand reached out to touch the gravestone, missing it by a few inches. I pushed her chair forward. Her fingers outlined the letters of her daughter's name. Slowly and carefully, she followed each line and curve of the letters and breathed deeply with each movement of her hand.

"Eighteen years old," Ora Mae said. Her head and voice shook. "Just a baby, my baby."

"Tell us about her," I whispered, bending down near Ora Mae.

"She was a fussy little baby. Had the colic for months. Never could sleep with that baby, always fussing. A pretty little thing. Always smart. Taught her the ABC's myself. Always a smart child, too smart sometimes."

Ora Mae reached out for Lola's hand, and with her other hand she touched her own throat.

"Water, Miss Chapman?" Lola asked.

Ora Mae's head nodded. Meticulously, Lola poured water from the thermos into a plastic cup, as if she were pouring Communion wine, and she held it for her to drink. Beads of clear water slowly dripped from her quivering chin. "Thank you." Ora Mae's head nodded with those words.

"Would you like to tell us more about Ruth?" I asked.

"Never did have much of a chance to raise her myself. My mammy took her and raised her like she was her own. I had to go out and find work and send money back home. I did. Found work cooking, cleaning, and caring for other people's children. Never a chance to care for my Ruth, always tending to white folks' babies."

"You showed a lot of love to those children," I said.

"How did your daughter die?" Rachel asked.

"She's a high school graduate. First one in my family to graduate—all twelve years, not eleven years."

"You were proud of her," I said.

"Graduated with the best of them. She had a new pretty white dress, polished patent leather shoes, hair greased and pulled back, and a little gold-filled chain around her neck. My baby looked like a somebody. Walked up there and got her diploma just like everybody else. Nobody . . ."

Ora Mae's voice stopped as though she were in another place and in few moments she returned to us. "Nobody gave it to her, she earned it herself. Earned it herself." Her cotton patch black hair shook in the wind like a proud dandelion, making her declarations to all who would listen. "Earned it herself."

"You must have been very proud," Rachel said, moving nearer to Ora Mae.

"I was. My Ruth was going to be somebody. Been accepted at a college in Atlanta, Georgia. Miss Estelle helped her find the college. My baby was going to be a college girl in Atlanta, Georgia. The preacher helped her some, but she did it with the good Lord's help."

"What happened?" Rachel asked.

Ora Mae continued to tell the events of Ruth's short life and the details of her last day and night as though it were yesterday. She described how she sat proudly in the outside bleachers that Friday night and how the stars shined brightly from God. It was like the stars wanted a peek at her baby's graduation. Most of the faces there were black, but there were white ones, too. Ruth Chapman's name was called out. Ruth marched straight as an arrow up to that platform and took that diploma from that white man. She stood tall and she sat tall in the metal chairs on the football field.

"My whole family was there," Ora Mae recalled. "The screen door swung and slammed all afternoon and evening. Couldn't keep the flies off all the food. It was just like a family reunion—children running through the yard, men smoking on the porch, and women working in the kitchen. When Ruth got that diploma, it was like it belonged to all of us."

Ora Mae paused. Tears clouded the sparkle in her alert eyes. "Are you all right?" Lola asked, holding Ora Mae's wrist.

"I'm okay. We had all gone home that night. Ruth stayed behind, wanting to talk to her teachers. One of her teachers gave her a little book of poems. Ruth went back to thank her. We lived about a mile from the high school. Ruth said she would walk home alone. Never should have let her go by herself. She said, 'Mama, I'm a big girl now, going to Atlanta.' She never came home. The police came and told us that she had been shot on the way home from her graduation."

"Oh, God," Rachel said, turning away from Ora Mae.

"Never knew who shot her. Neighbors said some men were driving and drinking, throwing cans out the window. A shot was heard. The car drove away. They left Ruth on the side of the road, like some piece of trash. Somebody shot my baby's brains out!"

Ora Mae's eyes turned back to the headstone and once again stroked her hand gently on it as if she were caressing the head of her child. "I buried her with that little book of poems. I promised you, baby, that I would never forget you. I'm coming soon to be with you. I've told the story. People will remember Ruth Chapman, Ora Mae's daughter. I always loved you. Love you now just like the day you was born. Soon we'll read the poems together."

A few minutes passed before Lola said, "Miss Ora Mae, we need to be getting home." I moved to the wheelchair to take the handles and move Ora Mae back to the driveway.

"Not yet. One more visit," Ora Mae said.

"We need to get you home," Lola insisted.

Ora Mae raised her head, resolute, and spoke with a steady voice. "Next time I come here, I won't be rolled in no wheelchair. The undertaker will be rolling my coffin over here. I said I got one more visit to make."

I gripped the bars of the chair. "Which way, Ora Mae?" She pointed to the opposite end of the cemetery.

Once again Ora Mae guided me, up and over curbs, and around trees, headstones, and park benches. Ora Mae's entourage of three followed her as though she were royalty. "I think it's over there."

I looked at the headstone where Ora Mae had pointed. My back stiffened and my soul froze as I read the inscription, "Wayne Ray Daniels." Our stares, like bullets, darted around each other.

Lola took charge of our confusion. "Now, Miss Ora Mae, why do you want to come here? It will just upset you."

"Something I need to say to Mr. Wayne."

I bent down to Ora Mae, touched her hand and asked, "What do you need to say to Wayne Daniels?"

Ora Mae stared at the headstone and did not touch it. "You was wrong, Mr. Wayne, for not letting me bury my baby here."

Ora Mae went on to describe how she took Ruth here on her visits to Caruthers' Gap and how her daughter enjoyed running through this well-kept section of the cemetery.

"It was the prettiest place to be in Caruthers' Gap. I wanted my baby to be buried here. My family said I was crazy. They knew that no one would let a black girl be buried in white folk's cemetery. I said I was going to try."

"They wouldn't let you bury Ruth here?" I said.

"Mr. Wayne worked at the cemetery. I went to him. I had worked for him and Miss Winnie for years, mostly on weekends. I begged him to let me bury my girl here. He laughed at me, saying people would run him out of town for burying a black girl with decent white people. I pleaded with him. Somebody called the police and they took me off. The last thing he said to me was, 'Stop acting like a Martin Luther King nigger. What happened to your daughter might just happen to you. We'll be looking for a place to bury you.'"

"Ora Mae, I'm so sorry," I said, feeling ashamed for the injustice done to her.

"Mr. Wayne, I want to say that I'm sorry for what happened. Sorry that you weren't laid to rest with your people. I didn't want this to happen. All those years I hated you. I kept working for you because of Miss Winnie and Laurel. If I could have gotten my hands around your neck that day you wouldn't let me bury Ruth, I would have choked the life out of you, but I can't afford to be unforgiving. I forgive you for what you did and what you said. I ask that you forgive me, too."

Lola interrupted, "We've got to get you home." Lola took the handles of the wheelchair and began pushing it toward the car.

The ride back to Ora Mae's house was silent, no more comments on the places we passed. From my rearview mirror, I saw Ora Mae falling asleep, almost as soon as I started the car.

Once Ora Mae was safely inside her bed, Lola thanked me for taking them. "Tell her that I'll see her tomorrow," I said.

Rachel and I walked silently to our cars. "I have a class; otherwise, I would stay with you," Rachel said.

"Pretty devastating information," I said. "I knew about Ruth, but I knew nothing about Ora Mae's relationship with Wayne Daniels."

"Dinner tonight?" Rachel asked.

"What?"

"Dinner tonight?"

"Yes, that would be good. What time shall I pick you up?"

"I'll pick you up, say around seven at your motel."

I watched her car leave my line of vision. Now I understood for the first time why Ora Mae was accused of killing Wayne Daniels. When your children are hurt, whether it is a rejection or a physical attack, parents—all parents—have the ability to protect and to kill. I understood now that Ora Mae could have killed Wayne Daniels. I could not blame her, nor excuse her, but I understood.

I had made arrangements to visit with J.D. in the early afternoon about my contract with Hunter-Harwell. J.D. must have alerted Ruby because she motioned for me to go back to his office. I smiled, not wanting to interrupt her crossword puzzle endeavor. His office was filled with tobacco smoke and cigarette stubs, which were especially disturbing if his office had been cleaned the previous night. Through the smoke I saw him seated at his desk, immersed in books. Behind J.D. was his computer with a waving U.S. flag screensaver displayed.

"Very patriotic of you," I said, pointing toward the monitor.

"Dad's idea," J.D. said.

"J.D., I appreciate your seeing me," I said.

"Did you bring the material?"

"Yes."

I handed him my contracts and the Hunter-Harwell University Policy and Procedures Manual. "When do you think you would be able to let me know something?

"Today's an unusually light day." J.D. laughed. The open books and papers looked anything but light. "I should be able to get back with you by late afternoon."

"I do appreciate your reviewing the materials."

"You really want to leave your current job?"

"It's a chance of a lifetime. At my age, good positions are difficult to find in academia."

"I hope it works out for you, buddy," J.D. said. "It's good to be free to do what you want to do."

"Is something wrong?"

"No." He was quiet.

"It was good to see you and Laurel last night," I said.

"It was like old times. Rachel is a real beauty."

"Yes, she is."

"Look at that grin on your face," J.D. said. "Come on, tell me. What happened after you took her home?"

"Nothing."

"Either nothing happened or you're holding out on your old friend."

I offered J.D. no further information about Rachel. "How's Laurel handling her mother's condition?"

"Like Winnie, Laurel has good days and bad days with it. Laurel's very protective of her mother."

"Thought I might go by and visit Miss Winnie," I said.

"That would be nice. Just don't upset her, especially around Laurel. It's like Laurel becomes another person when she's around her mother. I've always known that mothers protect their daughters. Well, it's like Laurel is the mother and Winnie is the daughter."

The phone rang, interrupting our conversation.

"Yes, Ruby," J. D. said. "Yes, I understand. Tell her that I'm with someone."

I motioned to J.D. that I could easily leave. He shook his head in agreement. "Okay, send her back," he told Ruby.

"I'll speak with you later." I got up to leave.

"Wait a minute and you can see one of your old teachers. Estelle Cameron."

"She's still around?"

"Just like an old Timex watch, keeps on ticking. She comes by my office periodically, demanding that I clear Ora Mae Chapman of murder accusations."

"She also believes in Ora Mae's innocence?"

"Yes, she's one of the few who do."

We heard her footsteps outside the door. As J.D. opened the door, Estelle walked through it.

"Miss Estelle, do you remember Adrian Stockwood? He was in my class."

"Stockwood, yes, I remember. He always turned in his assignments."

"Now, I'm working on mine, Miss Estelle. What can I do for you this fine summer day?" J.D. asked.

"You can exonerate Ora Mae Chapman of all murder charges."

"You believe in her innocence?" I asked.

"I do."

"Now, Miss Estelle," J.D. began, "You know I can't do any more for Ora Mae than I'm already doing. I'm allowing her to die peacefully in her own home."

"Horse feathers," Miss Estelle said. "It's my fault that she's been accused of murder. It's all my fault."

"What do you mean?" I asked.

"Adrian, don't get involved. We've been over this time and time again," J.D. said.

"Why is it your fault?"

"I was the one who arranged for the septic tank in Ora Mae's yard to be replaced," Miss Estelle said.

"You were?" I asked.

"Yes, she was in the hospital. I knew she had been having difficulty. It was to have been a surprise for her."

J.D. moved me toward the door. "Adrian, I'll be in touch with you later today. Leave a number with Ruby where I can reach you."

"Okay. Goodbye, Miss Estelle."

"Come by and see me if you really want to help Ora Mae," Estelle added.

Leaving the room, I could not escape from Estelle's words "if you really want to help Ora Mae."

When I arrived, an older Cadillac was parked in Maggie's driveway. Familiar inside voices reverberated to the front porch as I knocked on the door.

"Come on in, Adrian. Guess who's here? The Cobbs," Maggie giggled. Maggie always had the annoying habit of answering her own questions.

"Is Caroline ready?"

"Just a minute. You have time for a cup of coffee? We always have time for coffee at this house."

Maggie ushered me to her kitchen and dining room table. The tablecloth was spotless. My eyes glanced at the open trashcan. A large plastic wrapping paper with a tablecloth label peeked over the can's rim. Just like our own mother would do, Maggie had taken out a new tablecloth for her special guests. In Maggie's thoughts there was no one grander than Samuel T. Cobb and his wife. Samuel T. had been instrumental in Maggie's husband's Christian conversion. Both Maggie and the local law enforcement would be eternally grateful.

"It's so good to see you," Mrs. Cobb said. Her small frame had not changed in years. The last time I saw her was at my mother's funeral. In this very room, Mrs. Cobb filled mismatched plates with food for family members, and hungry neighbors.

"Nice to see you too, Mrs. Cobb," I said. Mrs. Cobb rose from her seat and gave me a hug.

"Reverend Cobb," I said. "Good to see you, too."

"Adrian," Samuel T. Cobb said, neither rising nor extending his hand. "What brings you back to Caruthers' Gap?"

"To visit his family," Maggie said. "Coffee, Adrian?"

"No, thank you," I said.

"More for you, Reverend Cobb?" Maggie asked.

"Yes, Precious."

"I didn't hear you say why you were visiting Caruthers' Gap, Adrian," Samuel T. Cobb said.

"To visit family, as Maggie said. And to visit Ora Mae Chapman."

"Why would you want to visit her?" Cobb demanded.

"She's my friend and she asked to see me. She wants me to help her."

"That interference will lead to trouble, Adrian. Sounds more like some of your liberal learning and practice," Cobb said.

"Liberal learning? I don't understand."

"The table of a friend isn't the place for such talk," Mrs. Cobb said.

"Strange that you should now become the Good Samaritan, Adrian, especially when you refused to come back and help me build a Christian school as we had planned when you were in college. Never should have helped send you to that school. All their graduates are such liberals. Should have insisted on sending you to one of our Bible colleges. Your life would have been different then."

"Yes, sir, it would be different."

"What do you hope to accomplish by visiting this woman?" Cobb asked.

"I hope to give her some peace of mind, and I promised to help her with the murder accusation."

"Help her. The only way the woman can be cleared is to confess her sin, repent, and ask God's forgiveness. The plan is simple. It's been the same plan since Cain and Abel."

"That's provided she's guilty. If she's innocent, another must confess and repent."

"Another?" Cobb asked.

"If Ora Mae didn't kill Wayne Daniels, then someone else did," I said.

"That talk may be safe around some kitchen tables, but in the wrong kitchens, it will get you in trouble, son."

Caroline's appearance at the kitchen door could not have been better timed. "Daddy, let's go," she said.

"Let's." I turned to Maggie. "I'll bring her back for the sleep-over later."

We hastily parted from Maggie's kitchen, leaving my sister alone to enjoy the company of Claire and Samuel T. Cobb.

When Morriah returned late that afternoon from her bowling excursion with Caroline, I told her abut my visit with J.D. and his subsequent phone call. "Exactly what did he say," Morriah asked.

"Looks like the university holds the best hand. Unless they choose to release me from the contract, I am bound by the agreement."

"What would happen if you just didn't show up for class?"

"The university could sue me."

"What would they get?"

"Very little, as you well know," I said. "But it would damage me more than just financially. No university would hire a prospective faculty member who did not honor his contract."

"Any other options?"

"J.D. suggested that I offer to buy my contract from the university."

"Buy it?"

"My thoughts exactly. I need to go and talk with Adams again and try one more time to be released from the contract. I'll call his office tomorrow and arrange a meeting as soon as possible."

"Anything else?" Morriah asked.

"You've always had the ability to read me, haven't you?" I said.

"It's not difficult reading," Morriah said. "What is it?"

"Something that a former school teacher said to me today."

"Choke or spit it out. What did she say?"

"She asked me if I really wanted to help Ora Mae."

"Well, do you?" Morriah demanded.

"Of course, but what can I do?"

"You can start by believing in her," Morriah said. "Caroline does."

"What does Caroline know about any of this?"

"Caroline believes in her because she raised and loved you. For Caroline, it's that simple."

"We'll talk later. You're going to take Caroline over to Maggie's house for the night, aren't you?"

"I said I would."

"I may be out late tonight," I said.

"I see." Morriah's eyes scanned my attire. "Well, please use some discretion and protection, if you know what I mean."

Caroline stuck her wet head through the door. "I'm through, Aunt Morriah. It's your turn."

"I'm coming," Morriah said. Before she closed the bedroom door, Morriah turned to me. "Adrian, think about this. Has anyone ever believed in you, even when circumstances seemed to indicate otherwise? Just think about it."

CHAPTER EIGHT

The next morning I awakened early and refreshed. The freshness was not without some anxiety. I had taken a risk spending such late hours with Rachel. What if something had happened to Caroline last night and I could not be reached? She would not have been able to reach me. Thankful that I had insisted on driving my own car to her apartment, I had left Rachel and arrived back at the motel around two in the morning. I had fumbled with the keys and raced to the phone. The message button was not lit. No phone messages. Morriah, if she were awake in the next room, kept quiet.

Winnie Daniels' nursing home was a modern complex, clean, efficient, and disinfectant scented. The receptionist, a young girl, possibly a high school or college student working for the summer, walked me to where I would find Miss Winnie. Along the way, I observed there were no patients sitting in wheel chairs in the hallways, always a good sign. Through the glass partition overlooking an inner courtyard, I saw men and women working in a small garden area with two attendants present.

"They love to work the soil. It's good for them to feel useful. Of course, we carefully wash the dirt from under their fingernails," the young girl said.

I nodded.

"Mrs. Daniels has another visitor, her daughter, Mrs. Morgan."

I looked up and saw Laurel on her knees in the soil along with an older woman. The receptionist left as I approached Laurel. "Good morning," I said.

"Adrian, what are you doing here?" Laurel looked at me, puzzled.

"I just wanted to visit your mother. It's been a long time and I don't know when I'll be back."

Laurel moved toward me with her back to her mother. "I don't want you upsetting her, Adrian. Don't ask questions about Ora Mae or Dad." Her tone of voice told me that she would not allow any compromise of her position.

"I'm here only out of respect."

"Then you may stay," Laurel said.

Laurel put her hands on her mother's shoulders and guided Miss Winnie as she stood up and turned her to face me. "Mother, do you remember, Adrian? We played together as children."

Miss Winnie tilting her head to Laurel, remained silent. Laurel again said, "Mother, do you remember Adrian? We played together as children." Miss Winnie showed a childlike smile, her mouth open wide conveying a mixture of surprise, wonder, and silence.

Miss Winnie was the woman that I remembered falling in love with at first glance. She was beautiful, reminding me of a picture of a Greek goddess that I had seen. Her blonde hair was pulled back on her head, her eyes dark brown, and her skin porcelain white. She always wore pearls and at home, she always wore an apron. She made the best peanut butter cookies.

Her smile and sweet soft flowing words had enchanted me with their calmness and warmth. Words in my family were few and loud, often burning body and soul. Words from Miss Winnie were a delight and an enchantment, nourishing my mind and spirit. I had toyed with the fantasy of either marrying her or making her my mother. Either way I loved her.

When Miss Winnie turned and bent to work in her garden spot, I was sad. "Your mother's still lovely with her pearls and earrings," I said.

Laurel nodded her head. "I suspected you were always in love with her."

"You both stole a part of my heart years ago."

"Did we?"

As Laurel motioned for me to sit near her on the concrete bench, I felt that our old friendship had been restored. While we were good friends in elementary school and junior high school, we had drifted apart in high school and college. Only a few kind words had brought us together again.

"We've changed a lot since those early years, grown older," said Laurel.

"Yes, but you look just as young to me."

"That's only because you've gotten older." That was the first time that I had heard her laugh on my visit. "College, marriages, trips abroad, divorce, children, death. We've experienced first hand all those events that seemed so remote when we first read about them in literature class."

"Divorce?" I asked.

"You don't know my secret, do you? You were away. I married while in college to a law student. The marriage lasted only a few years, until I had financially supported him through his last years of law school," she said with no bitterness in her voice, only flatness.

"I had no idea."

"Life has lots of surprises," I said.

"Our only child died shortly after birth. We drifted apart. He turned to his law practice and his secretary. I went back to school. In the end, it was friendly enough. Neither one of us cared enough to fight."

"Laurel, I had no idea."

"We kept it a secret."

We both watched her mother work in the soil, planting her marigolds. We listened to the faint words of a song that she sang to herself. The others around her were planting flowers, but Miss Winnie moved the soil with her bare hands, as if living in her own world.

"How did you and J.D. get together?"

"In Columbia. I was doing graduate work and J.D. was at the law school. Davis helped get us back together."

"We came back when Mother's condition became more serious. Then last year, J.D.'s mother died."

"Lots of travel back to the same place," I said.

"Enough about me. So how are you handling mid-life? Any crises?" Laurel asked.

"None that I'll admit to."

"Sounds wise."

The receptionist interrupted our conversation. "Mrs. Morgan, your husband wishes to speak with you. The nearest phone is at the desk."

"Adrian," Laurel said, "will you watch Mother?"

"Of course."

I watched Miss Winnie move her hands among her flowers. Laurel had told me earlier that some days she was less angry and more coherent than other days. Today was a good day for us all.

"Your flowers are looking pretty, Miss Winnie."

"Who are you?"

"Don't you remember me? I'm Adrian Stockwood."

"Never heard of you. Never heard of you." Her voice and head were resolute.

"I played with your daughter Laurel when we were children. I came over to your house and you would give us chocolate milk, peanut butter cookies and, sometimes, ice cream."

"Never heard of you. You're here to get me, aren't you? You're here to take me off to the jail. Going to lock me in the pen. A jail bird." Miss Winnie's voice was becoming higher and higher. Fire burned in her eyes and in her voice.

Suddenly she marched around the courtyard, oblivious to her steps, sometimes missing and other times stepping on the flowers planted and unplanted. Her movement was like a lively dance to the chorus as she shouted, "Jailbird! Jailbird! Jailbird!" The words she cried were like the sounds of a little train picking up stream, moving ahead. Each word, spoken a little louder, energized her. Her momentum increased and increased as she ran around the courtyard. She had not made it around the courtyard once before a male attendant stopped her. His thick arms, hairy and tattooed, grabbed and restrained her.

Miss Winnie pleaded. "Please don't hurt me! Please don't hurt me!"

I moved to her, wanting to reassure her that she was safe.

She screamed, "Don't take me away! I didn't mean to do it! It was an accident! It wasn't me. Was it? Please don't punish me! Don't hurt me!"

The next sound I heard was the movement of running high heel shoes on the tile floor outside the courtyard. "What's happened?" Laurel demanded.

"Mrs. Daniels has gotten a little agitated. She'll be all right. Mrs. Daniels, let's go back to your room now," the orderly said.

"Laurel, one minute your mother was fine and the next she was screaming," I said.

"You see why we can't let anything upset her."

The attendant walked away with Miss Winnie. Laurel turned to me before joining them. "You see why I don't want your talking about Dad or Ora Mae? I can't bear to see her upset!"

"I understand."

"I've lost my mother. She's dead. I have no one. Her mind wanders. Occasionally, she's coherent. Other times, she doesn't recognize me. She's dead, Adrian. Dead, but alive."

Laurel hurried off with the attendant, leaving me to walk out alone. At the desk as I was leaving, I saw a familiar figure, Davis Morgan. He was an older man, in his sixties at least. His white crew cut hair was a 1950s nostalgic advertisement, the kind my father wore.

"Davis," I said. He looked toward the sound of my voice.

"Adrian, it's good to see you! I was glad to hear that you were coming. You should have called me when you arrived."

"I know. I have been busy. It was good to get your phone call."

"Likewise, boy! You need to get back here to see your family and friends more often. You're looking great!"

"Thanks. What are you doing here?"

"I make visits to the nursing home for the church. You'd be surprised how many people a man my age knows in nursing homes. What are you doing here?"

"I came to see Laurel's mother."

"I see."

"She was such a good friend."

"And a good teacher. Kept J.D. in school. How's she doing today?"

"Not well. Laurel's become real upset. She's with her mother now."

"Too bad. Such a shame for a beautiful and smart lady. What about your visit with your family?"

"It's been good to see everyone. I've been visiting Ora Mae Chapman."

"How is she doing? We hear she's eat up with cancer."

"Good days and bad days."

"The town's been a turmoil since they found Wayne's body. Upsets everybody."

"Apparently Miss Winnie, too," I said.

"Of course, it would. She was Wayne's wife and he was Laurel's step-dad. Adrian, we owe it to them to help them get through these days."

"I know."

"We have to do what we can for everybody. Look at the time. I'll be calling you soon to get together for one of our lunches. I want you to stay and participate in our July 4th church services."

"I'd love to have lunch with you."

"What about the church services?"

"We'll see. I'm not sure how long I'll be in town."

"Good to see you, son," Davis said, casually turning and moving easily down the hall.

That afternoon Caroline and I went to visit Ora Mae. Lola had said that Ora Mae might have strength for a brief afternoon visit. It had been years since Ora Mae had seen Caroline. She was sitting up in the iron bed when we entered the bedroom.

"I brought Caroline to see you," I said.

"It's about time," she said.

"Daddy's slow about some things," Caroline said.

"I know it, too," Ora Mae said. "Come here, girl."

Caroline moved, inch-by-inch in fear and in awe, to where Ora Mae's head rested. Ora Mae reached out her hand and Caroline cradled Ora Mae's hand in her own. "You look like your daddy," she said, "except a lot prettier."

Caroline muttered a soft thank you.

"Tell me something good about yourself."

Caroline looked to me. I nodded. "Soon I'll be thirteen. I like music. I like to read. I like being here and visiting my cousins."

"That's good. You need to get to know your family. I always told your daddy that."

Once again Ora Mae had made her position known, often talking to adults through carefully chosen words to children. For the next half-hour, Ora Mae shared stories about my family and me with Caroline. Caroline asked questions, but mostly she listened.

That evening after we had returned from our visit with Ora Mae, Morriah knocked at my door.

"What, no date tonight?" Morriah asked.

"No, not tonight."

"Going to spend some time with Caroline?"

"Yes. She's in the next room watching television. I'm catching up on some computer work."

"Her watching television and your working on that computer is not time spent together."

"What do you mean?"

Morriah closed the door that separated my room from the room that she and Caroline shared.

"Adrian, I don't like to tell you how to run your life."

"Since when?"

"Caroline is my great-niece and Meredith is dead. I have to speak my mind. You need to spend more time with the girl. If you don't spend time now, you'll pay for it when she's older. If you don't start spending some time together, and I don't mean watching television, you'll lose her. You'll both lose in the end."

"Morriah, I'm doing the best I can."

"Are you?"

"Yes, I'm trying to make a life for Caroline and myself. I've got to work on my career or I can't support her. I'm trying to give her opportunities that I didn't have."

"Opportunities for whom?"

"For her—school, art, concerts—things I never had."

"That girl doesn't need just things, Adrian, she needs her father."

"I'm doing the best I can."

Morriah shook her head. "I'm going out for the evening. It's up to you." Morriah went to the door, paused, and turned back to me. "You're depriving her of something that you've always fussed about."

"What's that?"

"You're depriving her of your attention, just like you said your daddy did to you." With those last words, Morriah slammed the door behind her.

CHAPTER NINE

Winnie Daniels' outburst at the nursing home was disturbing not only to Laurel but also to me. How coherent was she? I phoned Laurel for the stated purpose of apologizing for being present at her mother's outburst. I was pleased with her response to my phone call, inviting me to her home. The maid directed me through the Morgan house to the backyard pool. Approaching the pool, I noticed the lawn chair with a black and white striped towel carefully folded over the seat of the chair. From the deep end of the pool, Laurel called out to me, "Bring me my towel, Adrian."

I never knew the right words, especially adjectives, to describe Laurel, I thought. She was like a flavor that could not be named, only experienced. You could taste it, but were unsure what it was that still lingered on your tongue. Was it sugary, spicy, tangy, bitter or something in between? I had never known. I only knew that she had been a candy of my youth which I had once secretly longed to taste. Even now as a middle-aged adult whose taste buds were diminished and yet more knowledgeable and refined, I still could not name this piece of untasted candy, this Laurel.

Bending down and grabbing her towel, I discovered that it hid the top of a woman's two-piece bathing suit. Immediately I looked up toward her, scanning her frame. Laurel was topless and treading water. I did not move.

"Guess I'll have to come to you," Laurel shouted. She turned over and floated on her back toward me, her hands pushing the water back and forth from her hips. While I waited at the shallow end of the pool for her, my eyes watched her slender and bronzed figure emerge from the pool. Her wet breasts glistened in the sun.

"Embarrassed?" she asked. "Well, you shouldn't be. The three of us used to go swimming at my granddad's place. Give me the towel."

We had never swum like this, I thought, tossing her the towel. She moved up the pool stairs, taking the towel and hanging it around her neck. Depending upon her body movement, the towel teased my eyes, both hiding and revealing her flesh. Laurel looked nothing like the twelve-year-old girl, in the white choir robe, I remember coming from the baptism waters at Sydney's Creek.

"Have a seat," she said, sitting in the lounge chair.

"Sorry to have interrupted your swim," I said. I twisted in my seat, not knowing in which direction I should face.

"No, it was over," she said. "I always enjoyed swimming in the morning. It works up my appetite for lunch. What about you?"

"I don't swim much anymore."

"I didn't mean swimming, silly. Your appetite? Would you join me for an early lunch in the pool house? Lucille can make us something light."

"No, I need to get on to Brunson as soon as possible."

"What can I do for you, Adrian?"

"I wanted to talk about your mother and Ora Mae?"

"Mother? Why?" Laurel reached for another towel and began drying her hair.

"Well, Ora Mae worked for your mother."

"Like she did for yours."

"Laurel, do you really believe that Ora Mae killed your stepfather?"

"It's not important what I believe. The evidence points to her."

"I asked if you believe that she killed your step-father?"

"Adrian, I've learned it's safer to be detached. Just the facts, no emotions. J.D. taught me well. I'm not the same person you once knew."

"I understand your wanting to protect your mother."

"Protect my mother from what? Mother's lost her mind. You can't believe anything she says. She doesn't need protecting, but I would if I needed to." Laurel picked up a hairbrush and stroked her hair.

We were both quiet. "We're not going to get anywhere with this, are we?" I asked.

"Not about Ora Mae. But we could go elsewhere." Laurel dropped her brush.

I bent down to pick up the brush. Laurel moved toward me, putting her hand on my knee. Slowly she stroked my leg, moving her cupped hand up my thigh. I breathed deeper, enjoying her attention. It could only have been for a few seconds, but it felt longer.

"No, Laurel." I moved her hand away. Her face was close enough so that I could smell her breath. "You've been drinking," I said.

"I drink a lot, Adrian. It helps relax me. I can help you relax, Adrian."

"No, Laurel. J.D. . . . ."

"What makes you think he cares?"

"Laurel, you're his wife."

"J.D. has had his own interests."

"Own interests?"

"You'd be very surprised. Come, to the pool house."

"No, I can't."

"Don't kid yourself, Adrian. Sure you can. You're just not yet willing to admit it."

"Laurel, I'm going now."

"Just like little Adrian, little boy with big dreams and no guts, always trying to live within the lines. I've lived within the lines, Adrian, and it doesn't work for long. Go to Rachel. Hope it satisfies, if you've got the courage to pursue it, but stay away from my mother." Her voice frightened me like the taunts of childhood bullies on the playground. I left her by the pool.

The phone rang. "Hello, Davis," Maggie said, "give me a sec." Maggie went to the portable dishwasher connected to her sink and turned off the machine. "That dishwasher makes so much noise. One day I'll have a big kitchen with a quiet machine. You don't care about my old problems. What can I do for you? Tom's not here. You want me?"

"Do you know where I can locate Adrian?" Davis asked. "I want to arrange to have lunch with him."

"Well, Adrian left Caroline with us this afternoon. They're out in the backyard in the old tree house, talking about boys, I imagine. Where is he? He said he had to get back to Brunson. I think something about going to visit Hunter-Harwell. He's trying to get out of his teaching contract there. He wants to leave and go somewhere in North Carolina. I forget where. I hate to see him go off to North Carolina. We'll probably never see him or Caroline. Adrian's girl reminds me so much of me when I was little. Caroline and I have the same color hair, same texture. Not like my own little girls, bless their hearts, but they got their daddy's black hair and brown eyes."

"Did he mention who he was going to see?"

"It was a Bible name, an Old Testament name. Somebody named Adams, I think. Tom tells me that you're thinking about making him manager of your shop."

"It's under consideration, Maggie. Tom's a good man, someone I can count on. Know what I mean? It's important that everyone who works with me plays with the team. I am the team."

"Tom's the same way, Davis. The same way. Okay. Talk to you later now."

Maggie reset the portable dishwasher. Its noise of whirling flowing water filled the air and Maggie's ears. "I hope Tom gets that promotion. I'm getting tired of mama's old dishwasher. Getting tired of all these old things," she said. "I want some new things."

By afternoon I was at Hunter-Harwell and outside of Adams' office. Seated behind his massive desk, Adams did not rise when I entered the room but motioned for me to have a seat directly in front of him. "What can I do for you, Dr. Stockwood?"

"I still wish to be released from my contract with Hunter-Harwell," I explained. "I received your letter. I hope you and the Executive Council will reconsider my request."

"When do you wish to be released from your contract?"

"Immediately."

"Immediately. I assume that means to be released from the fall schedule."

"Yes," I said. I could have taken a chance and asked for a spring release. Duke University would possibly agree, but I would try for concessions if my initial request were denied.

"That creates a very difficult dilemma for us, Dr. Stockwood."

"In what way?" It was my turn to make him be more specific.

"Good instructors are difficult to find at best but given these eleventh-hour changes, it would be virtually impossible."

"Surely you could find a full-time instructor or contract the classes to an adjunct. We've done that before," I said.

"As I said, good instructors are difficult to find at the last minute."

"You're denying my request," I said.

"As presented, yes, I'm denying your request."

We both sat in silence. He used the words "as presented." Adams was the most carefully articulate individual I had ever known. Knowing Adams' preciseness and deliberateness in language had proven valuable to me on more than one occasion.

"You said 'as presented.'"

"That's correct."

"Are you open to other possibilities?"

"We're both men of the university, which means, of course, we're open to possibilities."

"What will it take to be released from my contract?"

"You've learned the art of directness."

"I'm waiting for the same, in turn," I said.

"I've had our legal advisor review your contract, as well as the contract signed by you for your sabbatical in England. You are under obligation to us for two years."

"Go on."

"Those wishing to avoid contractual obligations can purchase their contracts."

"How much?" I asked.

"Forty thousand dollars."

"You're joking," I said.

"I'm not attempting humor."

"Forty thousand. My annual salary is not much more than that!"

"That's true, but it would compensate for our investment in your sabbatical and it would allow you to pursue career plans elsewhere."

"I don't have forty thousand dollars cash."

"Don't underestimate your resources. Assets can be liquidated."

"My other option would be to leave and break my contract by not appearing in class," I said.

"Theoretically, yes. We both know that you won't do that. You're one of those men who still has glimmers of honor about fulfilling a commitment. Besides violating your idealism, pragmatically, your career would be placed in jeopardy."

"I suppose that ends our discussion for the moment," I said.

"You have choices to make. Either you will be in class as scheduled for the fall or you will be forwarding a check for forty thousand dollars to Hunter-Harwell. Good day, Dr. Stockwood." Adams had not moved throughout our visit.

On the drive back to Caruthers' Gap, I mentally reviewed my situation. The farther I drove away, the more I wanted to leave Hunter-Harwell forever. My best professional future was to go to Duke. My only option was to buy my contract. To raise that much would involve cashing in the value of some insurance policies, and using money from Meredith's insurance policy that had been designated for Caroline's college education. Only then would I have enough money.

Two figures were near the motel pool when I returned from Brunson.

"Adrian," Claire Cobb said. "Over here."

"Mrs. Cobb?" I said. I saw Caroline in the pool and Claire's feet swishing in the water.

"Hi, Daddy," Caroline said. "Watch me."

Caroline began swimming underwater from the shallow end of the pool to the far side.

"She's a good little swimmer, Adrian," Mrs. Cobb said.

"She's made real progress from last summer. Where's Maggie?" I asked.

"Maggie had some errands to run in preparation for our July 4th celebration. I offered to bring Caroline back to the motel. I wanted a chance to talk to you. Caroline wanted to swim. I hope that was all right."

"Thank you for bringing her back. She couldn't have a better lifeguard than you. Do you still give the youth swimming lessons?"

"No, not anymore."

"You were one of the best," I said. "Not everyone can have a prize swimmer as a water instructor."

"Well, it was fun. Good going, Caroline," Mrs. Cobb said. "Now practice six consecutive dives. We'll watch."

"Still the coach," I said.

"It comes back now and then, I guess. It's good to see you, Adrian. Maggie keeps us posted on you, when she knows anything."

"I have not kept in touch much since Mother died."

"The death of parents often breaks up families forever. Honey, that's real good." Her two thumbs went up toward Caroline in approval. "I'm glad that the two of you are working on family relations."

"How are your boys?"

"We get cards every now and then from both Paul and John Mark. They live in Dallas. They work with advertising and computers or something like that."

"I see."

"And Reverend Cobb?"

"You saw him last. What do you think?" Mrs. Cobb asked.

"He seemed the same as I last remembered him—still angry with me that I didn't follow him into his ministry."

"That was a disappointment to him, especially after Paul and John Mark didn't follow the call, either. Good going, Caroline. Now sit and rest."

"All three of us disappointed him," I said.

"Samuel T. always had high hopes for having a ministry group around him. It hurt him that our own boys and you didn't follow. He's really a good-hearted man, Adrian. He's always taken his responsibilities seriously since his conversion. The Lord delivered him from gambling."

"I never knew that."

"Samuel T. spoke about it a lot in the early years."

I smiled. "He always gave glorious testimonies."

"Still does." Claire Cobb glanced at her watch. "I must be going. Please take some time to visit with Samuel T. He needs to feel that he's been successful in some young person's life."

"I'll try, Mrs. Cobb."

"Thank you," Claire said.

After Claire had given her farewells and praises to Caroline, she left. Caroline went back to the room to get ready for supper. I sat there for a few minutes, pondering what Claire Cobb had said. Samuel T. had told me many times that his own two sons had run away from God and not yielded to the call to preach. I promised him that I would be faithful. I, too, had lost the call, failing him once again. I was sad for Samuel T.

CHAPTER TEN

In numerous ways, Estelle Cameron gave the outward appearance of the stereotypical old-maid teacher, having taught in the same school system for forty-five years prior to retirement. Teaching social studies had been her first life and light to the world. Her own mother had been a suffragette before her marriage to Miss Estelle's father. Her father, a conservative banker, had encouraged their daughter in the same love of government and democratic processes. Estelle lived her life in the home of her childhood, guarding its presence as though it were alive.

Her words, "if I really wanted to help Ora Mae," troubled me. Her lingering words drew me to her. Her appearance was unsettling, a rare mixture of a Chinese dowager empress and an Anglican nun. She was dressed as always—navy blue skirt, white silk blouse and black orthopedic shoes, and a large garnet brooch, her own signature attire. She wore those garments and her single jewel as faithfully as any novitiate.

Sitting in a white rocking chair, she was enthroned on her wrap-around front porch when I visited her. On either side of steps stood massive and cracked concrete lions, as though protecting the house and occupants through the decades. Behind the lions was Miss Estelle with two Pekingese dogs at her feet.

"Who are you?" Miss Estelle demanded. "I don't have my glasses on."

The little dogs awoke from their slumber stood alert by her side. Their barks were silenced by one word from the teacher—"hush." I suspected, apart from a bite to my shins, their own real damage potential was to my eardrums and pride. I, too, stopped and replied, "Miss Estelle, I'm Adrian Stockwood, a former student."

"Once a student of mine, you say."

"Pardon me," I said. "I'm still your student."

"That's correct, young man. If you were ever a real student of mine, you shall always be. You graduated in 1970."

"'71."

"You should know. Are you a registered voter?"

"Yes, Miss Estelle, in Brunson County."

"Do you vote?"

"Every chance I get." I said, crossing my fingers behind me.

"Do you vote your conscience? Now tell the truth."

"Yes, when I understand the issues."

"It's your business to understand the issues. If you do not spend time studying the issues and voting as an informed citizen, those Russian or Chinese Communists would love to take over the United States."

"Yes, Miss Estelle." Miss Estelle was still fighting the Cold War.

"What are you doing here?"

"I've come to visit with you about Ora Mae Chapman."

"Good. Ora Mae needs all of the assistance we can provide."

"Of all the people I've talked to, you're one who believes strongly in her innocence. Most everyone believes she's guilty."

"What color are those faces you've been talking to?"

"White."

"Of course, white faces are most apt to believe anything about black faces. Likewise, black faces are most apt to believe anything about white faces."

"It's still that way?"

"It's that way when it is convenient, Stockwood. Race is a powerful word for Southerners who have little left. Issues of race can be used to avoid the real issue. Come up and sit in that chair. It is much too hot to stand in the sun."

"Thank you," I said taking a seat beside her. "Ora Mae sent for me. She wants my help."

"It is good that you're willing to live up to your obligations."

"Ora Mae mentioned that you visit her."

"As much as I can," Miss Estelle said. "Cancer is a terrible villain to witness. Both my mother and grandmother died as its victims."

"How did you come to know her?"

"Come to know her? I've known Ora Mae practically my whole life. As a young person, she worked for my mother.

Her people have been involved with my people for over one hundred and fifty years."

"Involved? You mean, slaves."

"Yes. A quarter of the blacks in this county could trace their roots back to my mother's people. Grand plantation days were long gone before I was born, but a few slave descendants worked for my family through the years."

"She worked for you," I said, not knowing what was the appropriate comment to make."

"More than just worked, Stockwood. They were a part of the family. If the truth be known, some of my blood flows through her veins." Her eyes glanced sideways. "That was a long time ago."

While I had never made the comparison before, the two of them, Ora Mae and Estelle, were kindred spirits. The only differences were skin color, education, and money. Now I understood. Estelle and Ora Mae were related not only by spirit but also by blood. "You've been friends a long time," I said, not knowing what to say.

"As I said, since childhood. Ora Mae taught me how to smoke. Don't look shocked. I'm not canonized. I've had tobacco. In return, I taught her how to read and write and helped her register to vote."

I smiled. "I'm trying to help with the murder accusations. Can you tell me anything about Wayne Daniels?"

"He was an active member of the church, but he always seemed odd. He appeared clean and sweet on the outside, a little too sweet and clean. He spent too much time with children."

"What do you mean?"

"Well, I enjoyed teaching children, but all in the correct proportion. When three o'clock came, I was ready for adult company or just my own company. Daniels was always volunteering to accompany school or church groups. He did not spend enough time at home with his wife and own daughter. Winnie and Laurel spent too much time alone. They were neglected."

"You didn't like him," I said.

"Like him? I did not trust him. He flaunted his religious airs," Miss Estelle said. "People should talk less and live more."

"It appears he was a complex man."

"He was. Stockwood, you must be careful. People do not like others prying into their secrets."

"What do you mean?"

"Wayne Daniels has long been dead, but he was popular. To many who remember him, he was good man. He did well for the town and the church. His reputation will always be less examined and be more spotless when compared to a sick, old black woman."

"I see."

"What are you plans now?"

"Talk to more people. I need to know more about his death. Do you recall any specifics?"

"It was the summer of 1964 and there was a boating accident. Everyone thought he drowned. His body was never recovered—until a year ago." Estelle stopped.

"Until they found it beneath Ora Mae's septic tank."

"Unfortunately, yes. We cannot deny that his body was discovered. Either he fell in or somebody buried him."

"Anything more?"

"Let me do some research. I have a collection of church bulletins that I kept for all those years when I played the church organ. I used to take notes on the page about the sermons, my reflections, and other things going on that week, especially when my mind wandered during Samuel T.'s sermons. I'll try again with Ora Mae. So far, she has not been willing to talk."

"Thank you."

"Stockwood, tell me, why are you willing to help her?"

"A private debt between us."

"Good reason. Now, if you will excuse me, I must prepare luncheon for my girls."

Dutifully, the attending Pekineses followed her wobble through the double stained-glass doors. My hour and my audience with her had ended.

Davis' phone call and invitation to lunch was no surprise. I was already seated at a familiar steak house in a strip mall when Davis walked through the door. His white shirt and tie that I remembered had now become an expensive two-piece suit with black alligator shoes. Matching his financial prosperity, his walk was a steady, confident one.

Several minutes passed before he came to our table. Pausing at tables and talking with the patrons, Davis shook hands and laughed. Slowly, he worked the room until he reached the small table I had chosen.

"Good to see you, son," he said. "Glad you could work me into your schedule. Sit back down. Sit down."

"You're looking great," I said.

"Have you got enough room?" he asked. His question made me think I had chosen a table too small. He had become more accustomed to larger tables, more prominent and visible.

"I'm fine," I said, feeling smaller now that he was with me.

"Good, good. Now tell me what's going on in your life."

"I've just returned from two semesters in England and I'm here visiting family and friends. I've had a chance to see J.D. and Laurel. They look great."

"The kids are doing fine. J.D. has political aspirations, you know. I encouraged him to come back home for a few years. Let the homefolk get reacquainted with him before he runs for state office. Maybe one day a national office. What do you think of the plan?"

"Sounds like a good plan," I said, even though I had never imagined J.D. in national public office.

"Glad that you agree. Where's that waitress?" Davis looked up, raised his hand and motioned for a middle-aged woman to come to our table. "Honey, could we get something to drink and some menus? Time is money for both you and me." He smiled, showing his polished upper teeth.

"Yes, sir," she replied.

Attentively and silently she took our order. Only her head nodded. "Thanks, hon," Davis said.

As we waited for the meal to come, Davis moved the table condiments closer to him. "Just want to give you plenty of room," he said.

While we ate, I continually requested the table items from him. Each time I waited for him to pass me the item and he waited for me to return it. "I'll get you all that you need," Davis said. "After all, you're our 'Hometown Star' who's come back for a visit."

"Hometown Star." I had not been called that since my undergraduate years. In fact, I was identified by that designation twice a year, at Christmas and summer breaks. Davis always used that phrase to introduce me and other college students to the congregation. "Hometown Star" had become a cue for us. We were then called upon to say a "few nice words for Jesus," in the words of Samuel T., our pastor. There was usually a small group of us, fewer than six, the "Hometown Stars," who said our words about Jesus and then waited for the collecting of the love offering.

The love offering was divided among those who had given their testimony. At the time, it felt natural and unrehearsed, a matter of testimony, witness and affirmation. When I now reviewed those scenes in my mind, I used the vocabulary of psychology. What had happened in those student worship services could be described in terms of social modeling, rewards, operant conditioning, and reinforcement. Simply say the right word and get the reward.

"We've been very proud of you, Adrian. Going off to school with so little money. We know your parents weren't able to help you much."

"Yes," I said.

"Now you're a college teacher. You've made something of yourself."

"I've been very fortunate . . ."

Davis interrupted me. "Don't make much money in teaching, do you?"

"No," I admitted. "You don't go into teaching for money. Some measure of security, yes, but not money."

"I'm surprised that you haven't remarried since your wife died," Davis said.

"I hope that one day I will. You understand how hard it is to find love again and to trust in love."

"Some loves never let you escape," Davis said.

I was amazed at his unexpected insight into how I felt. Before I could ask him to explain, Davis changed the subject.

"Never had a chance to go to college. Little money and I wasn't school smart."

"You apparently have done well," I interjected.

"Real estate made it possible. I've always had the Midas touch with investments. I know what is going to rise in value and I've invested early."

"Buying low and selling high."

"Exactly. Real estate made me successful and I made real estate successful."

I nodded, not knowing what to add. My business acumen was limited.

"I made my money without, what do you call them … college credits?"

Again I nodded.

"It's made it possible for me to help J.D. and Laurel."

"J.D. seems very successful. A huge house."

"Yes, I got it for them. Real good deal, a nasty divorce situation. I bought the house for seventy cents on the dollar. It was a present for J.D. and Laurel."

"A very generous gift."

"I want J.D. to go further in life than I ever did, further than Caruthers' Gap."

"No doubt he will."

"I wonder at times. J.D.'s ambition is too small. I have to give him a prod every now and then. You're a parent. You know what I mean?"

"Yes."

"J.D. and Laurel don't have any children. They need children. People want to elect a man with children. You can trust a man who has children. It shows responsibility."

I smiled and silently remembered the folk wisdom. My own family never regarded me as an adult until I married. Otherwise, I was always sitting at the children's table at family get-togethers along with my unmarried second cousin, Serena. Only when Meredith and I had a child did I become one of them, a "real adult."

"Couples are having children later in life now. There is still time."

"Don't get me wrong. Laurel's a great asset for man in politics. She's the perfect hostess—beautiful with real style. She's a great fundraiser—a natural. Still, a man in politics needs all his assets and limited liabilities." He stared at me. "Do you know what I mean?"

"I'm not following you."

"All this business about Laurel's father has come at a bad time."

"Bad time?" I took a drink from my iced tea.

"Yes, elections are about a year away. We need to get this matter settled."

"I'm still not following you."

"For a college man, you're green. Any hint of scandal could hurt his chances of election."

"Scandal?"

"We all thought Wayne died in a boating accident years ago. Now we've discovered that that black woman, Ora Mae, murdered him."

"That hasn't been proven," I added quickly. "Maybe something else happened."

"It's talk like that . . . that could hurt J.D. and Laurel."

"Hurt them? How?"

"Let's just say examining skeletons could be a political nightmare for anyone seeking public office. Leave it at that. Besides, the woman is dying. Wayne has been dead for almost thirty years. No good can come of this. She's the one to take the responsibility." He quickly added, "She did it."

"That hasn't been proven."

"Why are you so interested in her?" His voice sounded not so much a question as a demand.

"Ora Mae was my childhood friend and she's asked for my help. I don't know what I can do, but I am here to help her."

"Adrian, Wayne was my friend, a good man. He did a lot of good for the community and for the church. Now, he wasn't perfect. He had his faults like we all do, but he didn't deserve to be buried secretly under a septic tank. I've never asked you for anything, Adrian. Have I?"

"No, sir," I answered.

"I'm asking now. Let it pass. Let nature and the law take its natural course."

"You mean let her die with the town thinking that she murdered a man?"

"I know it sounds harsh, Adrian. When you've lived as long as I have, you learn to balance things that you thought you'd never have to balance when you were young. Which is better for all? Ora Mae will be dead anyway. We can't change that. We can spare the living, Adrian, from needless pain."

We both stared at each other.

"J.D. tells me that you've gotten an offer from Duke to teach?"

"That's right. A real chance of a lifetime," I said. He must have noticed that my inflection did not match what I was saying.

"You don't sound real excited about it."

"I'm not sure that I'll be released from my teaching contract," I said, looking down at the soiled tablecloth.

"Why not?" Davis asked.

"Hunter-Harwell is refusing to release me from my contract."

"I'm a 'let's get the job done kind of man,' Adrian. What will it take to get you out of Hunter-Harwell and into Duke?"

"Forty thousand dollars," I said.

"Forty thousand? That's a hefty buyout," Davis said, bringing a toothpick to the corner of his mouth.

"It's a fortune to me," I said. I picked up the empty sugar envelope and examined it.

"Adrian, I'm known for being a tough negotiator. Who's the lead dog in this show? Who's the one I should negotiate with?"

"That's kind of you. But I don't think it would do any good. Harper Adams is a tough negotiator, too," I said.

"Is this Adams man the one to talk to?" Davis asked.

"Yes."

"Put the sugar package down, Adrian. Let me talk to him."

"I don't think it would work."

"Let me be the judge of what works. I've been blessed to have the means to help J.D. and Laurel. Maybe I can help you, too."

"I don't know what to say," I said, looking into Davis' eyes.

"Just say, 'yes.'"

"Okay," I said. "Just talk with them."

"The Lord says, 'to whom much is given much is required,'" Davis said. "I like investing in people and in real estate. You're going to appreciate in value, Adrian. I've already invested in you. Let me invest a little more."

"Thank you," I said.

"Can I get you gentlemen anything else?" the waitress asked.

"Just the check, honey," Davis said.

"I hope you liked your service," she said.

"Couldn't ask for anything more." Davis smiled at her and turned back to me. "Good," he said. "Now, let's get out of here."

He picked up the check and examined its contents as though he were mentally re-adding the figures. "I'll take care of this."

I knew the meal was an expensive one. "Let me take care of the tip," I said.

"No, it's mine. He stood, reached into his pocket as though he were drawing a gun from his holster. He drew out a money clip and pealed off an inside bill. Getting up I noticed one lonely wrinkled dollar left behind on the table.

Outside the restaurant, a group of children and a woman sat behind a table covered with a plastic tablecloth printed in a pattern of large daisies. Plates of brownies, cupcakes and a few cakes, all carefully wrapped with clear plastic wrap, stood on display. A young girl asked loudly, "Sir, would you like to buy some baked goods? The money is to help us go on a youth trip."

"No, thanks," Davis said, "I just spent all my money inside." Davis smiled at her.

"Your brownies look good. Here you are," I said. I placed a dollar on the table, smiled, and walked away toward the parking lot.

A moment later, I heard Davis' voice and turned to him. "Adrian, here, you forgot your brownies." Davis handed me two tightly wrapped brownies.

When I arrived at Maggie's house to pick up Caroline from her shopping trip, Maggie told me that they had purchased a swimsuit. "It looks real good on her," my sister said, "and it was half price." In my family, half price had the power to turn any sow's ear into a silk purse. We were seated at the kitchen table when Caroline emerged from the back bedroom.

"What are you wearing?" I shouted. My eyes were fixed on the tiny bikini. The size of the suit and her developing figure made her look older, at least sixteen.

"I think they call it a swimsuit, Daddy." Caroline said, curling down her lips.

"I don't need your arrogance," I said.

"Daddy, there's nothing wrong with this swimsuit. Is there, Aunt Maggie?"

"I didn't think there was," Maggie said.

"Caroline, put a towel around you. Get your things, we're going to the motel."

"Daddy, this is no worse than the swimsuit that your girlfriend Rachel would wear. Why can't I wear what she would wear?"

"Caroline, wrap yourself in a towel and get in the car," I said.

"Daddy, you're embarrassing me."

"Get in the car."

"I hate you. I hate you," Caroline screamed.

"Whether you hate or love me, get in that car now!"

"Daddy!" Caroline screamed. Caroline ran from the kitchen toward the bedroom.

"Adrian, you're making too much of this," Maggie said. "It's just a two-piece swimsuit."

"Maggie, this is my business. I don't want Caroline exposing herself that way. She's only twelve years old."

"Almost thirteen."

"Almost thirteen, then. That's too young for such a swimsuit."

"It's not too young if she has the body to carry it off. Whether you like it or not, she does have the body for it, Adrian."

"Maybe she does, but she's a little girl."

"Adrian, she's a developing young woman. You're too protective of her. She told me that you don't want her to grow up."

"She told you what?"

"She told me that you don't want her to grow up."

"If this is what it means to grow up, then I don't want her to grow up."

"Is it because it makes you feel old?" Maggie asked.

"No, that's not it," I said.

"You should have had your children earlier. You waited until you were almost thirty to have the poor girl. No wonder you're afraid to watch her grow up. You're getting too old."

"Sorry, but I thought it best to wait until marriage before conceiving a child."

I paused, but it was too late to retract my thoughtless words.

"Not like me," Maggie said.

"I'm sorry, Maggie. I didn't mean to say that. I wouldn't hurt your feelings."

"What you said is true, Adrian. But what I said is true also."

"Caroline is only twelve. Twelve-year-olds dressed like that attract trouble. I want her to have more of a life than just having babies and waiting on tables."

"Like the girls do here," Maggie said.

"I want her to have a chance," I said.

"Not like me and my girls," Maggie said.

"I didn't mean it that way, Maggie. Maybe I am too protective of her," I said. "It's just that I don't want her to grow up too soon. She looks so much like her mother. I don't want to lose her too soon."

"Adrian," Maggie began.

We both heard the front door slam.

"You better go to her," Maggie said. "She needs her daddy."

In his real estate office, Davis Morgan closed the door and sat in his chair. On the desk were framed photographs of his life—Davis at various business sites in the community with ribbon cutting ceremonies.

"I need to leave town for a few days," Rachel said.

Davis Morgan stared at her. "Why?"

"I've an opportunity to fill in as co-facilitator at a national conference. It's a chance of a lifetime."

"What about your other responsibilities?" Davis asked.

"I'll have coverage with the university, and my hospice assignment shouldn't be a problem."

"What about your private assignment?"

"I'll just be away for a few days," Rachel said. "Surely there shouldn't be a problem with just a few days."

"Shouldn't be, but we can't take a chance. Can we?"

"What are you suggesting?"

"Go along on your conference. Take Adrian with you."

"*What if he won't go?*"

"*Then, my dear, you don't go.*"

"*What if I refuse?*"

"*I don't think that you'll refuse,*" Davis said. "*You still have debts to pay, don't you?*"

"*We both know that I need the money. What if I can't get him to come with me?*"

"*Don't underestimate your considerable charms,*" Davis said. "*Now tell me, what's really going on with Adrian and Ora Mae?*" Davis leaned back in his chair.

CHAPTER ELEVEN

"Why don't you come with me to Chicago?" Rachel asked, seated next to me in my car outside the Social Sciences Building.

"I don't know about that," I said. "I came to visit Ora Mae. I just can't go off and leave her."

"Adrian, you know as well as I do that she could linger for several months. Some patients do. You and I have so little time together. It would just be for a couple of days. You would love Chicago. You told me that you've never been there. It would be a chance to go to the next level in our relationship."

"I'd love to spend time with you," I said.

"You would enjoy visiting Chicago."

"I would have to make arrangements for Caroline. She can't stay alone."

"Your friend, Morriah, would take care of her. You would have only to ask."

"She probably would," I admitted.

"I promise you that it will be one of the best, if not the best, times of your life," Rachel said. Her firm body moved closer to mine. She put her head close, moved her face toward my ear, parted her lips, and kissed my ear. Her warm breath summoned my body to full consciousness.

My mind wandered as I enjoyed her breath on my neck. Always controlled and dutiful, I had lived within the lines of my moral and religious code. What I hoped and imagined to experience with Rachel in Chicago was neither controlled nor dutiful. Purely passion. I had to pursue the relationship to learn if I could love again. My response was simple. "You win."

"We both win," Rachel replied. She continued to nibble at my ear.

My small canvas suitcase was open on my bed in the motel room.

"Of course, I'll keep her," Morriah said. "I've always helped Caroline."

"You seem less than sympathetic," I said.

"I typed your counseling tests long enough to recognize a reflective statement when I hear one. Now cut it out," Morriah said.

"Just tell me what you're thinking. I know you want to."

"Stop packing for a moment." Morriah pointed toward the pajamas that I held in my hand.

"What?"

"I doubt if you'll need those."

"Is that what this is about?" I asked. "You don't approve of Rachel?"

"I'm not approving nor disapproving. Every time I see her, I see a 'red light.'"

"Not the 'red light' again," I said.

"Stop shaking that smart head of yours. You're forgetting that my 'red lights' are usually right."

"Not always," I said. "You told Meredith that you got a 'red light' when you first saw me. That turned out all right, didn't it?"

"The jury's still out on you. I'm watching. Whether we like it or not, we're joined at the hip because of Caroline."

"I see."

"Rachel's out for something," Morriah said. "What does she want?"

"Is it inconceivable that she might just want me?"

"No, that's not it. I know her type. She's after something. You can't see past her bosom. Behind that pretty façade is a calculating woman."

"If it is a façade, it is a pretty nice one," I said.

"A façade is probably all you'll get. Course, you're a man, that may be enough for the moment."

"Have you finished?"

"I'll be the one to decide if I'm finished. Besides that, Ora Mae's dying and you came to be with her. And what are you doing? You're hauling your ass, if you'll pardon the expression, to chase some ass in Chicago."

I paused from my packing. "I'll only be gone for a few days. There is no way to predict Ora Mae's condition. She could go on for weeks like this. I've spoken with Ora Mae and she's fine with my going Chicago for a few days."

"She said it was fine?" Morriah asked.

"Besides, Morriah, I don't know what more to do here. I've spoken with people. I have nothing to go on. I don't even know what I'm supposed to be doing."

"You're just going to leave her?"

"For a few days. I need some time to sort things out. I care for Rachel, more than I have for anyone in a long time."

"I see," Morriah said.

"I'm only asking that you watch Caroline while I'm gone. I'm not asking you to sit in moral judgment of my behavior."

"I told you I would. Do you need a ride to the airport?"

"No, we'll be traveling with some of Rachel's colleagues."

Estelle Cameron rose early on Sunday, as was her custom. By six-thirty she had drunk her cup of hot tea and reread the Scripture passage of her Sunday school lesson. Still in her house robe, she walked to what she still referred to as the drawing room where she sat at her mother's desk. She pulled out unlined stationery from its special cubbyhole and reached for the fountain pen filled with blue-black ink. Like each day, the next thirty minutes she would spend in letter writing. Except for letters to public officials all of Estelle Cameron's personal correspondence was by hand. She was reaching for a stamp when the phone rang, interrupting her daily ritual.

"Miss Estelle, this is Lola," the voice said.

"Yes, Lola," Estelle Cameron said.

"Miss Ora Mae wanted me to call you. She's having a real bad time with nausea, real sick to her stomach."

"The medicines aren't working?"

"No. Only one thing seems to give her any relief."

"Well, I'll do what I can. Tell her that I will be there after dinner."

After she hung up the phone, Estelle turned to the Pekingeses at her feet. "Pickles, Peaches, appears as though I'm going to go shopping. I don't like buying on Sundays, but I'll need to call Leon."

Estelle spent fifteen minutes finding Leon's telephone number. Her head shook as she dialed. "Who is this? What do you want?" Leon asked.

"This is Estelle Cameron. I wish to speak with Leon Goodman."

"This is me, Miss Cameron."

"It is I," Estelle said.

"I know it's you, Miss Cameron. This is Leon."

"Yes, I know Leon. I could always recognize your grammar and logic."

"Thanks to you, Miss Cameron."

"Please, I deserve no credit. Leon, I do not have much time. I need to purchase the agent from you again."

"Agent?"

"Yes, remember what I purchased from you several weeks ago?"

"Oh, yeah. You want some grass. You're out of grass. I understand. I understand."

"I don't like slang, Leon. However, I do wish to make an additional purchase for medicinal purposes."

"Sure thing," Leon said.

"Can we make this transaction during the ten o'clock hour? You don't have plans for Sunday School, do you?"

"No, ma'am. I don't go to Sunday School any more."

"I'm not surprised. Can you make the delivery between nine-thirty and ten?"

"Sure thing"

"I'll meet you at the backyard gate this morning. I'll be sitting in the swing with Peaches and Pickles," Estelle said.

"Peaches and Pickles. Those the two strippers I knew in Charleston? What are they doing at your house? They took a fifty from me last time. Never did give me my change. Let me talk to them."

"Peaches and Pickles are my dogs, Leon."

"Oh. Where am I going to meet you?

"At the backyard gate. The one in the back, Leon."

"Gotcha. See you then."

"Until later, Leon," Estelle said, hanging up the phone and turning to her pets. "No, you were not named for two strippers in Charleston. You were born the summer that Ora Mae and I made forty quarts of peach pickles." The dogs made no response to their mistress' words.

"Do not look at me that way," Estelle, her head shaking, said to Peaches. Peaches was sitting up, looking at her as if she were about to question her mistress. Next to Peaches, Pickles rested her head on the floor with her two paws under her chin. "I know what you're thinking, Peaches. You're thinking that I shouldn't break the law by buying marijuana. Well, there is a higher law that sometimes must take precedence. Ora Mae is sick, like my own mother. If I had known then that a little marijuana would have eased her pain, I would have bought a whole field of it. I would have planted it myself." Still Peaches had not moved. "Just stop thinking about it, Peaches. You always try to second-guess me. Be more like Pickles. Get over it. We've got more important things to do than to debate the law. Come now, I say. I've got to find Daddy's tobacco paper. Almost time to get ready

for morning worship. Leon will be here soon. I never thought Estelle Cameron would be on a first name basis with a drug dealer."

The aging teacher and church organist, with Peaches and Pickles following her, chuckled and walked to the pantry. "What would mama and papa think if they knew?"

The ride from Chicago's O'Hare Airport had the grace of an unpracticed musical piece with starts, hesitations, jerks, and stops. I could only hope the driver knew where we were going. The airport shuttle was full of Rachel's colleagues, conversing in their special jargon. One middle-aged woman sitting near the driver, whose name I had learned was Louise, turned to one of the other women in the van. Louise said, "I knew we should have taken a cab."

Another middle-aged woman seated behind the torn vinyl seat responded, "Let go of it, Louise."

"Louise, we have some issues of power re-emerging," another woman said.

"Oh, shut up," Louise said laughingly.

"Sounds like withdrawal symptoms to me. How long has it been? Twenty-four hours?"

"Almost. I'd give any two of you away for one 100 mm cigarette," Louise said.

The women laughed. Except for the driver and me, everyone seemed to have the same tiny gold-rimmed glasses, single strands of pearls or gold, black or blue suits, and walking shoes.

"Empowerment, that's what we need to stress," the obvious leader of the small entourage said. Her glasses were the thickest and her pearls the longest. "Use it throughout the session. Whether it's in the engagement, assessment, problem solving, implementation or evaluation phase of our presentation. Good idea, matching content and form."

"I knew it would come to us," Louise said. "Good group processing."

I knew enough about social work to understand their own particular jargon. I glanced at Rachel. By far she was the loveliest and the youngest of the group of women professionals. Although she was seated next to me, I felt distant from Azure Eyes.

Her eyes followed their words and gestures. Her head mimicked their nods, her eyes their expressions and her body posture their stances. Rachel even rubbed and stretched her pearls when the others rubbed and stretched theirs.

I felt alone—the only male in the shuttle—even the shuttle driver was female. I moved my hand closer to Rachel. Before, she had always responded to my gesture by moving closer. This time, she placed her hand on my wrist, guided my hand away from her. Her face did not move toward my face, as it had always done before, but she followed her colleague's conversation, entering only to say a few words of affirmation to their ideas. Louise was right about the choice of transportation. Rachel and I should have taken a cab.

After morning worship, Estelle drove herself to Ora Mae's house. Normally, she shared Sunday lunch with four women at a nearby cafeteria, but not today. "I want to see Ora Mae alone," Estelle said to Lola. After Estelle closed the bedroom door, Estelle plopped her two bags under the window. She swayed side to side, as though she were still carrying her bags, when she approached Ora Mae's bedside.

"Girl, how are you doing today?" Estelle asked.

"The pain comes and goes."

"It is a pretty day. The sun is shining brightly," Estelle said.

"Not many more sunny days for me," Ora Mae said.

"Since when did you become God? Only the Creator knows our number of days," Estelle said.

"Did you bring it?" Ora Mae asked.

"I did. Let me open the window," Estelle said.

After the window was raised, Estelle pulled a cigarette from her purse, placed it in her cracked red lips and lit the cigarette with a lighter. Estelle inhaled. "Finally, I understand what the kids were talking about in the early seventies," Estelle said.

Estelle placed the cigarette between Ora Mae's lips, permitting her to take a drag on it. Estelle removed the cigarette, allowing Ora Mae to exhale.

"Thanks," Ora Mae said, "it helps the nausea."

"I know it does."

The next few minutes were spent with Ora Mae inhaling, Estelle inserting and removing the cigarette from Ora Mae's lips and Ora Mae exhaling. "That's plenty," Ora Mae said. Estelle turned on the overhead fan.

"Best afterglow I ever had," Ora Mae said.

"It's the only afterglow I ever had," Estelle said.

Both women laughed.

"I want you to take those candlesticks on the living room fireplace," Ora Mae said.

"Take them where?"

"They're yours. I want to you have them. I worked in a fine house once. The lady gave them to me. One is chipped on the bottom but I glued it back."

"Keep your candlesticks," Estelle said.

"No, take them with you today. Promise me," Ora Mae said.

"All right. Now it is time to be serious. Tell me what happened to Wayne Daniels. I've asked you for a year. I must know so I can help you."

"I wanted Adrian to help me."

"Where is he?" Estelle asked her old friend.

"Gone to Chicago!"

"What's he doing in Chicago?"

"He and his new woman friend, Rachel, have gone to a meeting."

"He should be here," Estelle said, "helping you."

"I had hoped he would."

"Tell me, Ora Mae," Estelle said. "I'll help you. Only death will keep me from helping."

"I didn't want anyone to know. I made a promise that I'd never tell."

"We're family," Estelle said, "You can tell me. I will not hurt you."

"Turn the fan off. Too much air."

Ora Mae motioned with her hand for Estelle to draw near her. Softly, she told her well-kept story.

"Is that everything?" Estelle asked.

"The truth, so help me God," Ora Mae said.

"What do you want me to do, Ora Mae?" Estelle said.

"I don't want people thinking me a murderer. Don't want that," Ora Mae said.

"You said that Samuel T. Cobb knows the story?"

"He knows," Ora Mae said. "He knows. The man of God knows."

"Well, I will see him very soon," Estelle said. "I promise that I will take care of this matter. It is my fault for replacing your septic tank without your knowledge. If I had not interfered, no one would ever have known."

"Try to let Adrian help you. He needs to help me, not just for my sake, but for his, even though he doesn't know it yet," Ora Mae said.

"I'll give him one chance," Estelle said. "Regardless, you will be helped."

We arrived at the hotel late Sunday afternoon and planned to return to Caruthers' Gap later in the week. Rachel had suggested that we stay past the conference for a few days, but I insisted that I had to get back to Caruthers' Gap. Her presentation was scheduled for Monday afternoon. After that our time would be our own, she said, except for opportunities she would need to network.

I looked forward to an uninterrupted evening with her. No phone calls from Morriah and no concerns about Caroline. This was going to be my time, I thought. It had not been since my early days of marriage with Meredith that I felt and wanted the excitement that being with Rachel offered. I needed to discover what directions our relationship might take, whether temporary or permanent.

Rachel had made it clear at the registration desk that she wanted one king-sized bed in our room. The room originally had two full beds. Rachel was insistent, "I'm sure that you will find numerous people for this conference who would prefer two doubles to one king. Please try again."

"The only room we can offer you would be a smoking room," the clerk said.

Rachel looked at me. I nodded. Exposure to passive cigarette smoke was a small price to pay for lying with Rachel in a king-sized bed.

"That will be fine," she said.

The desk clerk, a bald man of fifty, gave a half smile, handed the door cards to Rachel and said, "I hope these accommodations will be satisfactory. If we can be of further service, please let us know."

The room held its promise—a king-sized bed with a quilted coverlet that matched the drapes and lingering aroma of tobacco. A television with in-house movies and a hospitality bar completed the room.

After we had unpacked our bags, I sat down to read the complimentary newspaper and Rachel went to the bathroom to freshen herself. Before I had finished the paper, Rachel emerged with a new scent of perfume.

"Wouldn't you like to go downstairs for dinner? Later we could go dancing," Rachel said.

"We can go downstairs," I said. "But I don't dance."

"You don't dance? Why not?"

"I just never learned. Not much sense of rhythm, I guess," I said.

"I could teach you," Rachel said.

"No, I don't want to learn. But we can go out if you would like."

"Okay, but don't be surprised if I dance with someone else," Rachel said.

The hotel restaurant was filled with dozens of conferees scattered in every corner of the restaurant and corridors in the hotel. Everyone seemed to have a nametag but me. After almost two hours we returned to our room. Rachel had chosen not to dance.

After closing and locking the hotel door, Rachel said, "I want to get to bed early tonight."

"Tired from the flight?"

"Not tired at all," she said. "I just said I wanted to get to bed early."

She came closer to me. Her hands moved to my shoulders and then under my sports jacket, pushing my jacket to the floor. Rachel unloosened my tie and unbuttoned my collar. Slowly, she unbuttoned my shirt and began moving her hands across my bare chest. I was glad I had not worn my traditional undershirt that morning. I liked her fingertips and nails pressed against my skin. She guided her hands over my ears and brought my head closer to hers. The kissing began. First, soft and subtle and then, hard and provocative.

I muttered, "Now. I want you now."

"No, not now," she said, moving away from me. Rachel pulled a jade garment from the chest and flung it over her shoulders. Walking toward the bathroom, she glanced back at me still standing with my unbuttoned shirt. "Anticipation," she said. Before she closed the door, she added her last words, "I hope you aren't too tired."

I wasted no time brushing my teeth at the lavatory outside the bathroom. One thought rushed through my mind. What should I wear or what should I not wear? It had been a long time since this question had come up. Socks were always awkward. Take off the socks. I did. No undershirt. I was again glad I hadn't worn one. It would look natural that I didn't have one on when she returned. Boxer shorts. If I took the shorts off too quickly, it would seem as though I had only one interest. Leave the boxers on. Having completed my mental checklist, I got in bed and waited.

When Rachel came back into the room, the only light on was a small floor lamp. She first went to the chest of drawers for a few minutes as though she were putting away something. It must be cosmetics, I thought. She then joined me under the covers. My arms were around her and her jade teddy.

"Now, you didn't let us go dancing," Rachel said. "I've something else in mind. I'll take the lead."

Afterwards I awakened. The digital clock radio showed that two hours had lapsed since Rachel crawled into bed with me. Her crumpled teddy was on the foot of our bed. Once again, I placed my lips on her neck. My slow kisses did not awaken her.

Conversation in lovemaking did not come naturally to me, but it apparently came easily for her. She was always asking questions, giving directions and making requests. She was always asking me how I felt about what we were doing. She demanded descriptions of my thoughts and emotions. Usually, my conversation level had been limited to pleas of "yes, no, and ah." In light of what she offered, I was willing to expand my vocabulary and self-expression.

Lying there next to her, I didn't want the night to end. Somehow I must convince her that this relationship was worth pursuing. I was willing to make myself vulnerable to her. I could not let love and Rachel escape me. I lay beside her thinking of the rightness of our being together.

The next morning, the phone rang and I reached for it before it awakened Rachel.

"What are you doing in Chicago?" the voice demanded.

"Who is this?" I asked.

"Estelle Cameron."

"Miss Estelle." I held the receiver to my chest. "Someone from Caruthers' Gap," I said to an awakening Rachel.

"Your sister gave me your phone number. What are you doing in Chicago?"

"Oh, seeing the sights," I said, looking at Rachel's naked backside.

"What's wrong, Miss Estelle?"

"I have information that could be used to give Ora Mae some peace of mind."

"What is it?"

"I don't trust phones nor elevators. I hope to see you here soon. If not, I plan to go to J.D.'s office myself. Ora Mae has the mistaken idea that you're trying to help. Up to now I haven't seen much evidence of your helping her."

"Miss Estelle, please tell me what you know."

"I'll tell you tomorrow in Caruthers' Gap. I have someone else to visit before we talk. Hope you enjoy the sights," Miss Estelle said.

I heard a quick click as Estelle hung up the phone and I turned to Rachel.

"What was that all about?" Rachel asked.

"Apparently some new information that might help Ora Mae."

"You seem doubtful," Rachel said.

"No, I just don't want to get my hopes up."

"Well, let's see if I can get your hopes up," Rachel said, pulling me closer to her. "Besides this always relaxes me before a presentation."

CHAPTER TWELVE

When the doorbell rang, Claire Cobb answered it as promptly as she had done for the forty plus years she had lived in the parsonage. The parsonage, originally a white frame house with a brick veneer added later, was located within the shadow of her husband's church. "Estelle," said Claire, "please come in."

"Thank you," Estelle said. Estelle put one bag first through the door and then the second.

"You must have come about the plans for the Caruthers' Gap High School Reunion Dance."

"No, Claire," Estelle said. "I've already delivered my contribution to the high school auditorium."

"I know the class will enjoy newspaper articles from their teen years," Claire said. "No one else but you would have thought to keep all of those articles. I'm sure that it will be just wonderful."

"Now I remember. That's where they are!" Estelle exclaimed.

"Beg your pardon?"

"I just remembered some information that Adrian Stockwood wanted. I made those posters weeks ago. I'd completely forgotten. My blood sugar level must really be off," Estelle said.

"You need to take care of yourself, Estelle. Would you like some juice?"

"No, thank you."

"At least sit down for a moment," Claire said. Claire reached out and pointed to a nearby chair.

"No, thank you. May I speak with Samuel T.?" Estelle asked.

"Yes, he's in his study. Let me tell him that you're here."

A moment later Claire returned.

"Samuel T. says to come on back," Claire said, walking Estelle to her husband's study, formerly the back screened porch.

"Good afternoon, Estelle," Samuel T. said.

"Samuel T. Are you working on your Sunday sermon?" Estelle's eyes scanned the books on the shelves.

"Yes, preparing myself so the Lord can use me," Samuel T. said. "What brings you to see me?"

"I've had an interesting visit with Ora Mae Chapman."

"Hmm. Part of your Christian charity, I suppose."

"She's my friend, Samuel T."

"I hope you're not here again asking for my help, Estelle. The woman's guilty and she's dying. Let it rest. It will keep the peace for us all."

"I've known you for more than fifty years—long before you became a preacher. I've known you to be at times narrow-minded, opinionated, and too literal. However, I've never known you to be a liar until now."

"Estelle, I could easily say the same about you. You're often narrow-minded, opinionated, and not literal enough," Samuel T. responded. "But why are you calling me a liar?"

"Ora Mae tells me that you've known all along what happened to Wayne Daniels. You have it within your power to help her and you have refused."

"I don't know what Ora Mae Chapman's been telling you, but I have nothing to say about her or Wayne."

"Are you denying what she told me?"

"I don't care what she told you. I don't want to know what she told you. The Lord will have His judgment. We don't always understand His ways, but we can follow them," Samuel T. said, rising from his chair. "Good day, Estelle. You need not come back to this house again."

Estelle walked closer toward Samuel T., placing her finger on the open Bible on his desk and tapping her finger as she spoke. "As the Lord is my witness, as long as I live, I hope I will never hear you preach from this Bible until you correct the error of your ways."

Estelle left the house, passing Claire in the hallway. Down the sidewalk Estelle walked, balancing the two bags.

Later that afternoon Samuel T.'s study, knotty pine paneled and covered with religious pictures and artifacts from around the world, was quiet when Davis Morgan entered. The books were neatly erect with unbroken spines. Samuel T. was silently looking at his Bible, which was turned to the portion of Scripture from which he had planned to preach and where Estelle Cameron had pointed her finger hours earlier.

"Samuel T., what can I do for you? I was surprised to get your phone call."

"Davis, have a seat," Samuel T. said. He closed his Bible.

"What's up?" Davis said.

"*Estelle Cameron visited me this morning. She started talking about Ora Mae Chapman. Then she asked about Winnie and Wayne Daniels.*"

"*What did you tell her?*" *Davis asked. He leaned forward in his chair.*

"*Nothing, I told her nothing,*" *Samuel T. said.*

"*Good. There's no problem then.*"

"*There is a problem, Davis. My heart is heavy with all those secrets. I'm not sure we're doing the right thing.*"

"*Heavy heart?*"

"*Yes, I'm troubled. Maybe it was wrong to keep quiet all these years. If we told the truth . . . ,*" *Samuel T. started.*

"*Told the truth. If we tell the truth, we tell the whole truth, Samuel T. or the whole gospel as you like to say,*" *Davis said.*

"*What do you mean?*"

"*How are your boys doing?*" *Davis asked.*

"*The boys?*"

"*Yes, they must be past forty years old?*"

"*Almost.*"

"*It would have been such a shame if charges had been brought against them for stealing church money.*"

"*I've offered years ago to pay you back for those funds, Davis.*"

"*Nonsense, Samuel T. I was glad to be able to help you cover those missing funds, to save the boys from going to jail and to save you from public humiliation.*"

Samuel T. stared into space, not focusing on Davis any longer. His vibrant voice, that had filled the pulpit for decades, dropped to a low monotone. "I traded my silence about Wayne Daniels for your money to reimburse the church."

"*Nonsense, there was no trade. I merely helped my pastor and friend. And you helped several members of your congregation, like a pastor should.*"

"*I see.*"

"*It's interesting that scandal, no matter how old, can still create problems for people years later. People in churches aren't always as forgiving as I am.*"

"*I understand,*" *Samuel T. said.*

"*Good. Now let's go to Claire's kitchen for some coffee.*"

Among Davis Morgan's business ventures was a small hardware store located in downtown Caruthers' Gap. Like its customers, the shop was friendly

and familiar. Inherited from his maternal grandfather, the shop under Davis Morgan's ownership had minimal yearly profits. While he would have easily liquidated other businesses with more profit, sentimentally Morgan Davis held on to this shop. An hour or so before closing, Davis was concluding his conversation with Tom about the business.

"You're doing a great job," Davis said. "The books for the month look fine. The shop's making a good profit."

"Yes, Davis. Business is doing fine," Tom said. Tom paused and raised his hand, pointing to the store's entrance. "Did you notice how I rearranged the shelving in front? Selling more parts this way."

"Good idea."

"Thought we might want to have a monthly drawing for a tool. Specialize it with the season. You know, garden tools for the summer."

"Tools."

"Nothing real expensive. Just something to give the customers something to look forward to. They have to come in the store to write down their names on an entry slip. The more they come in, the more times they can write their names on entry slips. Each time they're in the shop, the more likely they are to buy something."

Davis paused and said, "I like it. I like it."

"I'm glad," Tom said.

"How's that brother-in-law of yours doing?"

"Adrian? He's doing fine. Maggie and the girls are enjoying him and Caroline. He's in Chicago for a few days."

"Chicago?"

"He said something about attending a conference."

"Conference?"

"Personally, I think he's chasing a woman, a nice-looking woman. Her name is Rachel."

"Hope he catches her. He needs loosening up. Too uptight. Know what I mean?"

"Yeah, I know."

"That's what I like most about you, Tom. You're a man I can work with. Hometown boys who stay hometown are always easier to work with and to promote."

"Promote."

"I'm going to need a general manager for the store. You've been doing a good job while Harris has been away. Harris is going to retire in a few months. I'll need a man I can depend on."

"You can depend on me, Davis."

"Just one thing," Davis said.

"One thing?" Tom asked.

"I'm working hard to help J.D.'s career in politics. It's not good that Adrian's been talking to Ora Mae. Never know what might be stirred up. Know what I mean?"

"I think so."

"Best to let sleeping dogs lie, like I did with you and the Cobb boys and the church money."

Tom stared at Davis.

"I don't like to mention it now. I wish that I could get Adrian to leave alone all this business about Wayne's death. No need to stir things up. I'm going to need a good general manager, someone I can depend on. Can I depend on you?"

"I think so. You can depend on me," Tom said.

"Good. Now tell me more ways I can make more money out of this little shop."

"One moment. I'll see if Dr. Adams is available for your phone call." Phyllis Brown put the caller on hold and pressed the extension of Harper Adams.

"A Mr. Davis Morgan is on the line."

"I'll take the call," Adams said.

"I'll connect you now."

"Haven't heard from you in a long time," Harper Adams said.

"Has been a while."

"Still wish you'd let me submit your name as a trustee for Hunter-Harwell," Adams said.

"No, I can't do that right now. Too many other commitments. Besides, I'm a believer that trustees should make substantial financial contributions to the schools they run."

"Yes, I know. That's why we'd like you to be a trustee," Adams said.

They both laughed.

"I have a boy from my church who teaches at your school. Adrian Stockwood."

"Yes, Dr. Stockwood is one of our more prized professors."

"I know he has an opportunity to go somewhere else."

"Yes, I believe that is correct."

"He tells me that there's a problem with his teaching contract with you."

"He is under contractual arrangements with us, Davis," Adams said.

"I'm really interested in that boy. Want to see him go places and do things," Davis said.

"We've prescribed to him certain conditions that would allow us to release from his contract."

"Forty thousand dollars."

"That's the correct amount," Adams said.

"That seems like a lot of money. As I said, I'm real interested in that boy."

"Well, since you're a potential trustee, a generous potential trustee at that, I'll be glad to ask the administration if they would reconsider the conditions in light of Dr. Stockwood's years of devoted service."

"That would be good," Davis said.

"What about twenty-five thousand dollars?" Adams asked.

"Twenty thousand."

"Twenty thousand. I'm not sure," Adams said.

"Of course, if he paid you twenty thousand dollars, I would be pleased to make an additional contribution of ten thousand dollars," Davis said.

"Ten thousand." Adams repeated the figure.

"Ten thousand, paid directly to you as you see fit."

"That would be helpful. So many miscellaneous expenses don't fit under a regular budget account."

"Good, when he's released from his contract, I'll send you a personal check."

"Wonderful, I shall go ahead and contact Dr. Stockwood today."

"I have a number where he can be reached in Chicago," Davis said.

"Chicago? I thought he was in Caruthers' Gap."

"He's away in Chicago for a few days. A little rest and recreation."

"Give me the number and I'll call him as soon as possible. Just one more point of clarification. You are comfortable with my submitting your name as a potential trustee?"

Davis laughed. "Adrian said you would be a tough negotiator. Yes, I'll let you submit my name."

"Wonderful for all of us," Adams said.

"Yes, you'll be having your dinner soon," Estelle said. She dropped the potato slices into the hot frying pan. The sizzle of them in the hot grease must have *sounded like a musical accompaniment to the Pekingeses. The dogs danced and barked to the crackles from the pan. "Yes, I'll share some with you. Be patient," she said.*

The sound of the frying potatoes was interrupted by the sound of the front doorbell. "Wonder who that could be?" Estelle said looking at her dogs. "I'll dismiss them and then we'll have dinner." Estelle turned off the stove and removed the skillet from the burner.

She walked toward her front door. Stopping at the side window, she pulled back the curtain and stared at the man on the porch. The man nodded to Estelle peeking through the curtains. J.D. held up a folder. "I've got the essay, Miss Estelle. Ready to complete my assignment."

Estelle heard his voice and said, looking down at her dogs, "Twenty plus years late. How much should I deduct for tardiness?"

As she reached out to open the door, Estelle's arms waved in the air before she fell forward and knocked against the small table where she had placed the candlesticks given her by Ora Mae. J.D. heard the shrills of the Pekingeses. When the door did not open, J.D. yelled, "Miss Estelle, is something wrong?" The dogs barked louder and louder. J.D. put down his portfolio on the wicker chair and yelled more forcefully, "Miss Estelle! Miss Estelle!" J.D. waited for another moment and then unsuccessfully tried to open the door.

Within ten minutes after J.D.'s summons, the police broke through the door. The dogs were still barking at Estelle lying on the floor. Near the place where she lay were two candlesticks, one intact and one broken. "Weak pulse and respiration," an arriving paramedic said.

"I'm pleased I was able to locate you," Adams said.

"I'm surprised that you did," I said.

"I have some good news for you."

"What's that?"

"I *was able to persuade* The Executive Council to reconsider your request for release from your contract," he said.

"You're releasing me from the contract?" I asked.

"Upon the receipt of certain conditions, yes, we are."

"Certain conditions?"

"Yes, the amount of money to be compensated to the university has been renegotiated from forty thousand to twenty thousand dollars," he said.

"Twenty thousand?"

"I'm pleased to be able to offer you that good news."

"Why the change?"

"In light of your years of faithful service to the university and community, we want to reward you with this reasonable release."

"Reasonable release," I said.

"Adrian, it is reasonable considering your fully paid year's sabbatical and the subsequent two-year teaching contract obligation."

"I see."

"Let us know as soon as possible about your decision. Until we are informed otherwise, we anticipate seeing you in your office and classroom this fall," Adams said.

Hanging up the phone, I rehearsed each of his words. I rehearsed those words as much as I imagined he had in the delivery. Considering the sabbatical leave, the time of the year and the contractual obligations, the offer wasn't unreasonable. It was reasonable, although I never knew anyone at Hunter-Harwell having been subjected to such restrictions. It would make leaving much easier.

Something did not feel quite right, something in his voice. He called me Adrian, I recalled. He called me Adrian. It would have been more credulous had he called me Dr. Stockwood. He only called me Adrian when it served his purpose.

Maggie and Tom's bedroom was one of competition for attention. The competition was not between the married couple, but between the king-sized bed and the big-screen television that was located at the footboard of their pine bed. Tonight's television watching had ended.

"Davis is thinking about making me general manager of the shop," Tom said.

Next to him in bed, Maggie closed her magazine. "I knew he would, Tom. He likes you. Besides, you're the best man for the job. It would mean a raise, wouldn't it? It would have to."

"Yes, I suppose it would."

"I sure would like for us to remodel the kitchen. Do you think we could?"

"We'll see. It's not a done deal, Maggie."

"What do you mean?"

"I've known Davis since I was a boy. He's unpredictable. He could change his mind."

"Don't let him change his mind, Tom. Keep him happy."

"Are you sure that you want me to keep him happy?"

"Of course, I do. It can't hurt to keep Davis happy."

"Even if it involved your family?"

"My family?"

"Davis wants me to discourage Adrian from meddling into Wayne Daniels' death."

"I wish that Adrian would stop meddling. I know Ora Mae was our family's maid. Adrian was always too close to her. I'll speak to him myself."

"Are you sure?"

"Tom, our family's future is important. Ora Mae's dying anyway. Lord bless her soul. But we need the extra money. We've done without for so long. Besides, it's not like there's anything to find. Is there?"

Tom was silent.

"We need to get some sleep. Good night," Maggie said. Maggie turned off the ceramic bedside lamp and kissed Tom good night.

Tom did not turn toward her and hold her that night as he usually did.

Peaceful exhilaration. Although Estelle would say I had created an oxymoron, I felt exactly that—peaceful exhilaration. I had spoken with Rachel and she agreed that I should return to Caruthers' Gap tomorrow. In fact, Azure Eyes insisted that she would return with me. Fortunately, she had completed her seminar responsibilities that afternoon. She was away downstairs saying goodbye to her colleagues.

Everything in my life was coming together like a intricate puzzle slowly crafted by many participants, some willing and others unwilling, during a long winter. Spring was near. I liked the total picture that was emerging, each piece of the puzzle having found its proper position. At last Ora Mae would be helped. With what Estelle now knew, Ora Mae might have the peace that she wanted. I was eager to discover what Estelle knew, just as she was eager to tell me.

Adams' unexpected phone call gave me the opportunity to leave Hunter-Harwell. While twenty thousand dollars was still a great deal of money, I could borrow it from Caroline's college fund and replace it as soon as possible. I would have the career opportunity that I had always wanted and I would have Rachel.

CHAPTER THIRTEEN

There in the hours spent in Chicago, it was like a fulfillment of the imaginations and fantasies of my adolescence—a place where no one would know me, a place where there could be new beginnings, and a place where I could ultimately discover myself. So many hurried lives had passed by me on the streets and no one seemed preoccupied with me and my own destiny. It was mesmerizing to be part of a crowd where no one watched. Chicago, popularly known as the Windy City, had been my Babylon in the words of Samuel T. Admittedly, I no longer gave any significant credence to his damnation pronouncements. Whether it was Babylon, Sodom, Gomorrah, or the Promised Land, I found it to be more than hospitable to my desires. While I knew I had to leave, I did not want to return to Caruthers' Gap. I wanted to linger longer in this city with Rachel.

When we left Chicago the next morning, I was confident that my life was moving to a crossroads. I had crossed the lines of self-prescribed conduct with Rachel and lightning did not strike. Like Adam and Eve, I did not immediately die. Morriah was to meet us at the airport when our commuter flight arrived from Atlanta. We were walking side by side, looking fondly at each other, when Morriah with a folded newspaper approached us.

"Your plane was late," Morriah said.

"Delays in Atlanta," I said.

"Thank you for waiting for us," Rachel said.

"I never wait for people at airports. They wait for me. I called ahead and learned your flight had been delayed. I only just arrived," Morriah said.

"How's Caroline?" I asked.

"She's fine. She's with Maggie's girls at Maggie's house. A lot has been going on since you've been away."

I felt awkward with Morriah's seeing my hand in Rachel's.

"I can see a lot has been going on with you," Morriah said.

"We had a wonderful time in Chicago," Rachel said.

"I bet so," Morriah said.

"What's been going on?" I asked.

"Most of the town's talking about Estelle Cameron," Morriah said.

"She called me. That's why we came back early. She has some new information about Ora Mae," I said. "I can't wait to talk to her."

"It's going to be a long wait," Morriah said.

"Why?" I asked.

"She died late yesterday at the hospital," Morriah said.

Morriah handed me the folded afternoon paper. Inside was a brief notice verifying what Morriah had said. Funeral plans pending, the article stated.

"I need to see Ora Mae," I said.

"Not until tomorrow," Morriah said. "I talked with Lola. When Ora Mae found out about Estelle's death, she became hysterical. On doctor's orders, Lola had to sedate her. She'll sleep till morning."

"Get your luggage now," Morriah said. "Better hurry, I'm double-parked. There's never enough parking at these airports. Also, a letter from Duke University was forwarded to the motel." Morriah began walking toward the parking lot exit.

"Do you have the letter?" I asked.

Morriah turned back. "It's in the room," she said. "I'll give it to you after we let Rachel off, wherever she wants to be let off."

Unlike Chicago, Caruthers' Gap was once again the familiar and the routine place, or so I thought. Inside the motel, after having dropped Rachel at her apartment, Morriah handed me the unopened letter and a letter opener. "Go ahead and open it," Morriah said. "It won't get opened any other way."

I tore the letter open without benefit of Morriah's letter opener. First, my eyes gazed through its contents. I reread the letter three times before I raised my eyes toward Morriah.

"What does it say?" Morriah asked.

"The dean has written to remind me that I have one week to accept or to reject the offer of a teaching position this fall. There cannot be any more extensions. It's now or never."

"What happens if you don't accept?"

"I may not ever get an opportunity like this again." I handed Morriah the letter and her eyes scanned the letter.

"Full block."

"What?"

"Full block. The secretary used full block to type the letter. Personally, I like semi-block. Seems more professional."

"Morriah," I said, shaking my head.

"What are you going to do?" Morriah asked.

"While I was in Chicago, I received a phone call from Hunter-Harwell. For twenty thousand dollars, I can be released from my contract."

"Twenty thousand. I thought you said it was forty thousand."

"Adams had a change of heart, Christian charity, I suppose, because of my years of faithful service."

"Christian charity?" Morriah said. "There's an angle there."

"Maybe so. But it comes down to twenty thousand dollars."

"You're going to pay it?"

"Yes," I said.

"How?"

"If I temporarily transfer some assets, it can be done."

"Don't touch Caroline's college fund."

My silence must have betrayed me.

"That's what you're going to do," Morriah said repeating herself, "that's exactly what you're going to do."

"I may," I said. "It would be a good investment for all of us."

"Wait at least forty-eight hours before you make a decision,"

"What will forty-eight hours do?"

"It may give you a chance to cool down."

"Cool down?" I said.

"Men, like dogs in heat, don't make good decisions when they're hot and bothered. It is Caroline's money from her mother's life insurance. Please wait forty-eight hours."

"Alright, Morriah, but I can't imagine that I will change my mind."

"Thank, God. The red lights are flashing."

Driving to Ora Mae's house, I passed what would be called the old home place, now owned by Maggie and Tom. The place looked smaller with a few of the surviving white pine trees that I had planted one spring. My parents had received free seedlings from a friend who had ordered the plantings from an agricultural agency. I thought I had to plant everything that I had been given. I planted those seedlings close together with little more than two feet between them on such a small plot of land that only then seemed much larger. It must have looked like a would-be fortress of trees between our house and the surrounding houses. However, nature intervened. Some would die from thirst and others from carelessness. These surviving pines had escaped the pains of summer droughts and the hapless encounters of children with menacing lawn mowers. These seedlings were now taller than the roofs of the nearby houses. Where grass once grew, were now carpets of pine needles and pinecones on the landscape.

This impatient gardening philosophy of my twelve-year-old mind—the more the better—had followed me to adulthood. Often I had not allowed new plants enough room to grow. Much time was spent transplanting and loosing mature plants that should have been given more space to grow in the beginning. Space and patience did not occur naturally to me.

I arrived at Ora Mae's house. A medicated night's sleep had renewed her energies, resulting in the familiar alertness in her eyes and the wit in her voice. "I want to see Miss Estelle," Ora Mae said. "No more excuses. Are you going to take me or do I call a yellow cab," Ora Mae said.

"Calm down," I said. "I'll take you."

Lola accompanied Ora Mae and me to pay respect to Estelle at the Thomas MacInvale Funeral Home in downtown Caruthers' Gap. While I pushed Ora Mae in her wheelchair, Lola walked in front and carried the walker as we went inside. "Bring that walker," Ora Mae had demanded. As soon as we went through the doors, a clean-shaven young man in a navy blue suit approached us.

"May I help you?" he asked, looking directly at me.

"We would like to view the body of Estelle Cameron," I said.

"This way please. The slumber room on the left," he added. His eyes turned once again to me alone. "Would you like to sign the guest registry?"

Ora Mae nodded her head. "Yes, I would, young man."

He stood frozen and pointed his hand to the registry high enough to be out of Ora Mae's reach. "There's a pen," he said.

Waiting for Ora Mae to respond, we stood by silently. By saying nothing, Ora Mae was communicating.

"Please hand her the registry and pen," I said.

His eyes stared at me once again, making me feel colder from his glance. He opened the book, picked up the pen and bent down to the wheelchair-bound woman.

Her withered hand shook as she guided the pen across the lined pages. "There, it's done," Ora Mae said. She placed the pen in the opened book and left it in her lap. Ora Mae's eyes gazed at the young man. She waited.

He bent down to her chair, retrieved the book from Ora Mae's lap and placed it back on the podium.

"Friends of the family?" he asked.

"No," Ora Mae said.

He raised his eyebrows. "Oh?" he questioned.

"Family . . . on my father's side," Ora Mae said.

"Well. If you need me, I will be close by," he said, leaving the three of us alone.

"Wheel me closer," Ora Mae demanded.

I wheeled her closer to Estelle's casket. I stood on one side of Ora Mae and Lola on the other side. A few minutes passed as we watched Ora Mae stare at the body. I read the cards on nearby floral arrangements that filled the room. I suspect florists were always busy when old maid schoolteachers died.

"Give me that walker," Ora Mae said.

"You shouldn't stand," I said. "You're weak."

"Got to stand," Ora Mae said. I guided her hands to the bars of the walker. She stood, looking down into the open casket.

"Always stand in the presence of a lady," Ora Mae said. "Never should have told you. Never should have told you. Miss Estelle said she would take care of me in the end. I should have taken better care of her." Her head shook as she talked.

Tears collected around her nose and mouth. Once more, her eyes looked tired, the brightness having left.

"Are you ready to go, Miss Ora Mae?" Lola asked.

"Time to go," Ora Mae whispered. "Help me down."

After Lola and I guided Ora Mae back into the chair, I turned her chair from the casket. "Stop," Ora Mae said. "Wheel me backwards. Want to see her as I leave the room."

We were almost out of the room when Ora Mae said, "I'll be seeing you soon, girl. Joining you real soon."

After Lola had safely placed Ora Mae back in her own bed, my question had to be asked. "What was Miss Estelle trying to tell me before she died?" I asked.

"Can't say."

"Can't or won't?" I asked.

"Makes no difference," Ora Mae said.

"I can't help you if you won't tell me," I said.

"Nobody can help me, boy," she said. "I told Miss Estelle and look at her. She's dead now."

"Miss Estelle died because of her diabetes. She went into a coma."

"Maybe. Maybe not. All I know is that I told her something and now she's gone."

"Please tell me what you told her," I said.

"Makes no difference now, just a few more days. I've asked God to let me live to my birthday."

"I returned to Caruthers' Gap to help prove your innocence."

"Is that why you came back? Couldn't really tell. Sometimes I feel like a nuisance. Besides, nobody's all that innocent. We all share the shame, you and me, too."

Her words stung as deep as any summer wasp could. "I'm here now," I said. "Let me help you."

"Can't. I made a promise years ago to keep quiet and I kept it. I broke that promise a few days ago and now Miss Estelle's dead. Can't break it again. Can't let that happen to anybody else. You won't hear nothing from me. I need my rest, I'm tired."

I returned to my motel room to talk with Caroline about how our future was going to change. Caroline came into my room shouting, "Guess what? Some of my friends are going to be in my classes in seventh grade. You were right. It won't be so bad. I'll have my friends."

"How do you know?"

"Aunt Morriah called the school and found out. Let's go swimming. You said you would go with me."

"I want us to talk first. I have something to tell you," I said.

"What is it?" Caroline asked.

"I've been offered a teaching contract at Duke University in North Carolina."

"Well, we're not going," Caroline said.

"What do you mean we're not going?" I said.

"I'm not going to move away from Brunson and leave my friends and Aunt Morriah."

"Caroline, I've talked about leaving Brunson if I received another teaching opportunity."

"I don't care. I'm not going to leave my friends. You can't make me."

"Caroline, I don't want to make you, but it is for my career and what's best for all of us."

"It's always what you want."

"Stop it. You're acting like a spoiled, selfish child."

"Well, I am a child. You're always telling me that I'm a child."

"Be reasonable, Caroline," I demanded.

"I don't know anybody in North Carolina. In Brunson, I have friends and Aunt Morriah. Once we get there you won't have any time for me."

"What do you mean?"

"You're always working. You never spend any time with me. You're always working, reading, or writing. You don't like being with me."

Caroline began crying. I put my arms around her.

"Caroline, I'm sorry. I'm sorry."

"You like Rachel more than you like me," Caroline said.

"That's not true," I said.

"It is true. Look how much time you spend with her," Caroline said. "Why don't you like Corrine? She's the only one who spends time with me besides Aunt Morriah."

I said nothing to Caroline, pondering her words.

"What's the use! I'm going to the pool," Caroline shouted.

As Caroline left my room, Morriah walked through the open door from their room.

"You've been listening?"

"Yes," Morriah said.

"Go ahead and tell me. I've really blown it with Caroline, haven't I?"

"It's nothing that can't be corrected."

"What do you mean?"

"Just think about what she's said and remember what I told you. You're acting toward her the very way that you said your daddy acted toward you."

"I'm not like that."

"It's something to think about," Morriah said. "I'm going down to the pool."

Having failed with Ora Mae and Caroline, I needed to be with Rachel, my one ally. The social work suite of offices was empty, not an unusual occurrence. Summers and lunch breaks often meant few professors and less available secretarial help. The door to Rachel's office was open and I went inside to wait because we had planned a late lunch after her class. She should have been in her office by now, but could have delayed by a student's question.

Glancing about the office, I enjoyed its orderliness in sharp contrast to my own university office. I glanced toward her desk, where apparently she was involved in some research project.

I walked around the room looking at the neatly grouped diplomas and recognitions above her credenza. At first glance, I could not read the words on her diploma. Once I had my reading glasses on, I could read her date of graduation. When she was graduated from college, I had already been teaching with a master's degree for almost ten years.

Morriah's words still burdened me. What would Rachel see in me? I held a small gilded desk mirror up to my face. My flesh, drier than it had been fifteen years ago, was weathered but not completely destroyed. Fine lines, which soon would be thicker and longer, marked my face. I hoped someone, other than myself, would argue that I was still handsome. Still the vigor was waning, except when I was with Rachel.

I glanced down to her desk to an open folder with the top page entitled "The Sexual Behaviors of White Middle-Aged Men Reared With Childhood Maternal Substitutes." The title surprised me, interesting and provocative.

I sat down and began reading what I had first assumed was some type of research prospectus. I read her hypothesis carefully. She was studying sexual behaviors and practices of men who had significant experiences with substitute mother figures. Looking through the document, I examined her line of reasoning. She believed that males reared in certain critical periods with substitute mother caregivers were likely to have adolescent or immature sexual fascinations with females when they reached middle age.

As I continued reading, my insecurities and questions increased. Our sexual activity, the questions about my relationship with my mother and with Ora Mae, were these the subject of a study? Beneath the folder was an audiotape marked "Subject C" and had a clearly marked date corresponding to our time in Chicago. I put the tape into the nearby recorder and listened, but only for a few minutes. The voices, the breathings, the verbal encouragers were all familiar. There were other tapes.

I searched among the folders and found one entitled "Comments on Subject C." Within the folder were observations, methodically and detached, on our moments together. Unlike for me, what it had meant to her was not love, but only clinical observations.

When I left the building, my stomach felt as twisted as my thinking felt confused. How could a few chance moments change my life? When I left Chicago, I was at the brink of having everything I wanted—a new job and a new relationship. Now life was crumbling around me. Caroline was upset about moving; Morriah was right about Rachel; Rachel had been using me in some study; and Ora Mae was dying without my having helped her.

That afternoon I was back in Ora Mae's bedroom. I was there when Ora Mae opened her eyes from her afternoon nap.

"Didn't expect to see you again," Ora Mae said.

"Just needed to see you," I said.

"Hmmm." Ora Mae stared at me, like she stared at the young boy with a chocolate moustache who protested that I didn't take the chocolate milk from the refrigerator. "What's the matter?" Ora Mae asked.

"What do you mean?" I said.

"You haven't 'just needed' to see me for years," Ora Mae said.

"That's not true."

She was right. Only now had I found myself coming naturally to her when I wanted to talk.

"What's is it?"

It was like being a boy again and talking to the one woman who had always listened. I was at home with her. "I've been hurt by someone I cared about," I said.

"A woman?"

"Yes."

"Tell me," Ora Mae said.

"I cared a great deal for her."

"Didn't work out?"

"No, she was just using me. Morriah said she was just using me. I didn't want to believe it. I thought she cared."

"Do you love her?" Ora Mae asked.

"I'll never know now."

"You talking about Rachel?" Ora Mae asked.

"Yes," I said. "How do you know?"

"I'm dying, but I'm still watching and listening. Morriah and Caroline have been here while you was in Chicago. Morriah said you been sniffing around Rachel."

"That's not exactly how I would describe the relationship."

"Don't matter what you call it. Means the same thing."

"She betrayed me. She used me to get what she wanted."

"Men and women been using each other since the Bible times."

"Should I just forget it?"

"Not saying that. You're hurting."

"I am."

"Don't let your hurts sting you twice. Once, the hurt stings because it comes first. The second time it stings because you ignore it or feed it."

"Feed it?"

"Hurt is like a little bird that chirps when it's hungry. You can ignore, but it keeps chirping and gets louder. Or, you can feed it by fussing over it. Either way, the hurt grows and stings over and over."

"How do you deal with its sting?"

"Don't give it away but use it. You got to master it. Use it for yourself."

"When did you get to be such a good philosopher? I'm supposed to be the counselor."

"You don't learn everything at college. An old woman ought to know something."

"How old are you?" I asked.

"Not sure. My mammy said I was born the day after the white folks got their freedom, July 5th."

"Just a few days till then."

"Won't live much past my birthday," Ora Mae said with her voice fading. "The Lord willing, I will live till then, my Independence Day."

Her voice was beginning to fade.

CHAPTER FOURTEEN

I spent the next few days visiting Ora Mae and thinking about what I had discovered about Rachel, not only about Rachel, but also what I had learned about myself. I had always taught my students to analyze situations in terms of facts, avoiding overgeneralizations. No matter how I had tried to reframe what I had found in Rachel's office, the same original conclusion always returned. Although I felt angry and betrayed, I was still strangely and powerfully attracted to her.

Ora Mae's words "use the hurt" kept returning to me. My preoccupation with Rachel had diverted me from my original purpose in returning to Caruthers' Gap. The blame was mine, not Rachel's. I had lost valuable time and opportunity. Now I must follow what I had always instructed my students to do when they were overwhelmed with the demands of college. Added to this was Ora Mae's wisdom of using the hurt to deal with the hurt.

What I was going to do was again crossing the line. Once you've crossed the line, the second time is easier. I had purposefully avoided Rachel until I had decided upon my response.

"You seem distant," Rachel said as I sat down in her living room.

"Do I?"

"Yes, you do. I don't like not seeing you," Rachel said. "What have you been up to?"

"Just spending time with family."

Rachel moved closer to me and pressed her hands on my cheeks. "I've missed you," Rachel said, turning her head and kissing my neck. Instinctively my body responded to her familiar touch. She took my hand and led me to her bedroom, her touch had refueled my desire for her.

"Get undressed and wait for me in bed," she said. "I'll be back in a few minutes."

Rachel went into her bathroom as I undressed. A few minutes later I heard her voice.

"Close your eyes," Rachel said. "I want to surprise you."

"Okay," I said.

Only this time, as she said her seductive and familiar words "close your eyes," I kept one eye open. She carried some clothing to the top of her dresser bureau, pausing for a moment and carefully arranging her rumpled clothing on the bureau.

"Now, open your eyes," she said. Dressed only in a matinee-length string of pearls, she crawled into bed beside me.

"It's been too long," she said. "I've missed you." Rachel knew when I was ready for her and she resumed her typical position.

"No," I said. "Not this time. I'll lead this time."

She stared at me and then slowly complied, turning over on the bed. Rachel continued to ask me questions about my feelings, but I shook my head and said, "No, not now. Later."

An hour later Rachel was asleep. Determined that I would be the first to leave the bed, I left the bed and stood in front of her bureau and examined her rumpled clothing. In the midst of the clothing, I found what I had suspected—a tape recorder. I removed the cassette tape and replaced it with a blank one, hidden in my jacket pocket. Before returning to her bed, I turned on the overhead fan.

A few minutes later, Rachel awakened and moved closer to me. "It's cool," she said. "Don't go away. I'll be back soon."

Rachel left the bed and headed to the bathroom. When she returned, I was putting on my shoes.

"Why are you getting dressed?" she asked. "I thought we could cuddle and talk."

"I'm through," I said.

"Through?" she said, standing in her terrycloth robe.

"Through. Actually, it's equally correct to say that you're through," I said. Both shoes were now tied.

"What are you talking about?" she asked. Rachel pulled tighter the belt on her bathrobe.

"I know all about you, Rachel. I know all about your tape recorder," I said.

Rachel turned to the bureau and back to me. "What are you talking about?" Rachel asked.

I reached into my coat pocket and pulled out the most recent cassette tape. "Now will you admit it?" I asked.

"Yes, I taped our lovemaking. I like to listen to it when I'm alone. It makes me more responsive. It makes me want you even more. Surely you know how quickly I respond to you," Rachel said.

Her facial expressions appeared convincing, but not to me. "Good try, but not good enough."

"What do you mean?"

"I was in your office the other day. I heard the tapes and saw the notes on your desk. You were using me for some research. Why?"

"You seem to know everything. You tell me?"

"I haven't completely figured that one out. You've been using me sexually."

"And you haven't been using me? We're both over twenty-one. Adrian, men and women have always used each other sexually. Or is it that I've been the aggressor that makes it frightening to you?"

Her words skillfully sought my insecurities. "Again, Rachel, a good try," I said. "You've used me sexually and you've kept me away from Ora Mae."

"Ora Mae. Really, Adrian, you need some therapy. You're fixated on that woman. Maybe that explains some things. We really should talk about this. It's not normal."

"You've diverted me, perhaps unintentionally, from helping her. Now that is going to change."

"What do you mean?" she asked.

"You're going to do two things for me. First, you're going to help Ora Mae."

"I'm not going to encourage your fixation with her."

"Yes, you are going to help me or else."

"Or else?" Rachel asked.

"I've discovered the most important part of your life, Rachel. It's the one spot where you're vulnerable. You're preoccupied with your profession. If you don't assist me, I will inform the university and the licensing board of your sexual misconduct in the handling of your hospice case, and in unethically obtaining material without proper consent. I'll expose everything, and you'll lose your license and your academic credibility."

Rachel's reddened face and her silence confirmed that I had found her weakness. "You're not as indecisive as I thought," Rachel said. "In a distorted way, I find this side of you more exciting."

"Exciting or not, do we understand each other?"

"What else must I do? You said there were two things."

"You've already met one of my requirements. You made a payment in full for the past hour."

"You bastard," she said. Her words spoke fire.

"Perhaps. But I must admit that I did find something that was even harder than your body."

"What's that?" she asked.

"Your heart. I'll be in touch soon." I stood in the doorway. "Be ready or I won't hesitate to issue a formal complaint with the licensing board and the university."

I had left Azure Eyes behind and now only Rachel remained. When I got in my car, my head collapsed on the steering wheel, and my sighs were loud and deep. Finally, I could breathe calmly again. Through my last confrontation with Rachel, I felt like I had to hold in my breath as I held my hurts inside. Otherwise, I could never go through with the plan.

Now I was no better than Rachel. I didn't like blackmailing her, but I needed help in helping Ora Mae. Motives, I knew, were never pure and neither were mine. In spite of lingering sentiment for Rachel, I had to be tough with her, or I would give into my remaining passion for her. I had to be strong and firm with her. I was finally trying to put Ora Mae first.

It was always amazing how the informal messages and teachings of our childhood would return to us at moments of uncertainty. What was forgotten becomes powerfully remembered, from the unconscious to conscious awareness, to guide our steps. When someone departs from us, we keep them alive by rehearsing their words and their words help keep us alive and focused. Such were the words of my departed mother. Mother always said that if you wanted to find out the "dirt" in Caruthers' Gap, you had to go to Wanda's Hot and Curl, one of the town's oldest beauty shops. Mother always said that if you were feeling blue, go down to Wanda's. Once you heard about the troubles of those other poor women, you were bound to feel better about your own.

The owners of the Hot and Curl were rich in culture, history, and encouragement. Little Wanda was about fifty years old. Her mother, Big Wanda, had started the beauty parlor. When Big Wanda couldn't be on her feet anymore because of varicose veins, she gave the shop over to Little Wanda's care. Little Wanda, trained all of her life for that moment, assumed the responsibility for the bleach dispenser, hair dryers and permanent solutions.

About thirty years and one hundred pounds separated Little Wanda and Big Wanda. Little Wanda was a size twenty and Big Wanda was a size ten. Little Wanda had proven equal to Big Wanda in making women look good, feel good, and know the "goods."

"I don't want to go in there," Rachel said as we got out of my car.

"Not much choice. Either you cooperate with me, or else."

"Why do you need me?"

"I can't go into Wanda's shop without you. You legitimize my presence there. While they work on you, I can get them to talk about Ora Mae and Wayne Daniels."

"Will they talk?"

"No question about it," I said. "They always talk."

"Get in this place," a deep and friendly voice called. Little Wanda, dressed in a big print smock, called out to us from the back of the shop. In the shop were several women in various stages of hair styling.

Rachel and I stood by the cash register listening to the floors creek as Little Wanda wobbled toward the front. "My friend Rachel wants the works, Little Wanda. I told her you that you were the best beautician in town."

"You're right about that, honey. Don't I know you? Never forget a face. You're Norma Helen's boy, Adrian, the college professor."

"Yes ma'am, that's right." I grinned. Daddy always told me grinning got you a long way with women in beauty parlors.

"It's been a month of Sundays since I last saw you. Not since I did your mama's hair for the funeral."

"You did a fine job, Little Wanda." Little Wanda's faced beamed.

"She made such a pretty corpse. Just wanted to pinch her. She looked so good. Praise the Lord, I was able with His help to remove all the split ends. Just a work of the Spirit, it was."

I nodded.

"What can I do for the two of you today?"

"Tell Little Wanda what you want done, Rachel."

"I don't know, maybe, just a wash today."

"Honey, don't be shy around Little Wanda," I said. I turned to Rachel and then back to Little Wanda. I was using my best down-home language— sweet, fervent, naive and personal. The only thing lacking was a half-chewed matchstick rolling in my mouth. "Little Wanda, she wants the works from you. Just last evening she said how hard it was to manage her hair in this Carolina summer heat. Rachel's a professional woman. She needs a hair style that she can just comb through lightly and get on to work."

"I know what you mean, honey. We professional girls just have to comb and run sometimes. Still you got mighty pretty long hair. Are you sure?"

I glared at Rachel and she nodded and said, "I'm sure, Little Wanda." I detected that the words seemed to stick in Rachel's throat, like a too quickly consumed peanut butter sandwich.

"Say no more. You're in Little Wanda's world now. Go on over there now and have a chair."

Rachel's eyes gave me a permanent kiss-of-death look. "Selma, what are we going to do for this young lady?" Little Wanda asked. "Go ahead and sit yourself down, sugar." Little Wanda guided Rachel to the chair, draped a pink plastic sheet over her and turned her around to the mirror.

Little Wanda explained that Selma was another beauty operator who was on Little Wanda's first line of consultation. Having studied under Big Wanda, Selma was top notch. Selma rose from reading her soap opera magazine and walked around Rachel. "Let me see, Little Wanda." Selma paced around Rachel, scrutinizing Rachel from every conceivable angle, much like Joshua did around the walls of Jericho. Guttural sounds reverberated from Selma's mouth as she did her consultation.

"Come on, Selma," Little Wanda said. "I ain't got all day."

"Hush," Selma said with hands waving as if they were in the local Pentecostal church. "You can't rush artistic inspiration. It's coming. It's coming. Wait. I know."

Selma rushed to her operator's sink, bent down, and opened the cabinet. From the cabinet, she pulled out a magazine. "There it is." Selma brought the magazine cover over to Wanda. "What do you think?"

"Looks good to me. Rachel, what do you think about the 'Princess Di' look?"

I had been listening carefully from my seat. I was surrounded in the waiting area by overgrown snake plants and old magazines. Immediately, I went and stood beside Rachel looking at and admiring the magazine cover with the late Princess Diana. "That will make you look like a princess," I said. "That's the one, Little Wanda. Selma, you did it."

"Are you sure?" Rachel asked, turning to me.

"I'm sure. In fact, I'll pull my chair next to yours. You don't mind, do you, Little Wanda?"

"No, hon, that's real sweet," Little Wanda said, grinning at Selma.

"Let's get to work. Selma, my scissors." I watched as Little Wanda cut Rachel's long blonde hair. I almost felt sorry for her as the hair dropped to the oak floors. However, I kept reminding myself how Rachel used me. No, this hair cutting was a small price to pay, especially since it wasn't my hair being cut.

Needing to acquire information without drawing attention to my questions, I thumbed through the magazines that were dog-eared, torn and sometimes missing. I waited for my cue to shape the conversation.

Little Wanda asked, "Adrian, what brings you back home? Haven't seen you since your mama died."

"I'm here visiting Ora Mae Chapman."

"Sad, sad," said Selma, still hovering around Rachel and providing moral support and guidance for Little Wanda.

"Good a woman as you'll find, black or white," Little Wanda said. "Keep your head down, hon." Little Wanda now had Rachel's head over the sink.

"You know her, then," I said.

"Know her? Everyone around here knows Ora Mae."

"Do you think she did it?" I asked.

"Did it? You mean kill Wayne Daniels? No, not that girl. If she'd killed him, they'd never have found him. Ora Mae's not stupid. If she'd buried him, he'd stayed buried."

"I think she did," Selma said, who had stopped sweeping the blonde curls from the floor.

"I know what I'm talking about. Ora Mae's too smart," Little Wanda said.

"The woman's dying of cancer," Selma said. "She's not so smart. Should have gone for those yearly physicals. I tell every woman I know, 'Go to your doctor.' Sure, it hurts to have a stranger mash your breast. A mashed breast is better than no breast."

"I know, Selma. And a life without breasts is better than breasts without life." Both said the last line in unison, as though it were as familiar as a beloved hymn refrain.

"Still, she didn't do it," Little Wanda said. "No, ma'am. Ora Mae didn't kill him. Too many other husbands around here would have done the deed. Lord knows Wayne did the deed enough times."

"Wayne wasn't that bad. He talked a lot, flirted a lot, but I don't think he did near as much as he said he did. Lots of churchgoers are like that. They like to flirt, but nothing ever comes of it. Or did you have something to confess to us about, Little Wanda?" Selma asked.

"Get your mind out of the gutter, Selma. I wouldn't have had that old so-and-so. The way he treated his wife, I wouldn't be surprised if she did it."

"Don't talk about Miss Winnie that way," Selma said. "Never knew a better lady or teacher. If it wasn't for her, my Leon would never have passed the third grade the second time around."

"How is Leon doing these days? I haven't seen him in a while," said Little Wanda.

"He's now on weekend passes from Columbia. He does some kind of door-to-door sales."

"What's he selling?" Little Wanda asked.

"He's kinda vague on what he sells. I think it's some type of garden supplies. I heard him talking about weeds or something like that on the phone. He was at Estelle Cameron's place last weekend."

"What a shock that was! Estelle Cameron dead!" Little Wanda said.

"We all knew she was going to die sometime," Selma said. "The way she ate with that diabetes. Diabetes will kill you. Sure glad that Leon made his sale before she died."

"Selma, you tell Leon that he can set himself up a little table at the Hot and Curl. Right over there near the water cooler. We need to help Leon on the straight and narrow. I still care about that baby."

"I'll tell Leon. He's real sensitive. He sure loves you, Little Wanda."

"An unfortunate timing of justice," Little Wanda said, turning to me. "His best friend and girlfriend were involved in a convenience store robbery and some missing lottery tickets. Poor Leon. He happened to have been in the back seat of the getaway car with a six-pack of beer, yelling, 'We won! We won!' when the police pulled the car over for speeding."

Selma's head shook, saying, "Didn't see a dollar of those winnings."

"What about Miss Winnie? Do you think she could have been involved?" I asked.

"I'll agree she had reason. He was a fart," Selma said.

Little Wanda was rinsing Rachel's hair over the sink. "You know what?" Little Wanda asked.

"What?" asked Selma.

"Let's go lighter."

"Lighter?" asked Selma.

"Yes, her hair would look nice with a lighter shade of dye."

"Dye?" Rachel said.

"Honey, no need to be shy or ashamed. I can spot a dye job when I see one. Now it's a good one all right. Now raise up and look." Wanda guided

Rachel's head up from the sink toward the mirror and removed the towel. In the mirror, I saw Rachel's expression of disbelief when she saw her once long hair now reduced to a length above the collar.

"A shade lighter might be nice, Rach," I added.

"Does it really matter anyway?" Rachel said.

"Good. If you don't like it, I can always dye it back in a month or two," Little Wanda said. Selma and Wanda proceeded to work with Rachel's hair and I sat back watching and smiling with my satisfaction both for Rachel's hair and for my newly acquired information about Wayne.

While I continued to pretend to read the one un-mutilated magazine I found, I kept listening to Little Wanda and Selma. Rachel, I suppose, had become comatose, or at least had taken a nap, with what was happening to her.

"Little Wanda's given you a few extra curls, girl."

"Curls?" Rachel murmured, awakening from her apparent slumber.

"That's why it's called the Hot and Curl," Selma said. "Every girl leaves with a little extra curl."

"That's our motto," Little Wanda said. I had forgotten to inform Rachel about the motto and the practice.

"I've seen Miss Winnie at the nursing home," I added in one last attempt for more information.

"I go every two weeks," Little Wanda said. "I go and help do hair and share a little sunshine. Sometimes Miss Winnie knows me and sometimes she doesn't. That Alzheimer's a bad thing."

"Sure, she had retired, getting ready to enjoy the retirement when she got sick," Selma said. "Worked so hard all those years. And for what? Sitting in a nursing home, not knowing whether she's there or in Tahiti. I'd hate to think that I'd worked all those years like she did and for what? A nursing home."

"That Miss Winnie was always a good teacher," Little Wanda said. "She knew how to get them kids to learn their lessons, not like today."

I, too, remembered that Mrs. Daniels' classroom management was excellent. As a child, I could not name her behavioral techniques as I could now. In fact, I had even used Mrs. Daniels' techniques as illustrations in one of the educational psychology classes that I periodically taught. As a child, I could only remember that she made you feel safe and warm in the classroom and that she opened your heart and mind to learn. She did know how to work with all types of children to facilitate their learning and performance.

"That daughter of hers, Laurel, is always telling people about her poor mother's Alzheimer's Disease," Little Wanda said.

"She sure does," Selma said. "It's one thing to talk about other people's family skeletons, but don't volunteer talk about your own people. It don't seem right. Disrespectful."

"It's like that girl is trying to ruin her mother's reputation," Little Wanda said. "She should have taken her mama in her own home. It's the only way to save money and self-respect."

"I know what you mean," Selma said. "Course, Laurel's like two different people. Maybe it's her hormones. I was like that before the change."

"Them hormones are powerful," Little Wanda said.

"Sure enough."

"She didn't have to work," Little Wanda said. "Wayne left her a big insurance policy. She worked because she wanted to. Didn't need the money. In fact, she still lived in that same old house when she could have lived anywhere in Caruthers' Gap. Having money and being satisfied not to spend it, that's real class."

"She did, too, have to work," Selma added.

"Did not."

"She sat in that very chair." Selma pointed to a nearby chair and said, "And told me that she had to work to make ends meet for her and her girl, Laurel. I know what I'm talking about. Had to wait seven years before Wayne could be declared dead and get that insurance money."

"You're right about that. I forget. Some folks thought he skipped town from one of his deals."

"Seems like the only thing he skipped was the funeral. Had his own funeral in Ora Mae's backyard," Selma said.

"Beneath the septic tank. That's poetic justice," Little Wanda said. The roar of their laughter could be heard throughout the Hot and Curl.

"There you go, honey. What do you think?" Little Wanda asked.

A third beauty operator had joined Little Wanda and Selma, huddling around any customer who had received the works. It resembled, I suppose, an athletic team huddling together after a game for that final moment of bonding. They moved back so I could see Rachel's reflection in the mirror more clearly. There was a pause in the room as we waited for Rachel to comment on her new hairdo.

"Well, what do you think?" Little Wanda asked again.

"I'm speechless," Rachel said.

"Isn't it a little orange?" the third beauty operator asked.

"Just a tint. That's what happens when you start mixing dyes. I think it looks nice," Little Wanda said.

Quickly, I paid for the appointment and left a generous tip for both Little Wanda and Selma. Rachel was silent as we went through the front doors of the Hot and Curl. "I look like a cheap whore," Rachel said as she got in the front seat of my car.

"I think you're anything but cheap."

That night was the first time in my life that I had a captive date for the Caruthers' Gap High School Reunion Dance. Rachel looked as beautiful, except for her flawed hair, as anyone I had ever seen. Her dress clung to her body as though it had been applied by an artist's spray gun.

"You look wonderful," I said.

"I'm surprised you'd notice."

"Even your hair." I lied.

"Had to work all afternoon. Trying to salvage a bad hair job. Still too short. It will take months for it to grow out."

"Let's not spend the evening talking about what's behind us," I said.

"Why did you insist that I come? I imagine you'll be the envy of every man there, an older man with a younger woman."

"You certainly have a high, but accurate, evaluation of yourself. We're here to help solve the mystery."

"The mystery?"

"At first it was my attempt to try to help a dying woman save her reputation. Now, it's why do people not want me to pursue what really happened to Wayne Daniels."

"Let's get this over. I want to get back to my life."

"Me, too."

The high school gymnasium was filled with registration tables and booths commemorating various activities from our high school years. Athletics comprised the largest tables. Other groups were represented— student government, debate club, national honor society, glee club, and homemaking club.

My fears were realized at the first reunion I had ever attended. Everyone was older, waistlines were larger, hairlines were receding, eyes were dimmer, and auras were less grand. The people who had seemed beyond my reach seemed much more human. The stars of the class play, student government, or the athletic team did not seem as powerful. Everyone nodded and smiles were exchanged. Were it not for the nametags, I might not have recognized the people who had influenced my life.

"Adrian," Laurel said, "Over here." Laurel was seated at the registration table.

"Good to see you, Laurel," I said.

"And you. Hello, Rachel," Laurel said.

"Good turn out?" I asked.

"Fair. As much as you expect from these sorts of things," Laurel said.

"You don't seem excited about the reunion," I said.

"Well, I'm here because it will help J.D.'s career and because Davis thinks it's important."

"Rachel, would you please get us some punch?" I asked.

"Sure," Rachel said.

"Better not let her out of your sight. Shall we take bets on how many times she'll be hit on between here and the punch bowl?"

"Sounds as though you've already been to the punch bowl once or twice," I said.

"You're perceptive. But not *that* punch bowl. I have my own stock at home."

"What's wrong, Laurel? We were once so close."

"Time. Roads traveled. Not keeping in touch. You figure it out." Her voice was detached and flat.

"I've been trying to do that ever since I came back."

"You're a failure, like the rest of us."

"You're not a failure, Laurel."

"We're all failures."

"That's the alcohol talking," I said.

"No, it's me talking. The alcohol makes it easier and clearer. We're all failures. We've all failed in our dreams of youth. It happens to everyone. The sooner we face it, the better for all."

"Let's walk outside," I said.

"Sounds interesting," Laurel said.

Outside we saw small groups huddled together, couples and isolated individuals. It was like high school all over again, I thought. "We once talked about many things, Laurel. What should we talk about now?"

"What do you want to talk about?"

"About you, J.D., your mother, Ora Mae, or Wayne Daniels."

"Wayne Daniels. You don't know how I hate that name. I hated him. He made my life miserable. I thought we had escaped him when he disappeared. They say you can't come back, but Wayne proved them wrong. Only he came back dead."

"Why did you hate him?" I asked.

"I hated him because he took my mother away from me. We were fine before he married her. She loved him more than she loved me. He took away my mother," Laurel repeated.

"Laurel, your mother's marrying Wayne Daniels didn't mean that she loved you less," I said.

"That's how I felt. You can't deny me my feelings, can you, Dr. Stockwood?"

"No, I can't deny how you felt," I said.

"I need to have this all behind me, Adrian. I need this nightmare to stop. Can't you see that it's destroying my life? J.D. and I were happy before we returned to Caruthers' Gap. We had problems, but it wasn't like this."

"What do you mean 'like this'?"

"J.D. was happy practicing law in Columbia and teaching part time. Mother's condition worsened and she had to be placed in a nursing home. Davis began to pressure J.D. into a political career."

"A lot of change and pressure for you," I said.

"When they found Wayne's body, mother's illness grew, and the talk began about Wayne. I wanted to leave, to take Mother and return to Columbia. Davis said it would hurt J.D.'s career if we left. Here was the opportunity, he said. Here was the opportunity to show that J.D. was a moral leader for immoral times." Laurel laughed.

"I'm sure that Davis only wants what's best for you and J.D."

"Yeah, what's best for J.D. as interpreted by Davis."

"What do you want, Laurel?"

"I want peace, I want my husband, and I want to get away."

"There you are. I've been looking all over for you," Rachel said.

"It's time to get back inside. I want to look for J.D. He should be through working the crowd by now," Laurel said.

Laurel left Rachel and me outside. "Did you find out anything?" Rachel asked.

"Nothing, except that she's miserable. Something's tormenting her that even she doesn't understand."

"Not too insightful, Doctor," Rachel said.

Later that evening Claire Cobb found us, as we were about to leave the gymnasium. "Hope you had a good visit," Claire said.

"It was good to be here," I said. "I'm glad that I took your advice and came."

"I'm glad you came back to your school," Claire said.

"Thank you for all your work. I noticed your name on the program. You've worked hard helping the committees to organize the event."

"I enjoyed it. I only wish Estelle were here."

"I know."

"She'd been in borderline health for years. She didn't watch what she ate. Lots of complications can occur."

"Well, she was old," Rachel said.

"Yes, that's true, too," Claire said, giving Rachel a weak smile. "She visited Samuel T. the day she died. She was so upset. Emotions can affect your health and so can working too hard. Did you look at the display that she set up in the school library? It showed clips from your high school and junior high years."

"No, I didn't."

"You should. Lots of work went into that display. It will bring back memories. I guess it was her last gift to your class."

"Let's go see it, Rachel," I said.

"Adrian, it is late," Rachel said.

I smiled at Rachel. "I suppose you're right." Turning to Claire, I said, "Thank you again for a wonderful evening."

"Hope to see you in church, both of you," Claire said.

"Maybe," I said. Rachel didn't respond.

CHAPTER FIFTEEN

Calvary Memorial Baptist Church, Samuel T. Cobb's church, had not changed since I had graduated from university. No new additions were present. The walls were the familiar light beige and the same well-walked carpet separated the left and right pews all of which had burgundy cushions on the oak wood. The baptistery dominated the front of the church, symbolic of Samuel T.'s fervent insistence that we all be born of "living water."

My spiritual journey, at least my institutional one, had begun within the shadows of Calvary Memorial Baptist Church. While my parents were indifferent to church attendance, Ora Mae had encouraged me to go to nearby Calvary Memorial. Within those church walls I felt both love and acceptance.

Samuel T.'s training had been three years in a Bible College. A fundamentalist, although I had no real idea of what that meant at the time, Samuel T. took Scripture seriously and literally.

Supplemented by the church's Bible teaching program, Samuel T.'s preaching had nurtured and sustained my biblical knowledge and understanding. Samuel T. had encouraged me to go to his alma mater. Had not Estelle Cameron visited with my daddy, I would have gone to Samuel T.'s school. Instead, I suddenly found myself going to another private university.

While Samuel T. was disappointed with my decision, he along with Davis Morgan periodically encouraged the church to assist me in my education with occasional love offerings at Christmas and at the end of summer. For years, Samuel T. had talked about my returning to Caruthers' Gap to help him begin a Christian school for the saving of the minds of young people from secular and satanic influences. With my approaching graduation, Samuel T. had fully expected me to return with him to build his school.

At my graduation when I had firmly and finally said no to his plans of my return, I witnessed the rage in Samuel T.'s eyes. The years of university study, along with a new understanding of who I was, made it impossible to return. I had tried to explain my plans to him and to ask his forgiveness, but even though I carefully explained my interest in studying counseling and my belief that this was God's will for my life, Samuel T. was unmoved. His temper exploded with my decision, calling me an unredeemed secularist. Samuel T. left with his quoted Scripture still stinging in my ears, "And Jesus said unto him, 'No man, having put his hand to the plough, and looking back, is fit for the kingdom of God'" (Luke 9:62).

The last words of the one who had nurtured me spiritually were "not fit for the kingdom of God." Each time I gained a new insight that was different from what I had been taught under Samuel T., I heard again the words "not fit for the kingdom of God." Leaving Samuel T. and some of his teachings behind was one of the most difficult parts of my journey. I had found myself alone, facing the future and cut off from the past.

As Caroline and I entered the church's auditorium, the usher with the familiar single white carnation boutonniere handed us a bulletin containing the printed worship service. An American flag was on the bulletin cover. In a huge brass urn, the flowers in front of the church were white, red, and blue-dyed carnations. Beside the flowers on the communion table was a large Bible open to the text of the minister's sermon. On each side of the choir stood the flags— the American flag on the left and the Christian flag on the right.

We sat down near Maggie and her daughters. Caroline and I still had a tension between us. Caroline, sullen in private with me, was still avoiding the subject of our move to Duke. The only unfamiliar note came when I saw the name of the morning speakers—Davis Morgan and Tom Crowder. I turned to Maggie and said, "I didn't know that Tom was speaking."

"Isn't it exciting?" Maggie said, her eyes beaming with pride. "Brother Cobb has been real upset since Estelle Cameron died. He called yesterday and asked if Tom would be willing to bring a message. Davis is leading the services and Tom is going to preach. He was up all last night, practicing. I'm so proud of him," Maggie said. "Aren't you?"

"For both of you," I said.

The service proceeded familiarly and predictably. The hymns centered on Christian service and freedom and the women's trio sang. Davis read the morning Scripture, welcomed the guests, and made announcements about the dinner-on-the-grounds following the services. Caroline and I stood briefly when Davis welcomed us. As always, he referred to me as one of the Hometown Stars and jokingly said I was an aging star.

Seated back at Samuel T.'s church, I reviewed the changes in me over the years. No one present knew who I was and what I thought. New beliefs had emerged about the nature of Scripture, the relationship between civil government and religion, the role of women in leadership, and much more.

Like a female colleague whom I believe was paraphrasing Reinhold Niebuhr, I was no longer as certain of the climate and furnishing of both Heaven and Hell. Strangely, my lack of certainty posed no anxiety. What had been so important to know in my youth was no longer as important in my middle years.

Still there was the an ever-present tension between my own new ideology and the words of Samuel T., "not fit for the kingdom of God." My way of coping with the ensuing cognitive dissonance was to distance myself from Samuel T. and his church and his type of church. Distancing myself helped reduce the tension, but I was never sure where I belonged. As a young boy, I had first come to Samuel T.'s church as a seeker "not fit for the kingdom of God" and as an adult I had returned to church as a seeker still "not fit for the kingdom of God."

When Tom's turn arrived, I felt an unexpected mixture of pride in him and embarrassment for him. He had no formal training, but the tone of his words was filled with intense emotion and sincerity. He had some natural gifts of oration, an ease and rapport, that could be developed, I thought. His message was often ungrammatical, his metaphors mixed, his points repetitive, and his conclusions not always logical.

After the services, the congregation gathered around him with praises, kisses, and pats on his back. "Didn't he do good?" Maggie said, turning to me.

"He did very well." Maggie and I smiled.

Maggie went to join the crowd gathered around Tom. Caroline turned to me. "I thought it was awful, Daddy," Caroline said.

"Caroline, it was his first attempt. First attempts aren't always the best, but they are important."

"Sounds like something Ora Mae would say," Caroline said. "Were you ever like Uncle Tom?"

"Once, many years ago. I remember standing behind that very pulpit one Sunday night. I had carefully typed my words on unlined stationery. While my body shook, I read most of it. I finished my twenty-minute message in eight minutes."

We were both smiling at my confession when Maggie rejoined us.

"I made plenty of food for our family and that includes the two of you," Maggie said. "Caroline, go on with your cousins and the other young people out back near the picnic tables. I want to talk with your daddy."

"Adrian, walk with me," Maggie said. She led me to the front of the church that was now vacant. "I have a favor to ask of you. I know we've had our differences. We were never much alike. You were always the different one in the family. I don't mean that in a bad way. You were just different." Maggie stopped and moved closer to me. "I haven't hurt you, have I?"

"No, I understand what you're saying," I said.

"Well, Tom and I are finally getting on our feet after all these years. Tom's now a member of the church and he's a deacon. He's really changed his life. Davis has talked about him becoming the manager of the hardware store."

"That's wonderful," I said.

"Yes, it is. It could mean more money for us. We need the money. Our girls could have the chance to go to college or something. Maybe they could take some courses like learning the computer. I don't know what I'm saying, but I need your help."

"What can I do?"

"Davis wants you to stop asking questions about Ora Mae Chapman and Wayne Daniels. If you don't stop stirring up trouble, he may not give Tom that promotion."

"Maggie, you can't ask that I stop trying to clear my friend's name and get to the truth," I said.

"Yes, I can, Adrian. I've never asked you for anything before. Don't make me lose this chance. Please."

I stood there silent, not knowing what to say to my older sister. Having abandoned his suit jacket and revealed the sermon-soaked white shirt, Tom joined us in the hallway.

"Maggie, let's get out there with our friends," Tom said, putting his arm around Maggie's shoulder. "Adrian, you come on too," Tom said. "Speaking makes me extra hungry for some of Maggie's banana pudding."

After the dinner-on-the-grounds, Davis approached me. "Adrian, have you got a few minutes?" Davis asked.

"Sure," I said.

"We can step into the church library. We won't be disturbed."

The library was smaller than I had remembered. Framed pictures of Jesus, depicting his ministry in Galilee, adorned the walls. His face seemed less ruddy than I remembered. Books lined the shelves on which were also mementos from different parts of the world, including numerous black carvings of baby Jesus brought by visiting missionaries.

"I remember spending lots of time here," I said.

"Yes, you sure did like to read and think," Davis said.

"This was a special place to me."

"Yeah, you didn't spend much time with the boys in the gym. Now it's time to let all that learning start to pay off," Davis said.

"What do you mean?"

"What's your situation about going to Duke?"

"I think it's going to work out. There's no need for you to call Hunter-Harwell on my behalf," I said.

"Really?" Davis said. "How come?"

"I got a call from Harper Adams, the Provost at Hunter-Harwell, and he agreed to reduce the amount of money I must pay in order to break my contract."

"Great," Davis said. "Seems like everything's working out for you. You're getting everything you want."

"I do have one problem," I said.

"What's that?"

"Caroline is reluctant to go," I said.

"That shouldn't be a problem. Just tell her what to do. It's in her best interest to follow her daddy," Davis said.

"It's not always that easy," I said.

"Sure, it is. J.D. didn't want to consider running for public office, but I told him that he needed to. Now he's doing what's best for him."

"I'm glad it's working out for him," I said.

"There's just one thing, Adrian," Davis said.

"What's that?"

"Running for public office is hard these days, harder than ever before. People are always ready to pry into your past or your family's past."

"What do you mean?"

"I want you to promise me that you won't work against J.D.," Davis said.

"I won't work against him."

"That means then you'll stop trying to defend that Ora Mae Chapman."

"What?"

"Stop snooping around, trying to defend her. She's as guilty as sin," Davis said.

"If she is guilty, then my snooping will be useless. If not, then it will prove her innocence. Her innocence can't hurt J.D."

"It can," Davis said, starting to pace back and forth across the room. "It won't do any good to go snooping into Wayne's death. Wayne is J.D.'s father-in-law. Bad publicity can hurt J.D.'s election chances. On the other hand, this conviction would put him solid with the townspeople. He would be correcting a wrong done years ago. He'll be seen as a moral fighter, righting wrongs."

"Is that want he wants?"

"It's what he needs, if he's to be successful."

"What if Ora Mae's innocent?"

"You're a man now, Adrian. It's time to cut the bullshit. She's just a 'nigger.' She's dying anyway. She'll never serve any time," Davis said. "I bet J.D. would promise that."

Finally, he had said the "n" word. His anger and frustration had betrayed him.

"Am I hearing what you're saying?"

"Don't give me that holier than thou attitude!" Davis said.

"What?"

"You were born here, you and your family. You're just as prejudiced as the rest of us."

"Do you realize what you're saying? What you're saying is against everything I believe."

"It wasn't what you used to believe."

"What do you mean?"

Davis looked me directly in the face. "Don't forget that when the blacks tried to integrate this church, I stood at the front doors, along with the other deacons, and refused to admit them into this church."

"I remember."

"And do you remember where you stood?"

"Right behind you," I muttered.

"Yeah, you and the other youth were right behind us, holding your Bibles, and the Christian flag. What happened to you, boy? What changed you?"

His words stung me as swiftly as if they were poison darts. Davis had brought me back to my place, reminding me of those moments of young self-righteousness that I had displayed in this place of worship. Davis described a simpler time when being white and being Christian were synonymous.

"Answer me," Davis said. "What happened to you?"

"I grew up," I said.

"What would your daddy say?" Davis said. "Your daddy didn't have much to say about religion. Did he?"

Daddy had little to say about religion. In his words, he wasn't for it or against it. It just depended, he said. I had for years tried to get him to come to church with me. He came only once to surprise me. He had been there that morning when we stood with Davis in front of the church steps. On the Sunday that we refused to allow a black family to come into the auditorium, Daddy had accepted my invitation.

I remembered standing there with my eyes filled with clear Christian tears because we were standing up for God. Tears of the righteous, they were called. It was like being a part of a great Christian army standing up to forces of evil that would try to infiltrate and to dilute our Christian strength. Fighting desegregation was a holy Christian cause. I had never felt such power. The black family turned away. We didn't have to say a word. Our presence together had done the talking for us, I thought.

I recalled looking toward the parking lot, and there was Daddy, dressed in his only suit, watching us. I was proud, hoping he would be proud of me, too. He turned away as he looked at that black family walk past him back to their car. "Daddy," I called. "Daddy!" He looked back at me and shook his head. He never came back to church, and we never talked about God, church, or religion again.

"Are you listening to me?" Davis asked. His words called me back from remembering the only day my daddy visited the church.

"I'm listening," I said.

Davis picked up an offering plate on the library table. "We supported you in your education all those years. Don't you owe us, owe *me* something?"

"Owe you something?" I asked.

"Yes, I helped put you through school and so did the other white people in this place. Adrian, you're one of us. You belong to this place."

"Belong here," I said. Funny, I thought. No one in Caruthers' Gap had ever told me that I belonged there.

"You're one of us. It's time to pay your dues. Stay away from Ora Mae Chapman. You've already accepted my help."

"What do you mean?"

"If you can't raise the twenty thousand dollars to buy your contract from Hunter-Harwell, I'll give you the money."

"I never told you it would cost twenty thousand dollars."

"Son," Davis said. "You're awfully green for a man who's past forty. How do you think you got the money reduced from forty to twenty thousand? I made a phone call and sweetened the pocket of Adams in order to make it possible for you to leave."

"You made a deal," I said, standing up.

"Not a deal, Adrian, a gift."

"Gifts always have strings, don't they?"

"Not strings, just obligations," Davis said.

"Well, I don't accept your gift."

"Do you know what you're doing?" Davis asked.

"I think so," I said. I began walking away from him and then I stopped and turned to Davis. "I do need to thank you."

"For what?"

"Ever since I returned to Caruthers' Gap, I've been cautioned against helping Ora Mae because she's black and Wayne was white."

"Makes sense to me," Davis.

"It made sense to me, until now."

"What do you mean?"

"Estelle told me that when people are afraid, they often turn to racial issues. You protest too much. There is something that you don't want me to find. Do you know what that means?"

Although Davis was silent, my flesh felt the burn of his gaze. Waiting for his response produced nothing but a pounding within my chest.

"It means that it can be found," I said, breaking the silence. Walking away from Davis and the church, I felt as alone and unsure of my direction as I had ever felt before. I had now lost Davis, the man I had admired and loved like a father, who had encouraged me to get an education. No longer were the heroes and the villains so easily distinguished.

I spoke briefly with Maggie outside the church. It was hard to imagine, but when I saw her face, I knew where to go. This time I would go not out of obligation but out of need.

Half an hour later, I read the simple bronze inscription, my daddy's name and the dates of his short life. As a teenager I thought it was strange that my mother would come to his grave and talk to him. Now I knew that she was right—talking to the dead could make more sense than talking to the living.

In that next hour I stared and wept at his grave. Words and thoughts too precious and too frightening to say out loud to the living I said in that cemetery. Now that I was near his age at the time of his death, I spoke to him as a son to a father, parent to another parent, and man-to-man, confessing my failures and asking for his and God's forgiveness.

Loosening my black-and-blue striped tie, I pulled it over my head, held it in my wet hands, and examined its knot, a Windsor. Over the years I had owned and given away scores of ties, but I had tied each one with the only knot that I'd chosen to learn.

"It's funny, Daddy, but I've always made the Windsor knot, the one that you taught me when I first went to church. No clip-on ties for your boy, you said. Maybe it's been my way to carry a little part of you with me."

Holding the tie, I turned it over, noted its expensive London label, and thought how different it was from the one my daddy showed me how to tie.

"You wore mostly working man's clothes, except for your one suit. I was ashamed that you didn't dress like Samuel T. and Davis." I unfolded the tie, moving the fabric in reverse fashion, more slowly than I had that morning when I had first placed it on my neck. "I was blind. I couldn't see past your blue uniform to the man beneath the sweaty fabric. I didn't know quality when it was right before me."

I put the tie back around my neck, lining up its narrow end between the fourth and fifth shirt button. Looking up to the marker, I said, "I thought Davis and Samuel T. were the ones who helped me learn how to make a living, but you were the one who taught me what was important about living. You were the honest one. They wanted something from me. You gave out of love, wanting nothing in return."

My scanning the cemetery eventually became lengthy stares into space, I turned back to my daddy's grave. "I remember your telling me how you could not make payments on your car. You went downtown to the finance company, put your last quarter in the parking meter, and went inside to return the car keys. I never realized it until now that you were the one who taught me to be honest before any teacher did."

As I began to recall what he had taught me, other forgotten stories came to mind. I continued to work the tie back to its former Windsor knot.

"Do you remember when I made a neighborhood boy cry by telling him he was not invited to my birthday party? You invited that boy, his mother, and father to our house. I cried as I told him I was sorry for being so mean. I don't remember that boy's name, but I remember my resolve to never hurt another person's feelings."

I looked down at my college ring and smiled. "I remember your making me watch a television interview with a state government official on the importance of getting an education. I thought you were crazy. Whenever the television reported the American Negro College Fund motto 'a mind is a terrible thing to waste,' you always said that's right. An education was something that could never be taken away from me, you said. You wanted me to get a high school diploma, something that you never had. I did get that diploma, Daddy, and five more degrees besides. I never realized it, but it wasn't Samuel T., Davis or even Miss Estelle that had first instilled the importance of getting an education. It was you. If Miss Estelle had not convinced you to intervene, I would have gone to Samuel T.'s Bible College, and not a university. Daddy, you helped me get my education."

With the knot of the tie still loosely hanging from my neck, I sat there thinking more of what he had taught me. Each story was precious, revealing Daddy through his honest words and actions.

"Daddy, I'm sorry for being ashamed of you. I wanted you to be like Davis or Samuel T. I was wrong. I was so busy seeing who you weren't that I couldn't see who you were. You were honest, you cared about people, and you worked hard for us. You saw through the religious hypocrisy. When you walked away from church that Sunday when the congregation turned away that black family, you saw the hypocrisy. I should have gone with you. I thought I was so righteous, but I was just young and stupid. You were the wise one."

I pulled the knot closer to my neck, but not as tight as that morning. "God bless you, Daddy. Thank you for giving me values that couldn't be purchased. God forgive me for not appreciating you."

That afternoon, words of confession had a strange efficacy that rivaled any modern medical cure. The words, once they came from my lips, generated more words and more hidden thoughts, feelings, and disappointments. In a real but unexplainable way, I spoke to my daddy and to God. When I stood up from sitting near his grave I felt lighter, cleaner, and peaceful. I no longer had to run away or to be ashamed.

As I was leaving the cemetery, I saw Tom standing near the entrance. I rolled down my car window and Tom came up to me.

"Adrian, I overheard you in the cemetery, talking to your dad and praying," Tom said.

"What?"

"Maggie sent me to look for you. She thought you might be there. I overheard you talking."

"You must think it pretty silly, talking to a cemetery marker."

"No, sometimes the most honest conversations are one-sided," Tom said.

We both laughed. "There's just one thing," Tom said.

"What is it?"

"Davis doesn't want you to pry into Wayne Daniels' death. In fact, he wants me to discourage you," Tom said.

"I see," I said. "I've misread him. All those years, I idolized him. He cared for me like a son. I thought I loved and respected him more than I did my own daddy. I was a fool. I couldn't see he was using me, manipulating me."

"Davis likes to have his own way. But he wasn't always like that, Adrian. He did a lot of good for people and still does," Tom said. "Davis changed after Wayne disappeared."

"So he changed?" I asked.

"Adrian, I need to let you know one thing. I don't know what happened to Wayne Daniels, except for this. I was at the camp-out with the boys when Wayne disappeared. Wayne had gone out fishing by himself, but I saw him leave the camp right after . . . ," Tom said.

"Right after what?"

"Right after Davis left the camp."

"What are you saying?"

"Two people left the camp-out. Davis first, and then Wayne. The next day we found Wayne's capsized boat and we never found his body. Davis said he saw Wayne go out fishing that night alone."

"Thanks, Tom, for telling," I said. "No one will know what you told me."

As we walked toward our cars, Tom smiled and put his hand on my shoulder. From the boy I knew in my childhood to the man of today, Tom had truly been reborn.

After leaving the cemetery, I drove to Samuel T.'s home where Claire led me to her husband in his study.

"I'm surprised to see you here," Samuel T. said. "Although you once considered this like your second home. Why do you honor me with your presence?"

"Miss Claire told me that Estelle visited you shortly before she died," I said.

"That's right."

"Miss Estelle phoned me in Chicago. She told me that she had information about Ora Mae Chapman and Wayne Daniels."

"She did?" Samuel T. asked.

"Miss Claire also said that Miss Estelle was upset when she left your house and that you've been upset ever since," I said.

"What are you saying?"

"I believe that you know something that could help."

"Estelle told me nothing."

"What is it you know?" I asked.

"I know nothing!"

"You know something. Miss Estelle visited you. Ora Mae told me that she came to see you," I said. Ora Mae had told me nothing, but it was a chance I had to take, to persuade Samuel T. that I knew more than I did.

The preacher, who had always had a word to say, was silent.

"Is it true that Miss Winnie and Wayne Daniels were having marital difficulties?" I asked.

"I know nothing about that. People in my church, especially my deacons, don't get divorced. If they did, they would leave the church."

"What a comfort you must have been."

Words of protest did not flow from Samuel T. as I thought they would. Instead, he muttered, "I'm not feeling well. Please go. I have nothing more to say."

It was no use, I thought. Samuel T. wasn't going to tell me what he knew.

At the door to his study, I stopped and turned back. "When I was a youth in this church, you told us that we had to live with ourselves longer than any other person. I still believe that."

Once more there was silence until I spoke my final words to Samuel T. "Thank you for your encouragement and love that you gave me as a young adult. I am grateful for what you and your wife did. You once told me that I was 'not fit for the kingdom of God' and I want you to know that you're right. But none of us are, Samuel T., and that is what makes God's grace so powerful."

Outside the door, I saw Miss Claire standing there silent. "Thank you for your help," I said.

"Adrian, did you ever look at the posters that Estelle did for the high school reunion? She said that you would find them helpful. I don't know what she meant, do you?"

The two aging figures were alone in the parsonage, far away from public view of searching eyes and eager ears.

"You're not telling the whole truth, Samuel T.," Claire said.

"You have no right to speak to me that way. I am your husband and the pastor of your church."

"If what I think is true, you have no right to be pastor. If you don't tell me the truth, I'll not live with you any longer as your wife," Claire said before she left him alone in his study.

Early evening came before I was able to reach J.D. It reminded me of the times that I had called my friend, waiting for him to return home from his social and athletic engagements. Whereas my life was home and church centered, J.D.'s circle of life was much more pronounced.

"J.D., I need to get into the high school library," I said.

"You need to do what?" J.D. asked.

"Miss Estelle made some posters about our class. I need to see them. They're locked in the school library."

"Okay, let me see what I can do," J.D. said.

I phoned Rachel and said that I needed her help. An hour later, Rachel and I were waiting outside the high school when a man appeared around the corner. "I guess you're Stockwood," the man said. "Well, the Director of Maintenance called and said I was to come down and let you in the school."

"We appreciate it."

"Well, I'd rather be at home in bed with my wife, instead of up here at night. Most stuff can keep till morning for most people."

"We need to get into the school library."

"Follow me," he said.

Inside the library, Rachel and I searched for the posters in every conceivable location. Rachel said, "Maybe they've taken them down."

"It's no use. They're not here," I said.

"It might help if I knew what you wanted," the janitor said, reentering the library.

"Some posters that were on display for the reunion," Rachel said.

"I told them plain and simple. All of that stuff was to be cleared out of here by Sunday noon or else. I was to start my vacation tomorrow. I didn't plan on coming back."

"Who took the posters?" I asked.

"No one. I told them plain and simple. All the stuff was to go or else."

"Where is it?"

"In the dumpster. I told them I was going to throw away anything left behind. They said fine."

Rachel and I spent the next hour searching the dumpsters by flashlight. "Do you have any idea what we're looking for?" Rachel asked.

"Anything about the summer of '64."

"Here's some old cut outs about the youth."

"Let me see," I said.

My eyes scanned the articles. "It's one of those 'Youth Notes' that appeared in our Saturday evening paper. Bernice Oliver wrote it. You met her. Well, you saw her at the reunion."

"Oh."

"Yeah, she's been writing insignificant stuff for years."

"What kind of stuff?"

"Silly stuff. Back then it seemed important."

"Anything there?" Rachel asked.

"Articles about parties, sleepovers, trips out of town. Wait, here's one near the time that Wayne Daniels disappeared." I brought the flashlight closer. "Let's get to the alley light," I said.

"Read it to me," Rachel said.

"'While the boys went on their annual fishing trip, the young ladies of Calvary Memorial Baptist Church had a slumber party. All the young ladies stayed the entire night save one. Apparently she got homesick and went back to her parent's home. Who was the shy one? Her initials are L.D. L.D. braved her homesickness, however, and returned shortly after having left the party. The hostess of the young ladies, Claire Cobb, said the young ladies had a feast of hot dogs, brownies, potato chips, and peanut brittle.'"

"L.D.," Rachel said.

"Laurel Daniels. But that doesn't make sense. Laurel told me that she had spent the entire night at the girls' sleepover. Why would she lie?"

"Maybe she's not lying," Rachel said. "There's something you don't know about Laurel. When I knew them in Columbia, J.D. mentioned that Laurel was seeing a therapist. He made a comment that the therapist said he thought Laurel was repressing memories."

"Repression?"

"She's complicated," Rachel said.

"Repression could explain a lot of things. Maybe Laurel knows more than she's been willing or able to tell," I said. Puzzled, I looked at Rachel and said, "You didn't have to give me that information. Why did you?"

Rachel was silent.

This night in Caruthers' Gap was like my nights in Brunson when I was processing student's submissions, academic questions, faculty gossip and administrative decisions. What I was learning about my old friends and myself was new, uncertain, and disturbing. I was looking for the gestalt, putting the pieces together to arrive at solutions and recommendations. Absorbed in my thoughts, I was nearly asleep when the kaleidoscope would turn and a new pattern would come into view.

Morriah and Caroline were asleep when Rachel knocked quietly and asked if she could come in.

"I didn't expect to see you any more tonight," I said.

"I saw your light was on. I thought you might need some company. What are you doing?"

"I'm composing my letter declining the teaching offer at Duke," I said.

"Adrian, you can't be serious. You're throwing away an opportunity that I would do anything to obtain."

"And I almost did, too," I said.

"What changed your mind?"

"A little talk with my father."

"Your father's dead."

"Yes, but I still talked with him. It was therapeutic and not psychotic," I said.

"What did he say?" Rachel asked.

"He didn't say anything. He let me do all the talking. I have been running away from this place all my life. I wanted more than living and working in a cotton mill town. In this process, I turned away from some important parts of my life. I've been in denial."

"What has made the difference?" Rachel asked.

"I realized that I was becoming the very thing I disliked in my own daddy. I resented that he never spent time with me, always working. Well, I'm exactly like that, except he had to work long hours just to make ends meet, and I don't. I don't spend enough time with Caroline. Instead, I focus on my career."

"There's nothing wrong with a career," Rachel said.

"No, nothing wrong with a career, but at what price?"

"What do you mean?"

"I was willing to buy my contract and even to use the money that was for Caroline's future."

"You shouldn't give up the chance for Duke."

"I have to for now, not the right time. Maybe in the future."

"Maybe not."

"Maybe not," I said. "All these years I wanted this moment, and it's within my grasp. Davis' gift would set me free, but he would own me."

"I'm not following you," Rachel said.

"If I accepted Davis' help at Hunter-Harwell, I would have to drop the investigation. I would have to betray a person who loved me unconditionally."

"You mean Ora Mae?"

"Yes. I know it sounds melodramatic, but I couldn't accept his offer."

"Adrian, there is something I haven't told you."

"What?"

"Davis has been paying me to keep you occupied and diverted from Ora Mae to avoid finding the truth, whatever it is."

"Why?"

"Davis said your investigation would hurt J.D.'s election. He offered money I needed to pay college loans."

"So you were doing double duty. You were using me in your research project, and you were being paid for it as well."

"Pragmatic, but not very pretty, I know," Rachel said.

"Why are you telling me this now?" I asked.

"Watching you give up what I would sell to achieve. I don't know. It's just that I want there to be honesty between us."

"No more secrets?"

Before she could say answer, the phone rang and I heard Claire's soft voice.

"Adrian, I'm sorry for calling so late, but I appreciate your trying to mend fences with Samuel T."

"I'm afraid they're beyond mending, Miss Claire," I said.

"I overheard Samuel T. say something to you that's not true. I'm trying to think of anything that could help you and Ora Mae. I do remember something."

"What is it?" I asked.

"Winnie Daniels came to us—both of us—years ago and said she was thinking about asking Wayne for a divorce. Samuel T. was always so careful in his early years about being alone with women. I was always with him when he counseled women."

"What more can you tell me?"

"Samuel T. discouraged her from seeking a divorce. He said it was her duty to make amends in their marriage. She was to submit to Wayne and his leadership. If she left Wayne, he told her, there would be no place for her in the church."

"What did she do?"

"She left very upset. I really thought she would divorce Wayne, but then he died. Samuel T. said the Lord provided a way for Winnie."

"Thank you for calling. I know it wasn't easy," I said.

"Thank you," Claire said.

I hung up the phone and turned to Rachel. "Well, it seems that Miss Winnie was contemplating divorcing Wayne."

"His death made the divorce unnecessary. How convenient," Rachel said. "What are you going to do?"

"Tomorrow I go fishing."

CHAPTER SIXTEEN

Early morning was the best time of day for both fishing and answers. J.D. came to my motel before six with all the essentials—tackle, rods, bait, a six-pack of beer, and, I hoped, information. On the way to Lake Caruthers, J.D. pulled into the local donut shop, where we filled our thermos with hot coffee and added doughnuts to our provisions. It was like the outings of our youth, except we now drank coffee instead of milk. The burn of coffee was on our lips before J.D. started the car.

"Going to the old place?" I asked.

"No other place to go," J.D. said. We turned on a side road that led away from the covered eating areas. The smell of pines and lake water brought shared memories of past adventures.

"Here we are," J.D. said.

With fishing gear and provisions in hand, we walked up the hill on a path that only feet, not cars, could travel. Through the pines we marched ahead as we had done years earlier. The sounds of young boys laughing loudly, throwing rocks into the lake and running ahead of the adult sponsors had long vanished. Now we were men, approaching the middle years, walking slowly and feeling the pains in our legs. Now our growing pains had been transformed to aging pains.

Half an hour into our fishing had passed before we spoke. Davis had taught us the importance of silence when fishing.

"It's been good to be back here," I began, breaking the silence.

"Likewise," J.D. said.

"I had lunch with your dad the other day. He looks great."

"Yeah, Dad takes care of himself and everyone else." J.D. put out his cigarette.

"I was always jealous of you," I said. "Your dad was so interested and involved in your activities."

"Involved. That's a good non-judgmental word."

"What do you mean?"

"Dad was always pushing me to go to college and law school, things he never had a chance to do. Now he's pushing me toward a political office."

"I thought you liked the idea of going into politics."

"Well, I think I would like it, but Dad is so relentless. He's always pushing. I'm not a kid anymore. Some days I think I would like more responsibility, and other days I'd like less responsibility."

"I know exactly what you mean." We both laughed.

"Wives can be that way, too," J.D. said.

"Oh?"

"Wasn't your Meredith that way?" J.D. asked.

"Meredith didn't push hard, except where our Caroline was concerned."

"Well, Laurel is always pushing me."

"I didn't know that Laurel had been married before you and she married," I said.

"Well, we had lost touch with you. Laurel and I had gone our separate ways. Her marriage was short and unhappy. I thought I had lost her forever until Dad got us back together after her divorce."

"She was always your first love."

"What about you? Don't tell me that you didn't have an adolescent crush on her."

"Not me," I said. "My admiration was chaste."

We both laughed again.

"Those were good and simple days. Wish we could go back. Don't you?" J.D. asked.

"Not me. Adolescence was a once-in-a-lifetime experience," I said. "I would much rather look ahead."

"In the end we might be out of our minds and in a nursing home."

"Maybe so," I said, nodding in agreement.

"At least you'll have someone to visit you."

"You mean Caroline?"

"Yeah, we wanted children, but it never happened."

"You still have time."

"No. Laurel can't have children," J. D. said.

"I'm sorry, J.D."

"I'm okay, but I think Laurel's tormented by it. It must be that."

"Tormented?"

"Laurel was a wonderful elementary school teacher, even receiving statewide recognition."

"She doesn't teach anymore?" I asked.

"No, not any more. She wanted to teach until she became pregnant. Several years passed. When the doctor said she couldn't have children, she quit at the end of the school year."

"Why?"

"She said that she couldn't bear to be around children if she couldn't have her own. She quit teaching and began drinking," J.D. said. "We were separated for a while. She went to counseling, but I don't think it helped."

"I'm sorry for both of you, but I'm glad that you have each other. At least you will be together when you go to the rest home."

"Don't count on it. I wonder if Laurel and I will be together in the end."

"What do you mean?"

"Our marriage has problems. It's not satisfying," J.D. said.

"What do you mean?"

"The sex. When we were first married, everything was great. Now, it's on again, off again. Sometimes it's none for months and then it can be almost every day for a while."

"Have you been able to figure out why?"

"Laurel goes from being hot to cold. She can change her personality more quickly than any woman I've ever known. She can be just as soft, like the girl that we both knew. Then she can be hard and tough, like somebody you've never seen before. Seems to be getting more serious now."

"Why is that?" I asked.

"This whole business with her stepdad. It's stirred up all these emotions in Laurel. I want to get this mess behind us."

"Is that why you're pushing to convict Ora Mae?" I said.

"I didn't think we were going to talk about the case."

"You brought up the situation with her stepdad. Obviously it's important."

"I guess it is," J.D. said.

"What do you think is troubling Laurel?"

"She had always been so protective of her mother, all through junior high and high school after Wayne died. They were so close. It's like an obsession. Laurel is like her full-time protectress."

"Sounds like you may be jealous."

"Jealous? Yeah, I am jealous. Not very noble, I know."

"Understandable," I said.

"Well, I'll admit that our sex life has improved. Every time that Laurel wants me to do something for her mother, she becomes accommodating."

"What kinds of things do you do for Miss Winnie?"

"Straightening out her finances, taking care of her legal matters."

"I would imagine that life's been hard for her and Laurel, always working. I guess that Wayne didn't leave them well off financially."

"That's the strange thing. Miss Winnie actually has money. More money than I would have imagined. You couldn't tell by the way she lived."

"Wayne left her money?"

"What I've determined is that Wayne left her a large insurance policy. Of course that didn't pay off until Wayne was legally declared dead."

"Surely, she then used the money."

"Not until recently. The money was invested, but she never spent the interest nor the principal. She lived like the money wasn't hers, taking loans for Laurel's college. Laurel and I finished paying her college loans after we married." J.D. stopped and looked off to the lake. "Actually, Dad paid off the loan."

"I'm glad she has the money."

"It's slowly being drained by nursing home expenses. I'm just glad it's there. Otherwise, Laurel and I would be paying for it."

"Good she has the money," I repeated.

"Enough about Laurel and me. What about you and Rachel? You never did tell me about that trip to Chicago."

"How did you know about the trip to Chicago?" I asked.

"Dad told me."

"How did he know?"

"Dad makes it his business to know everything," J.D. said.

"You sound resentful."

"I may have made a mistake in returning to Caruthers' Gap. We were happier in Columbia, but we had to help with Laurel's mother."

"You could transfer Miss Winnie to a facility in Columbia."

"Maybe. Adrian, there's something I've wanted to ask you all morning," J.D. said.

"Ask away," I said.

"Adrian, would you speak with Laurel to see what's bothering her? She always would talk with you. She's become worse in the last year and won't even visit her mother's house anymore. She said it makes her uneasy. I've had to go by every week or so to check on the place."

I purposefully withheld saying I would talk with Laurel until I had asked a few more questions. "Why don't you sell it?"

"We promised Winnie that we wouldn't sell."

"You say that Laurel refuses to go to her mother's house?"

"Yeah, the few times we've had to go there, she gets real upset. In fact, she promises me anything, if you know what I mean, if I'll take her away."

"I'll be glad to talk to Laurel, if she'll talk to me."

"I think she will. Last night was a bad night. She's agreed to talk with you," J.D. said.

"Before I talk with her, take me by Miss Winnie's house. If Laurel is resistant to going there, it might help me to visit first."

"I don't understand why, but I will trust your judgment. What about now?"

"Yeah, I think we've caught about everything we're going to catch here," I said. I thought I made a good catch that morning, even if none of it were drawn directly from the lake.

A few hours later we were on our way to Miss Winnie's house. Earlier J.D. had dropped me at the motel where I had showered, changed, and pondered. I was unsure what we might discover, but intuition was leading me to unravel what had transpired among these strangely connected residents of Caruthers' Gap. The clues must be there, they always were, I thought. I hoped that I would not regret what I might find.

"Sure is hot in here," I said, once we opened the doors in Miss Winnie's house.

"Yeah, let's get some air on," J.D. said. "We'll need to walk through the rooms and make sure the vents are open." J.D. left me in the living room to open vents while he went into the hall to turn on the air conditioning.

We went through each room, checking the vents. Everything seemed fine.

"What's this room?" I asked.

"This is Miss Winnie's junk room. Laurel doesn't like it in here," J.D. said.

"Really?"

"Hand me that chair," J.D. said. "I need to open the ceiling vents. Looks like two of them, one on the floor and the other in the ceiling." J.D. opened the ceiling vent while I opened the floor vent.

"That's funny," J.D. said.

"What?" I asked.

"I can't feel any air out of this one."

"Air's coming out of this vent," I said, feeling the air from the floor vent.

"Well, it's not up here. Something else to repair."

"Let's go upstairs," I said.

We were outside a bedroom when J.D. said, "This was Laurel's bedroom. I can't remember where the vents are."

"Over here," I said. I bent down and opened the vent near the doorway.

J.D. walked around the room. "That may be the only one," he said, walking on the throw rug in front of the rocking chair. That doesn't feel right."

"What?" I asked.

"The floor," J.D. said. He bent down and picked up the throw rug. "No wonder," he said. "The rug was covering another vent. There. They're all open."

"We better go. It's getting late," I said.

"Okay." J.D. quickly tossed the rug into the corner.

Once outside I turned to J.D. "J.D., it might help if Laurel came and walked through the place with us. It might help if she talked about this place," I said.

"I'm willing to try anything," J.D. said.

"Hello," I said, picking up the phone back in my motel room.

"Adrian?" Her voice on the phone asked.

"Yes, who is this?"

"Adrian, it's Corrine," she said.

"Sorry, Corrine, I didn't recognize your voice."

"Nor I yours. Are you all right? You sound tired."

"A little."

"I'm sorry that it's taken me so long to get back to you about your e-mail message."

I had momentarily forgotten about the e-mail message telling me not to delve into Ora Mae's secrets. Every day I had checked my computer and there were no additional messages. "What did you learn?"

"Not much, I'm afraid. The message was sent through the Internet, and then the sender's address was stripped."

"Stripped?"

"Erased. Removed."

"Which means?"

"We cannot trace its source of origin."

"I see. Well, thanks for trying, Corrine."

"Have you received any more?"

"No. I've been checking my e-mail every day."

"Hmm."

"I know that 'hmm.' What are you thinking?"

"Your current e-mail address was issued about two weeks ago. In fact, you received the e-mail message a day or two prior to our officially posting the e-mail address on the Hunter-Harwell web site directory. While your e-mail address was active, no one knew the new address."

"You say no one knew about it?"

"Only myself and Morriah. She was doing new business cards for you and I gave her your new address for the printing of the cards."

"Morriah gave me the cards when I first returned from England."

"Maybe Morriah gave out the address."

"I doubt that Morriah would give out the address. She steadfastly refuses to have anything to do with computers of any sort. She still does some typing for me on her old electric typewriter."

"Well, maybe she gave out one of your new business cards."

"The box was wrapped when I got the cards. I put a few in my wallet. I've only given out one." And then I remembered. I paused.

"Are you okay?"

"Yeah, I am."

"Have you made a discovery?"

"You know me too well," I said.

"Probably so," Corrine said. "I don't know if this is important, Adrian, but do you remember Harvey Mullins, a former students of yours?"

"Vaguely."

"Well, Harvey's been working here this summer. He commented how he preferred working in air conditioning, unlike last summer when he worked in Caruthers' Gap for a septic tank company."

"Caruthers' Gap? A septic company?" I said, becoming increasingly interested in Harvey Mullins.

"Yes, he was on the crew that discovered the body at Ora Mae Chapman's house. I thought you would find that interesting."

"Did he say anything else?" I asked.

"He said the crew chief commented about the large willow trees planted around Ora Mae's property."

"At one time there were lots of willows there."

"The crew chief said that planting that many tress near the septic tank was just asking for trouble."

"Yeah."

"As if she wanted to have the tank replaced," Corrine added.

"As if she wanted to have the tank replaced," I repeated Corrine's last words. "Thanks, Corrine"

"Before you go," Corrine said, "how is Caroline doing? I've missed seeing her."

"She's fine. She's been enjoying visiting her cousins and seeing where I grew up."

"She needs that," Corrine said.

"Morriah and Caroline tell me that you spent a lot of time with Caroline while I was away," I said.

"I enjoy being around her."

"I'm sorry, Corrine, that things didn't work out for us."

"You've said that already, Adrian. No need to say it again."

"Thanks for your help. I hope to see you soon," I said.

"Me, too."

Caroline was lying on her bed and reading a book when I knocked and entered her room. "Caroline, there's something that I need to talk with you about," I said.

"What is it?" Caroline looked up from her reading.

"It's about my going to North Carolina to teach."

Her eyes turned back to her book. "What is it?"

"I'm turning down the offer. We'll be in Brunson this fall."

Caroline closed her book and placed it beside her. "I'll be with my old friends?"

"Yes."

"You're doing this for me?"

"No, I'm doing it for both of us. It's not the right time to move."

"Just the two of us?" Caroline asked.

"Just the two of us," I answered.

"I like that," Caroline said.

I sat on the bed next to her. "Caroline, I can't promise that we won't move someday."

"My concern is today," Caroline said.

"That's the way it should be. I'll be concerned about tomorrow. Now go put on the pink bikini. It's in the package on my bed. Let's go for a swim."

"You didn't take it back?"

"No, I didn't."

"Thanks, Daddy," Caroline said. "One day I know there might be three of us."

"Would that be okay?"

"It depends on the third person," she said.

"Sure it does. Now get ready. I need a swim with you."

Morriah, Rachel and I were in the motel room when the phone rang.

"I'm not sure if she'll make it through the night," Lola said.

"I understand. I'll be there as soon as I can."

"Who was it?" Morriah asked.

"Lola. She thinks Ora Mae won't last much longer."

"Are you going to her?" Morriah asked.

"Soon, but I must make one more visit and keep an appointment. J.D. and Laurel are going to meet me at Winnie's house at six o'clock tonight. But first, I have time for one visit. I have a theory to test."

"Would you like company?" Rachel asked.

"I hoped you would volunteer. Morriah, please take Caroline to Ora Mae's house. I'll be there as soon as I can. Watch over Caroline. I don't want this to be too painful for her."

"I know how to take care of Caroline. I've been doing it for years," Morriah said with her eyes bulging.

People were complicated and rarely purely good or evil, as I had been taught in my youth under the messages of Samuel T. In some ways, they might be easier to understand and control if they were such. However, the complexities of human nature made each one intriguing and not easily explained, even Rachel. Diagnostic and categorical thinking were often misleading and often incomplete. Giving credit where credit is due was the missive I had always left with my students. I, too, must practice what I had taught.

Rachel and I were on our way to Miss Winnie's nursing home. "You were the one who left me the e-mail message about not probing into Ora Mae's case," I said.

Rachel turned to me. "What are you talking about?"

"You sent me the e-mail about my not investigating Wayne Daniels' death. You're the only one who could have."

"Why am I the only one?"

"Rachel, don't answer a question with a question. I know that technique all too well. I didn't realize it until today, but I gave you a business card the first time we met. That card contained my new e-mail address."

Rachel paused. "I did send you the message."

"Why?"

"I didn't want you to cause problems for so many people, including myself."

"What do you mean?"

"I needed the money Davis was paying me to keep you distracted. I have personal debts and school loans. I sent you a warning."

"Why did you stop?"

"You were frightened enough by the message. I didn't need to send any more. Besides, I was able to keep you distracted from your investigation."

"Why didn't you tell me earlier?"

"I didn't think you'd believe me."

"I see."

"One more confession," Rachel said.

"What's that?"

"J.D. and I had an affair in Columbia. It was nothing serious, just recreational," Rachel said.

"Nothing serious," I said, shaking my head, and wondering how many more confessions and secrets she held.

When we arrived at the nursing home, the receptionist said that Miss Winnie already had a visitor. Rachel and I went to her room and found Davis and Miss Winnie sitting in chairs drawn close to each other.

"Adrian," Davis said. "I didn't expect to see you here."

"No, but I'm not surprised to see you, here," I said. I ignored Miss Winnie and focused exclusively on Davis.

"What do you mean?"

"You've worked so hard trying to keep me from the truth. You were skillful, I'll admit."

"You know nothing about truth. You've been ungrateful for all that I've done for you. You're more loyal to Ora Mae than to any of us."

"Ora Mae," Winnie Daniels said. The name seemed to awaken the woman. "Ora Mae's my good friend. How is she? I hear she's not well."

I bent down to Miss Winnie. "Miss Winnie, this is Adrian Stockwood."

"Adrian, yes, I remember." Winnie smiled.

"Ora Mae's not well, Miss Winnie. People are saying mean things about her. They say she killed Wayne Daniels. That's not true, is it?"

"No, it wasn't Ora Mae that killed Wayne, was it?" Miss Winnie looked up to the light fixture. "I wasn't a good wife," Winnie said.

"Hush, Winnie," Davis said. He reached out and gently rubbed her arms and shoulders. He turned to me. "You can't believe anything she says. Her mind wanders. Adrian, you need to leave. You're upsetting her."

"It's not my intent to upset her. Neither will I upset Ora Mae. I'm beginning to understand what happened. Wayne discovered that Miss Winnie wanted a divorce. There was an argument and Wayne was killed."

"Don't be ridiculous," Davis said. "That's part of your imagination. Ora Mae Chapman killed Wayne. It was her knife that was found with Wayne's body."

"The knife. So stupid. So stupid. The knife," Miss Winnie muttered.

"You're upsetting her. Get out or I'll call the police."

"Adrian, we had better leave. She's becoming upset," Rachel said, pulling me away.

"With or without you, I will discover the truth. There is still one other person who knows. I think Laurel knows."

"Laurel, Laurel," Winnie cried. "I wanted to protect you."

"Get out," Davis demanded.

"We'll go," I said.

Once we were out of the room and walking down the hall, the nurse at the desk looked up at us. Her smile conveyed sympathy, I thought. "I'm sure it must be hard watching patients with Alzheimer's," I said.

"It is. Oh, you mean Mrs. Daniels," the nurse said.

"Yes, so tragic," I said.

"Mrs. Daniels doesn't have Alzheimer's," the nurse said.

"What do you mean?"

"There's never been a diagnosis of Alzheimer's Disease."

"I don't understand," I said, looking at Rachel.

"Mrs. Daniels stays on our unit voluntarily. She does have early dementia, but the diagnosis of Alzheimer's has never been made," the nurse said.

"Her daughter said it's Alzheimer's," Rachel said.

"It's a common mistake that people make," the nurse said.

"Could someone like Mrs. Daniels live in monitored housing, rather than a nursing care facility?" I asked.

"Certainly. They do it all the time with an appropriate living environment. She would need understanding and loving caregivers."

"I see. Thank you," I said.

"Excuse me. You are family?" the nurse asked as we passed her desk.

"No, just friends of the family," I said.

"Forgive me. I've probably said too much," she responded.

"That's okay," I said. "I understand."

CHAPTER SEVENTEEN

"Winnie, it's Claire. Claire Cobb."

Winnie was silent.

"Don't you recognize me, honey? It's Claire Cobb, Samuel T.'s wife."

A smile emerged on Winnie's face.

"You do recognize me, don't you, Winnie?" Claire said.

"Claire, it's been a long time. How are the boys? It's been so long since I've seen them. They'll be graduating from high school before you know it."

Claire looked at Winnie.

"They're fine. Getting bigger every day." Claire wiped a tear away from her cheek.

"My Laurel is almost twelve," Winnie said. "Can't believe it sometimes. Seems like only yesterday when I brought her home from the hospital. Her daddy was in Korea. He only saw his daughter once."

"You loved Jim a lot," Claire said.

Winnie nodded her head.

"I hope Wayne is good to you," Claire said.

"Mustn't tell Wayne that I talked about Jim. He doesn't like Laurel or me to mention Jim's name. He's jealous, powerfully jealous. You won't say anything, will you?"

"No, I won't say anything."

"Wayne has been good to you, hasn't he?"

"Samuel T. says I must stay," Winnie said. "That's what I'm doing. I hope it doesn't kill us."

Claire shook her head.

"Claire, why does it hurt to do the will of God? I don't understand why it has to hurt so much."

"I know, Winnie, I know."

The two women sat there in silence until Winnie Daniels broke the silence.

"Claire," Winnie said, "do something for me."

"What?"

"Call Davis," Winnie said. "I remember now. I need to tell him before I forget."

Rachel and I were on route to meet Laurel and J.D. at Miss Winnie's house. In spite of apprehension about Rachel, I thought she was a competent therapist and I needed her skill for what we might find at the house.

"In cases like this, familiar places can trigger memories," Rachel said.

"Or it may induce further trauma," I said.

"You're right," Rachel said.

When we arrived, Laurel and J.D. were waiting on the front porch.

"Honey, are sure that you want to do this?" J.D. asked Laurel. I detected a deep and protective compassion in his voice.

"Yes, I need to get this settled. I don't want to be here, but I want this to be over. If Adrian thinks this might help, I want to do it," Laurel said.

"I don't know for certain that this will help, Laurel," I admitted, "but it's a start."

Laurel led us through the house, taking us through room by room. Laurel spoke few words as we moved through the foyer, the living room, the kitchen, the dining room, and her mother's bedroom. In each of these places, Rachel and I monitored Laurel's movements, her expressions, and her few words. As if we were in a clinical setting, we scrutinized her reactions. Nothing out of the ordinary.

"Laurel, let's go back through the rooms and I want you to talk with us about your memories of each one," I said.

Initially, Laurel hesitated as we went through the bottom floor rooms once again. She spoke about the dining room where once two of them ate alone; then Wayne Daniels joined her family and there were three. In the living room, she spoke about doing homework there with a set of encyclopedias and her mother sitting in the chair near the front porch window. In the bedroom, Laurel described sitting on the edge of the bed and watching her mother sit before the vanity.

"What is your mother doing at the vanity?" Rachel asked.

Good question, I thought. Wish I had asked it.

"Mother's putting on make-up. I loved watching her put on make-up. Sometimes she would let me play dress-up."

"Miss Winnie put on lot of make-up?" I asked.

"Mother cried at lot. Her make-up ran," Laurel admitted.

"Laurel, concentrate on your mother. Why is she crying?" I asked.

"She missed Daddy. No, she missed Wayne."

"Did she cry after Wayne disappeared?" Rachel asked.

"No, she didn't cry much after Wayne left," Laurel admitted.

"Is she crying while Wayne is still alive?" I asked.

"Yes," Laurel said.

"Can you tell us more?" I asked.

"No, I don't remember any more." The energy level in her voice declined. Obviously it was emotionally draining for her. As though it were my own, I could feel her exhaustion.

Rachel and I continued to prod her gently, but Laurel added little more. J.D. sat there in the corner of the room watching her strain to remember something that might help.

"Time to go upstairs?" J.D. asked. "Maybe the answer's upstairs."

One door, nearest the kitchen, had remained closed.

"What's this?" Rachel asked.

"Mother called it her guest room," Laurel said. J.D. began opening the door.

"I don't want to go in there," Laurel said.

"Why?" I asked.

"Mother didn't like for me to go in that room!"

"Why?" Rachel asked.

"She didn't want me to get into her things. Later, it was used mostly for storage."

"May we go in, Laurel?" I asked.

"I guess so," Laurel said. "Go ahead."

J.D. opened the door and entered the room. When he had found the light switch, Rachel entered next, followed by Laurel and then me. It was as Laurel had said—a storage room with dusty boxes lining the walls.

"There's a double bed here," Rachel said. A faded pink chenille bedspread covered the iron bed.

"Smells musty," I said.

"Yes, this room always smelled dirty, but Mother always smelled so nice to everyone."

"But your mother called it a guest room," Rachel said. "Yes, Mother used to call it the guest room. We rarely had guests. In fact, the only person I ever remember staying there was Ora Mae. No, Ora Mae always slept on a cot in the kitchen. Never in the guest room."

"Ora Mae?" Rachel asked.

"Yes, Ora Mae worked for us. Sometimes she would spend the night if someone was sick or if it was really cold. Her house had only a wood stove. Mother would let her stay with us. I told you there's nothing here."

"Why don't you like this room?" I asked.

"I don't know. Mother used to scold me for playing in the room. She said this was her one private place, her own world that only she could enter. She kept the door locked most of the time."

Rachel and I continued to ask questions in the hope of uncovering some hidden fact or scene. No use. Laurel recalled nothing more.

"Do we need to go upstairs?" J.D. asked. "This whole process is fruitless."

"Be patient. Let's not stop now," I said.

We went up the stairs. Three rooms were upstairs—one large empty storage room where J.D., Laurel and I played as children, and two bedrooms. We entered each room and painstakingly allowed Laurel the opportunity to tell us about the room. In each room, I hoped that we would find an answer, some answer as to what happened. Nothing.

"Only my room left. Let's get it over with," Laurel said.

Laurel led. As a young boy, I thought it was the bedroom of a princess, the white French provincial bedroom suite with the full canopy bed and lots of pink and yellow ruffles. A large white rocking chair, with stuffed animals and dolls, stood center in the room. The room was like stepping back into a picture book of long-forgotten fairy tales. I thought Laurel was the wealthiest girl in town with a room all to herself. The child saw the room as magic. Now, the adult knew the magic could easily be purchased from any furniture catalogue on credit.

"As I said, this is my room," Laurel said.

"Very lovely," Rachel said. "A wonderful room for a little girl."

"Mother decorated it. Said she always wanted a room like this when she was a girl."

"You never changed it," I said.

"No, I never did." Laurel bent over and pulled a stuffed bear from the rocking chair and held it close to her face. "I always liked the feel of this bear against my cheek."

Laurel stood, rubbing the bear on her face. Her smile stopped and she put her hands to her ears. "Did you hear that? Something dropped. J.D., it's gone. The diamond earring you gave me is gone. Help me find it."

"We'll find it honey," J.D. said.

"I see it," Laurel shouted.

Laurel stretched out her hand to the floor grate. "It's right here. Got it."

We each watched Laurel retrieve the diamond earring. "I'm always afraid I'm going to lose the earrings. I'm going to close this vent."

Rachel and J.D. had turned away to another part of the room. Only I was watching when Laurel reached to close the vent. She stood still, staring.

"Mother, no, don't do that!" Laurel shouted. "Mother, don't do that! Mother, no!" Laurel collapsed on the floor, crying like a wounded animal.

J.D. rushed to her side. "What's wrong, honey? You found the earring. It's okay."

Still Laurel cried, "No, Mother. Don't do that." Laurel clenched her stomach. "I can't help," she cried. She did not finish her sentence. Laurel gagged, turned her head away from J.D., and began vomiting.

"Get the wastebasket and a wet cloth," I said to Rachel, who quickly responded.

While Rachel and J.D. comforted Laurel, I had to see what Laurel saw. I looked at the open floor vent. Through the rusty grid, I saw a light. Two figures were walking in the room below, Davis and Miss Winnie. I could see them but not hear them. The view of a double bed was directly beneath the floor vent. Laurel's bedroom was above the downstairs room where Miss Winnie had her private and secret world.

At Ora Mae's house, Caroline, Claire Cobb and Morriah waited in the living room.

"Where's Daddy?" Caroline asked.

"Your daddy's taking care of some business," Morriah said.

"He'll be here soon, I'm sure," Claire said.

Morriah circled the room and dusted.

"What are you doing?" Caroline said.

"I always like to keep my hands busy when I'm waiting."

"Waiting for what?" Caroline asked.

Morriah glanced toward Claire.

"Your daddy, of course," Claire said.

Morriah looked at her watch. "I'm through waiting for Adrian. I'm going to get him. Caroline, I want you to come with me."

"No, Morriah, I want to be here with Ora Mae. I want to see her again."

"No, I don't want to leave you here," Morriah said.

"I'm going to stay, Morriah," Claire said. *"I'll take care of Caroline."* Morriah's eyes met Claire's. *"She's safe with me, I promise."*

"I'll be back soon," Morriah said. The front-door screen banged as Morriah left.

The four of us went downstairs where we found Davis and Miss Winnie in the living room. They were seated close together on the sofa, apparently waiting for us.

J.D. guided Laurel to an empty love seat and sat down beside her. "What are you doing here?" J.D. asked.

"Winnie insisted that I bring her tonight," Davis said.

"Mother, you shouldn't be out of the nursing home," Laurel said, having regained her composure.

"J.D., I may need a good lawyer. The nursing staff won't be happy that Winnie and I sneaked out of the nursing home."

"We've wasted enough time. It's time to tell the story and set people free." Miss Winnie tapped her cane to the words she spoke.

"No need to talk, Mother. It's okay. I'll take care of you," Laurel said.

"No. Davis, tell them."

"Winnie, no," Davis said.

"Now, Davis, now. For their sake and for our sake." Miss Winnie again tapped her cane. "For my sake, please." Miss Winnie patted Davis' hand.

"Laurel, J.D., Winnie and I want you to know something. We kept it a secret all those years." Davis hesitated.

"What is it, Dad?" J.D. asked.

"Winnie and I were in love when the two of you were children. We loved each other very much and still do."

The words electrified the room. All eyes stared at Davis and Miss Winnie. Miss Winnie's face had an expression on it that I could only describe as sorrowful happiness.

"Laurel, it was wrong, but it felt right at the time. Davis and I loved each other. Wayne was so busy with his work. I was lonely. We were both lonely. It happened. I failed Wayne as a wife, I know. It was wrong. It's been my secret ever since."

"Oh, Mother. It's all right," Laurel said. She paused and added the words, "I know."

"You know?" Davis asked.

Laurel made no response. We waited for her to say more, but she was silent.

"Laurel, tell them what you saw," I said.

"I can't."

"You can, Laurel," I said. "You now remember what you saw." I glanced at Rachel, and she nodded in agreement.

"I saw you, Mother. I saw you, Davis. I saw you together in the guest room."

"What?"

"Laurel, how did you see us?" Miss Winnie asked.

"He made me look. I didn't want to watch. He . . . he made me watch you together."

"Who made you look, Laurel?" I asked.

"Dad made me watch."

"You mean Wayne," I said.

"Yes."

"The son-of-a bitch," Davis said. "The son-of-a-bitch."

"My guess is that Wayne cut a false vent in Laurel's room directly above the downstairs guest room. You can see the bed from Laurel's room," I said.

"He made you watch us, Laurel?" Miss Winnie spoke to Laurel as she had spoken to me as a student, slowly trying to understand what had happened.

"Yes, Mama," Laurel said. I had not heard her call Miss Winnie "mama" during my entire visit.

"He covered my mouth with his handkerchief so I wouldn't scream. He held my head over the grill in my room. I saw you there with Davis."

"Oh, Laurel," J.D. cried. "No more. This is enough."

"I didn't know, Laurel. I didn't know, Laurel," Miss Winnie pleaded.

"I know, Mama. I never told you. Dad told me he would hurt you if I told you."

"Laurel, come here." Miss Winnie stretched out her frail arms to Laurel. Laurel left J.D. and sat next to her mother, placing her head in her mother's lap and Miss Winnie stroked her daughter's head.

"Davis, tell us what happened the night Wayne died," I said.

"Go ahead," Miss Winnie said, "or I will."

"All right, but what I say here I will never repeat again outside of this room," Davis said. "Adrian, do you understand?"

"I understand," I said.

Davis began to describe the night that Wayne died.

"It was a Friday night. Wayne and I had taken the church boys on a fishing trip, like we always did in the summer. The girls were at a slumber party at the Cobb's house." Davis stopped. "I left the camp for a few hours. Wayne was out in the boat fishing by himself, so I came to Winnie's house. We had so little time together." Davis stopped and turned to Winnie. "We loved each other," he said.

"Yes, we did," Miss Winnie said. Miss Winnie continued to stroke Laurel's forehead. Laurel nursed a strand of hair in her mouth.

"Wayne found you, didn't he?" I asked.

"Yes, later Wayne left the camp and returned to his house. He walked in on us in the guest room."

"What did he do?" I asked.

"He laughed. He laughed at us."

"Laughed?" J.D. asked.

"All he did was laugh. Said he hoped I enjoyed it more than he did," Davis said. "I started to fight him when he said that, but Winnie pulled me away."

"Go on," I said.

"Wayne said that he had known for a long time about us," Davis said.

"He let you go on?" I asked.

"That's what he said."

"I told him that I wanted a divorce. It didn't matter any more what the church said. I begged him for the divorce," Miss Winnie said.

"Again, he laughed at us." Davis said.

"'What do you want from us?' I asked him," Miss Winnie said.

"Nothing," Wayne said. "You can wallow in your sin and each other for all I care. I'll have my revenge."

"I asked him what he meant," Miss Winnie said. "He was almost out of the door before he turned to me. He looked at me and said, 'For every time you've had Davis, I've had Laurel.'" Winnie broke down in tears. "He did that to my little girl. I couldn't let him do that to my little girl."

"What did you do?" I asked Miss Winnie.

"I ran past him, out of the room toward the kitchen."

"What happened then, Davis?"

"We got into a fight. I beat him down pretty good. He looked up at me with his devil eyes and said, 'I'll have my revenge on you, old friend.' Wayne paused to get his breath and looked at me. He gave that smirk and said, 'you've been having my wife. Well, maybe I'll be having your boy. Who knows, maybe he'll grow to like it.' Wayne laughed. I lunged for his throat. I was going to choke him to death.

"Dad, you killed Wayne?" J.D. asked.

"Yes, son." Davis said. "I killed him."

"No, Wayne, we tell the whole truth now. We can't keep secrets anymore to protect each other," Miss Winnie said.

"No, Winnie."

"I came back from the kitchen with a knife. I ran behind Wayne and cut him deep because of what he did to Laurel. I'm the one who killed him," Miss Winnie said.

"How is Ora Mae involved in all of this?" I asked.

"Ora Mae had helped me all that afternoon to make treats for the girls' slumber party and for the boys' fishing trip. Ora Mae came back later that night for her knife."

"The one that killed Wayne." I said.

"Yes," Miss Winnie said. "Ora Mae saw me from the kitchen window pick up the knife and run out the door. She came inside. By the time she got into the room, Wayne was dead."

"The three of us talked. Ora Mae offered to bury Wayne in her back-yard. She was having a septic tank dug on her new place. We wrapped the body and I dug the hole deeper and laid the body where the tank would be placed. Later I capsized Wayne's boat to make it look like an accident," Davis said.

"The knife. Why did you bury the knife with Wayne?" I asked.

"I shouldn't have done it," Winnie said. She shook her fists in the air. "I threw the knife in the grave. Davis and Ora Mae didn't see me," Miss Winnie said, resting her head in her hands. "If they had seen me, they would have stopped me. After we buried him, Ora Mae asked about the knife. It was too late. We couldn't dig it back up."

"And you were going to let Ora Mae die with the community thinking that she killed Wayne," I said.

"I paid her all those years to help her keep our secret."

"Are you saying she blackmailed you?" I asked.

"No, she didn't. I just tried to help her out financially for helping us."

"Why didn't you go to the authorities when the body was found?" I asked.

"Miss Winnie's health was failing her," Davis said. "Ora Mae also had cancer. I thought Ora Mae would be dead before a trial could occur. And I had to protect Winnie."

"Davis has always tried to protect me," Miss Winnie said.

"You two never married." I said.

"No, the night Wayne died, our physical love died as well," Winnie said. "It had caused too much pain. We were never with each other again. I focused on Laurel, and Davis focused on his wife and J.D."

"You must tell the authorities," I said. "Ora Mae must be cleared and cleared quickly."

"No," Davis said. "I told you when I began the story, I'll never tell. No one in this room will tell the story."

"I'll tell the story," Rachel said.

"Won't matter. I'll deny everything. It's all hearsay. No one will talk. I know too much about anyone who would talk."

"I'll tell them, Davis," Miss Winnie said. "I was there."

"They won't believe you, Winnie, you're not well," Davis said. "She's been coherent now for a few hours. It won't last. It never does."

Davis was right. The courts wouldn't believe a woman with dementia.

"Are you still trying to protect yourself?" I asked.

"No, not me," Davis said. "Winnie, I'll protect Winnie."

"And let Ora Mae die with the community believing she was a murderer," I said.

Laurel raised her head from her mother's lap. "Mama, I came back the night of the slumber party. I missed you. I saw the three of you around Wayne's body. I never told anybody. I kept the secret to protect you."

"I'm so sorry, Laurel," Miss Winnie said. "So sorry for what he did to you."

"Mama, Wayne never touched me. Wayne never touched me. He made me look at you, but he never touched me. He never touched me the way he told you he did," Laurel said.

"What?" Miss Winnie asked.

"I was a good girl," Laurel said, tilting her head. "I never told that he made me watch you and Davis. He told me I had to protect you by watching. As long as I watched, Wayne said he wouldn't hurt you. I tried to protect you. I never told that I saw you at Wayne's body. I ran back to the slumber party and never said a word. I kept quiet to protect you. I did the right thing, didn't I Mama?"

Miss Winnie stared at Laurel for a few moments. Miss Winnie looked at each of us, as though she was bewildered. "Where am I?" We waited for her to continue. "This is my house," she said firmly. "Where's Wayne?" We said nothing. Miss Winnie's face grew sad. She turned and rested her head on the back of the couch and sobbed.

Davis broke the silence. "She's gone away, my lovely Winnie's gone again." Davis placed his hand on Winnie's shoulder and patted her gently.

"Laurel, why did you place your mother in a nursing home?" I asked.

"What are you talking about?" Laurel asked.

"You know what I'm talking about," I said. "You didn't have to place her in a nursing home."

"Mother and I agreed that the home was the best place for her."

"I know you love her, but why did you place her in a nursing home? Why have you told everyone that she has Alzheimer's?"

"Can't you see, I was protecting her? I put her in the home so no one would believe her when she said she killed Wayne. I had to protect her. If everyone thought she was just crazy, they wouldn't believe her ranting and raving about having killed Wayne. I had to protect her. I had to protect her."

"I know, Laurel," I said.

"Laurel, I love you so," J.D. said, reaching out to his wife.

"J.D., you believe me. Wayne never touched me," Laurel said, turning to J.D.

Rachel and I looked at each other.

"I believe you, sweetheart. It was all a lie," J.D. said. "It was all a lie."

"All these years," Davis began, "these secrets were based on lies?" Davis paused, put his hands to his forehead, and shook his head. No one spoke. Davis looked up to his J.D.'s stares. "What's wrong, son?"

"Dad, Wayne's threats were empty. I wouldn't have let him touch me. I would have fought back."

When Davis did not respond to his words, J.D. asked, "Dad, is that why you pushed me so hard?"

"I did what I thought you needed."

"Needed it?" J.D. said. Beads of perspiration were collecting on his forehead. "You were always on my back about everything. Whatever I did was never enough. I never felt that I was good enough to be your son."

"That's not it, J.D."

"What was it then?"

"Son, I was trying to make sure that you became a real man."

"A real man? A real man?" J.D. said again. J.D.'s head shook as he continued to speak. "Do you mean that you believed the threats of that asshole Wayne?"

Davis was silent.

"You pushed and interfered too much, Dad."

Davis bent his head, cupped his hands over his face and cried.

Ora Mae's words returned to me. Wayne Daniels was the meanest and lyingest man she ever knew. In that room I saw four people from my childhood who had lived years hiding what they thought was truth—a truth told by the meanest and lyingest man Ora Mae ever knew.

Each was there with his or her own secret hurt and shame—a middle-aged woman who had spent her life trying to protect her mother and who was being destroyed by her own secrets; my childhood friend who had lived his life being pushed by a father who feared his son was not a man; an old woman who lost her mental powers and had given up love because of the pain it had brought her family; and the old man whom I had admired for years who had become a man of greed and power, trying to protect the people he loved. Each was a victim, an isolated victim, closely intertwined in the lives of each other. Davis was correct. They would never be able to betray each other; their secrets were too deep and too tangled.

The silence was broken by the doorbell. Before I could get to the door, it opened. There stood Morriah.

"Adrian, you better go to Ora Mae's. Lola thinks she has only a few hours left. Ora Mae's calling for you."

Ora Mae had said she wanted to live until her birthday. I looked at my watch, only two hours away from midnight and her birthday.

"Where's Caroline?" I asked.

"I left her at Ora Mae's place with Claire. She insisted she stay with her. Come on."

"Can I leave them?" I asked.

"Why the hell not?" Morriah said. "There's the door." Rachel was the only one who knew what I meant. Emotional destruction and pain were so strong and pervasive in the room that even the air was heavy to the breath.

"Adrian, go ahead. I'll stay here. By the way, you're an effective counselor. You should resume your practice," Rachel said.

I had shared much with Rachel, and yet I was glad that I had kept the secret of why I no longer counseled from her. At least, on one deep level I had kept her from knowing all of my vulnerabilities. Regardless of what I had previously thought of her, Rachel had therapeutic skill. I had learned cautiously and selectively to trust her within limits.

"Thanks," I said.

CHAPTER EIGHTEEN

Peeking through the nylon curtains, Caroline was waiting for my return. Together the streetlight and the moonlight caused the oak and willow trees to cast great shadows over Ora Mae's front yard and porch. The bugs circled the white lights on the porch as though they were invited guests.

"Daddy, I'm glad you're here. Miss Claire said Ora Mae doesn't have much time left. The nurse thinks it may be soon. Daddy, she's dying, just like Mama died."

I bent down and held Caroline in my arms. "I know, sweetie," I said.

A few quiet moments passed between us as we shared our grief. "Do you remember what I told you when your mother died?"

"You told me that I didn't have a mother on earth anymore but that I still had a daddy."

"That's right. I'm here for you always."

"I know. I still hurt." She looked at me.

"There will always be some hurt and loss. As we get older, the hurt becomes less because we have new people to give our love to."

"Like Ora Mae."

"Like Ora Mae," I repeated.

Caroline turned away from me and looked once again into the summer night. "I don't want to grow up. I don't want to die."

"That will be a long time away."

"You said you didn't want me to grow up, Daddy." She stared at me.

"I know, but that was selfish on my part. I'll always love you, but you must grow up, too. It would be wrong for you to remain a little girl forever. Sometimes even daddies have to grow up."

"I guess."

"And it would be wrong for Ora Mae to live with so much pain."

"I know," she said.

"Let me go see Ora Mae. You stay in the front room for a while."

"No, Daddy, I want . . . "

"I'll come and get you when it's time," I said. "It's okay."

Claire motioned for Caroline to join her on the couch while I went to Ora Mae's room, where Lola greeted me at Ora Mae's doorway. Lola stepped out of the room into the small hallway, blocking my immediate entrance into the room.

"She's been asking for you," Lola said. "You need to know what to expect. Ora Mae will drift in and out of consciousness. Can't predict when it will happen. Sit and listen. Talk to her as much as you wish, say what you need to say."

"Will it be long now?" I asked.

"No one can say. My experience tells me it could be hours, but sometimes it could last for days. We can't predict, only wait."

"I understand."

"One more thing," Lola added. "Let her talk as much as she wants. She'll know when to stop. She's between two worlds now."

Going in, I sat down in the chair near Ora Mae's bed and Lola sat in a chair near the window. "Ora Mae, it's Adrian."

"You're here."

"How are you feeling?"

"The medicine helps. Makes me sleep. So far I always wake up."

"Rest now, I'm here to wait with you." I said.

"I know," she said.

"Just rest."

Once more Ora Mae drifted into her world of sleep and apparent peace, leaving me to my contemplations. It appeared that it was now truly a death vigil, even though I had fought against the reality. I knew what would happen; I had witnessed it too often. Sympathetic people would come and go, bringing food, some homemade and some store-bought, drinks and even toilet paper. As the time grew closer, the visits would last longer. Spoken words would be few, but unspoken thought plentiful in her small home.

"Got to talk to you," Ora Mae said, breaking the silence. She pointed to her bedside table.

"Whatever you want." I reached for an ice chip from the beige crock on the table and placed it on her lips.

"Tastes good."

"Tell me if you want more."

"I want to talk about your girl," Ora Mae said.

"You're her mommy and daddy now. You got to be strong and soft for her. Understand?"

"It's hard to be both mother and father to her."

"No, *mommy* and *daddy*," Ora Mae said. "You've always known a lot. You were born smart," she said pausing, as though she desperately needed to catch her breath one more time.

"I feel like there's a big 'but' about to come," I said, trying to fill in the silence.

"You don't feel the way you should," Ora Mae said, "always keeping your feelings locked up, scared to feel. You got to let yourself feel again."

Ora Mae had always known my vulnerability. "I've always had to guard myself, you know that."

"It was okay as a child, cause you had to get through. But you're no longer a child, you're a man now. Time to trust and open up your heart." She paused once more, not sleeping this time, but awake and focusing on her breathing.

I knew I had to tell her what I had discovered. She had to know what I now knew, I thought. "I've found out what happened the night that Wayne Daniels died. I know about you, Miss Winnie, and Davis. Davis and Miss Winnie told me. I know that you didn't kill Wayne. Miss Winnie did," I said.

"Is that what she told you?"

"Why wouldn't you tell the truth?" I asked.

"Not my truth to tell. I made Miss Winnie and Mr. Davis a promise that I'd keep to myself what I saw that night."

"One thing puzzles me, Ora Mae. You know a lot about trees and plants," I said.

Ora Mae nodded her head in agreement.

"Why did you plant willows in the backyard? You knew their roots would create problems with your septic lines."

Ora Mae did not respond. Moments passed and I wanted her to respond to me one more time.

"You wanted to be discovered, didn't you," I said.

Ora Mae broke her silence with intermittent phrases and short sentences, "Thirty years—a long time for secrets. Eats away at you, like cancer. Tears apart the good. Makes the bad worse."

I nodded, not knowing what words to offer.

"What happens now?"

"Because of Miss Winnie's mental state, no one would believe her, and Davis won't go to the police." I stopped, wanting to make sure that Ora Mae understood what I had said. "I'll do what I can to try to tell the story to make sure that everyone knows the truth."

Slowly Ora Mae shook her head. "Still not listening with your heart." She paused and then continued, "Do nothing. The people who matter know the truth." Raising her head slightly and regaining her breath, she added "Anybody else, they'll never be enough truth to make 'em believe."

"I thought you wanted me to help clear your name."

"Only with you. I got peace. The Lord knows what I did and why. Confessed my sins with the preacher. I did what I did," she said, drifting once more to her private rest.

Ora Mae closed her eyes and slept. Having kept her under her watchful eye, Lola went to Ora Mae took her pulse and softly rubbed her arms, hands and face. All the while Lola smiled.

Ora Mae's words and her closed eyes sent my mind away from that moment to another time and place, decades before. Guarding my heart. That's what I had learned to do. I remembered when she had taught me that lesson. It was the early fall when I came home with my shirt torn, my face bleeding and my back bruised.

"What happened to you?" Ora Mae asked as I entered through the screened kitchen door. She was the only one at home.

"They beat me up at 'phys ed'," I said.

"Come here, let's get you cleaned up." We went to the bathroom, where Ora Mae reached for the iodine and wiped away blood from my face.

"Ouch," I said. The iodine stung.

"Take off your shirt," she said.

Ora Mae must have seen the reflection of my back in the mirror. "What's that? Let me see," she demanded. Ora Mae ran her long hands over the marks on my back. "How did this get here?"

"It just happened," I said.

"Tell me the truth, the gospel truth, boy."

"The older boys did a belt line. They made me go through the line twice. The other boys went through only once. They made me go through twice. They took their belts and whammed me as I ran. I ran so fast the first time that they didn't give me many licks. That's why I had to run it twice. That second time they held me and whipped me hard."

"Where was the teacher?" Ora Mae asked.

"The coach, Ora Mae, the coach."

"Where the coach?" she asked again.

"He was there in the back of the room watching."

"He watched you get cut up like this?"

"Yes," I said, trying to keep back the tears.

"Go ahead and cry. We'll take care of this," Ora Mae said. "We'll tell your mommy and she'll call the principal. They'll take care of this."

"No, you can't tell them. I can't shame them. They're not proud of me. I can't do the things that other boys do. They think I'm a sissy. I'm no good at sports," I said.

"We got to tell them."

"No. If you do, I'll kill myself. I swear I will. I'll take a knife and I'll kill myself."

I must have convinced her.

"Okay," Ora Mae said, "but you got to promise me that you won't hurt yourself."

"I promise, but we can't tell them. It will make it worse. They'll hurt me more next time."

"I know" was all she said. At that moment, the difference in our skin color disappeared. She understood me. Skin color had lost its power to separate us.

We stayed there while she wiped away my tears and tended my cuts and bruises.

"You've got to learn to keep quiet," she said. "Don't let them know they can hurt you. Take what they give and say nothing. That's the way my people had to do to live. The time will come when you can talk, but now you got to be quiet and look down," Ora Mae had said.

She retold me the stories of how her mother, father, brother, and she had practiced that silent betrayal of soul in order to live.

"Time will come. You will know when, when you won't have to be quiet and then you can speak. Right now you must study, make something of yourself. Don't call attention to yourself. Let the attention come later when they can't hurt you. My girl Ruth wouldn't listen to me. She was always calling attention to herself and look what happened to her. They killed her. This ain't the time to be loud. Understand?"

Ora Mae opened her eyes and I left those former memories and returned to her in the present.

"You daydreaming?" Ora Mae asked.

"I was thinking about how you helped me with the coach and the boys. Thank you. You helped me survive."

"That was what you needed then. No one's going to do that again."

"It worked. They never again physically hurt me," I said.

"Something I never told you, " Ora Mae said.

"What?"

"I went to see the coach."

"I never knew."

"I couldn't help Ruth, but I could help you."

I nodded, tightening my lips and looked deeply into her face.

Ora Mae continued, "I told him, if he or any of his boys ever hurt you again, I'd call the police."

"What did he say?

Ora Mae began to tell me bits and pieces about her visit with the coach through her abbreviated phrases and half sentences, and frequent pauses for breath. I heard her describe what she did. She told him that if he or anyone else ever harmed me again, he would regret it. He called her "little black mammy." She said she was black alright, but she had boyfriends with blades who knew how to use them. In her own colorful language, she promised that she would have him castrated if this ever happened again. No doubt, she had his attention. I smiled, thinking that once castrated, priorities would assuredly be altered. She told me, in her own words, he better mind his little property if he valued it at all.

"You did that for me?"

"And for me and for Ruth. Only way I knew how to go on living."

"You did save my life," I said.

"Lives need saving."

"You helped give me that," I said. "You pointed me to God."

"And the church."

"That was when my life began," I said.

"I still say it. Stay close to God. Caroline told me that you don't go to church too much."

I nodded, wondering how much my precocious daughter had shared with Ora Mae.

"God's bigger than any church, black or white."

"I know that."

"Knowing and living are different. You made something of yourself. Trust God. You can love and not always agree."

I nodded. "When I first came back, it was because I had to," I said.

"You kept your promise that you would come back if I ever needed you."

"That was how it began, but not how it ended. Morriah said I needed to come to you. She was right."

"How" she asked.

"I've always tried to keep all the rules, but it wasn't enough. I haven't been able to keep relationships."

"Making something of yourself doesn't mean ignoring your past. Make peace with it, like I had to do with Ruth. I needed you to help me live on," she said.

"And I needed you," I said.

We were both quiet—I in the chair and Ora Mae propped against her pillow. She drifted back to sleep once again and left me alone to ponder what she said. I watched her closely, and hours passed. Lola continued to check her patient with her protocol that always ended in caressing Ora Mae's face.

Vaguely I was aware of the voices coming from the other rooms, sometimes with spontaneous loud laughter followed by hushed tones. I suppose they were experiencing their moments of sadness and sympathy along with the gentle humor. Ora Mae always liked people to laugh with her. Some even came briefly into the room, although I don't recall their names or faces. It was as though I, like Ora Mae, was in my own dazed state, gliding from the present moment to past memories.

"You still here? I guess I am, too," Ora Mae said, awakening from her slumber. Once more she appeared to have another momentary surge of renewed energy. I wondered each time if this were to be the last. Each brief interlude of revitalization was becoming shorter and shorter.

"Both of us still here," I said.

"Is it my birthday yet?"

"Yes, happy birthday."

"Close your eyes," Ora Mae said. "I want to see what you learned."

I tilted my head and closed my eyes.

"Hold out your hand," she said. I held out my hand with my palm up. She took my hand and placed her palm against mine.

"Feel my hand close to your hand," she said. "What color is my hand?"

"Black," I said.

"Do you feel the black?"

"No." I was about to open my eyes.

"Keep your eyes shut." Her voice was faint but firm. "What color do you feel?"

"I don't feel any color," I said.

"That's right. That's right. Does it feel like an educated hand?"

I smiled. "It feels like a hand, a hand of someone I love."

"Good. That's what it is," Ora Mae said.

I opened my eyes to her faint smile.

"Skin color and education don't matter if you love someone. Don't have to separate family."

Ora Mae reached up with her hand and touched my wet cheek. "It's all done now. Go get your girl. I need to say goodbye to her."

Caroline had fallen asleep in the other room. I brought her into Ora Mae's room.

"Sit and wait with me, girl," Ora Mae said. "Good for a young one to be with you. I've watched and loved your daddy. Now it's your turn."

"I will," Caroline said.

"Adrian, do what I said. I want to be buried near my girl. Keep our bodies together."

"You will be together. I promise."

Ora Mae reached out to Caroline's hand and held it. "Get this girl a real brassiere and let her dance. She needs... ," Ora Mae stopped, never finishing her sentence.

I held Caroline's hand as she held Ora Mae's hand. Caroline and I sat silently as we watched Ora Mae's mouth as she puffed out air. We listened and watched her breathing, the last music of her fading body.

I thought of what was going to be lost forever, the moments that I had foolishly taken for granted. No more the watchful eyes and heart of someone who had cared for me since childhood. Someone who had stood close with me when I needed defending and who stood away from me when I began to receive recognition as one of promise. She lived her life in the backstage of my own, only coming forward and being seen when needed. Ora Mae had been my supporting cast of one. Now her departure was near—one of the last adults linked to my childhood was leaving. No familiar older figure to give me encouragement and to show pride in me. I felt the chill of loneliness around me.

We must have listened to her breathing for what seemed like hours, even though it could have been minutes. I was no longer an accurate judge of the passing of time. Her breathing was irregular and much slower. There were rapid breaths and then silence with a loud rattling sound. Lola had called it the death rattle. Then the final sound came, as though Ora Mae were clearing her throat and going to say a word. No, it was like she was choking. Caroline looked at me.

"Is she going to come out of this?" Caroline asked.

I didn't know. Ora Mae raised her head as though she were rising to life and rejoining us. As quickly as she raised her head, she fell backwards and was silent. Instantly we knew. All three of us knew. Ora Mae met death.

Lola, who listened and kept quiet vigil, left her seat beside the window. All along in the background, she had watched Ora Mae. She came forward, took Ora Mae's pulse and checked her breathing.

"She's at rest," Lola said, looking at her watch, turning off the bedside lamp, and walking to the door. "I'll leave you alone for a while." Caroline wept, and I held her close to my chest. I rehearsed Ora Mae's words over and over, needing to remember so that I could understand them later. I mustn't forget those words, I thought.

I stood up and reached out my hand to Caroline. She stood as I brought her closer to me. I put my right hand around her small waist and she took her left hand and placed it on my shoulder. My left hand held her right hand. Awkwardly we moved together about the room. The floor sighed as if approving our dance. My feet were clumsy, but inwardly my spirit moved gracefully. Although our eyes could barely see from the tears, we each had a comforting smile. It was our tribute to Ora Mae.

Davis stood next to Winnie who was once more in the safety of the nursing home.

"We did the right thing. Didn't we?" Winnie asked.

"You were right. I didn't think so at first, but you were right, Winnie."

"Good," she said, clasping firmly to his hand.

"You convinced them," he said looking at Miss Winnie's smile and nod.

The sun was filtering through the Venetian blinds of her kitchen when Claire Cobb returned from Ora Mae's house. Soon the coffee was finished brewing. Samuel T. came through the swinging door.

"Coffee's smelling good," Samuel T. said.

"I'm glad. Have a seat. The paper's on the table."

"Thank you."

"I was worried when you weren't here when I went to sleep."

"But you slept anyway," Claire said. Her hands were firm as she poured the coffee into his favorite coffee mug.

"Yes, I did."

"Ora Mae died early this morning. I went walking to think, and I stopped by the store for a few groceries, including coffee."

"Think about what?"

"About us, Samuel T."

"What have you decided?"

"At our age, we don't have much time left. Life is short, no guarantees for how long we'll be here."

"What are you saying? Is anything wrong, Claire? You're not sick, are you?"

"No, dear. Not that I know of. It's just that watching Ora Mae die and thinking about Winnie, Wayne, Davis, and Adrian, it made me think about us and our family."

"What are you thinking?"

"About all the things we've said through the years, and the things that we haven't said. I've loved you all these years," Claire said. She put her hand on his hand.

"And I love you, Claire."

"Samuel T., I've loved you, but I haven't always been fair to you," Claire said.

"What do you mean, 'fair'? You've been the best wife a preacher ever could have," Samuel T. said. His hands were holding hers.

"No, I haven't been fair. I should have spoken up more and told you directly when I disagreed with you or when I thought you needed correcting."

"Correcting?" Samuel T.'s hand moved away from Claire's hand.

"Yes, correcting. You should have told what you knew about Wayne Daniels and Winnie Daniels years ago, Samuel T. You were wrong to keep silent when you could have done so much good."

"Claire, everything I did was for the church. I thought it best."

"I know you thought it best. Best isn't always right. Best is sometimes what's convenient. Some things have got to change."

"Change? What's got to change?" Samuel T. asked.

Claire was silent. She went about making the toast for their breakfast.

"I'm retiring from the church, Claire. Haven't I paid enough?"

"It's not up to me to say what the payment should be, Samuel T. This I do know. I will speak openly of my sons and will be a part of their lives openly. You may do whatever you like, but I'll no longer go behind your back to keep in touch with them. I'll talk about them with my friends and tell anybody who'll listen how proud I am of them."

"I see. You'll go against my wishes."

"Yes, I will and I will be your wife. It would be wrong for me to turn away from you, because I still love you. What becomes of us will really be of your choosing, Samuel T."

"I see."

"You'll have to make your own decisions, Samuel T. You'll decide about the quality of your life, just like you always have. I'll always be your wife, but I will no longer blindly follow you. I may not always be able to respect you, but I will show you respect."

Samuel T. was silent as Claire spread the jam on the bread.

"How's your coffee?" she asked.

"Good," he said, cautiously.

"Good answer. I'm glad cause it's decaffeinated. Coffee in this house will always be decaffeinated." Claire smiled.

The sun was vivid when we left Ora Mae's room. The funeral home had already come and taken her body away. Morriah was waiting outside. "How are you doing, honey?" Morriah asked Caroline.

"I'll be all right," Caroline said. "Daddy and I have been dancing."

"You two do the most unexpected things," Morriah said.

"How are they doing?" I asked.

"Well, Davis took Winnie back to the nursing home. He spent a lot of time talking to J.D. and Laurel. They went home. I took Rachel back to her apartment."

"Thank you."

"Did you get it?" Caroline asked Morriah.

"I said I would. I don't understand why you wanted it." Morriah handed a small brown paper bag to Caroline. Caroline opened the bag, looked inside and smiled. From the bag she pulled out a light bulb.

"A light bulb. Why do you want a light bulb?" I asked.

"Ora Mae told me that when she left her mama's house to move to her own house, her mama gave her an oil lamp to help light her way. I thought I would take a light bulb from Ora Mae's room back to my room. I got a new light bulb to replace the one that I want to take. May I?"

My mouth quivered. I could only nod. Caroline went to Ora Mae's room.

"I'll help her," Lola said.

"Rough night?" Morriah asked.

"Rough night," I said. "But I'm glad I came."

"Told you that you should," Morriah said. She put her hand on my shoulder. Morriah always preferred having the last word.

EPILOGUE

Grow, O little willow, grow!
Help us learn the art to bend;
Teach forgiveness, grace bestow
Till each foe we can befriend.

Grow, O little willow, grow!
Show us how to wisely spend
Time above and time below
Till this life we shall transcend.

The call of death, both past and impending, began my journey back to Caruthers' Gap that summer. Within my journey I encountered death on many levels and in many faces. I began by visiting the cemetery and now concluded my summer by standing with Caroline at Ora Mae's grave.

Numerous words, questions and thoughts still linger. I recall the words from John 12:24 that Samuel T. loved to quote, " . . . Except a corn of wheat fall into the ground and die, it abideth alone; but if it die, it bringeth forth much fruit." Interestingly enough, I saw some of its fruit that summer. Bless his heart, I wonder if Samuel T. knew the deeper meaning of the words he quoted so frequently.

This Labor Day marked the end of summer vacation and a return to a normal fall work schedule for children and teachers. Both old friends and new ones returned to their respective post-summer lives. Rachel left at the end of summer for another teaching position. We parted friendly but with finality. I could even joke with her in the end. We were not so different, having both sold a part of ourselves for what we pursued. She may have done hers with more honesty. I even asked her if Subject "C" meant I was the third participant, or if it were an evaluation of my performance. I did not let her answer.

I dreaded one day telling Caroline about what I learned about myself with Rachel and my moral failure. Just as Ora Mae had planted the willow trees that would one day force the telling of her story, I knew that I had already planted my own willows that would require my own confessions.

Redemption provides a way to be reconnected. Ora Mae had helped me find my way back to my family—to Maggie and Tom, to my deceased daddy, and even to Caroline. I was no longer bound by the past, but neither did I need to deny, reject, or run away from it. The past I learned with both my head and heart is always a part of the present.

Laurel and J.D. left Caruthers' Gap and returned to Columbia. Both had said they needed counseling to rebuild a life as a couple. My two old friends had journeyed long together, having lost each other, found each, lost each again, and now, perhaps, finding each other once more.

I knew that life would not be unstrained for them. Laurel was no longer the simple, desirable and untouchable candy of my youth. Quite frankly, I was now glad that I had not tasted her. For the first time, I had the ability to see not through the fantasy lenses of my adolescence. Instead, she was a woman with excessive emotionality and attention-seeking behavior. Her personality and behavior had the tendency, if not a full-fledged diagnosis, toward histrionics. It all made sense now. Rachel had helped me to understand in that hot summer in Caruthers' Gap. This tendency coupled with whatever trauma she experienced and then repressed would not be easy for both her and J.D. I would not hazard a prognosis for what their relationship would bring in the coming years. Only I would hope that they would find a mutual love stable enough and yet appealing enough to sustain and nourish their days and nights.

Behind in Caruthers' Gap were Miss Winnie, and Davis attending to her needs. Before I left my hometown, I visited once more with Samuel T. and Davis, thanking them for what they had taught me and had meant to me. I don't know that they understood, but I made my peace with them. Forever they would be a part of me. They would have to find their own peace.

I glanced once more at her grave. Ora Mae rested, as she had wanted, near her much loved daughter who would always remain eighteen. Unable to fully vindicate Ora Mae in the minds of everyone, my last gift to her was having Ruth's body removed and buried next to her mothers near willows in a place once reserved for whites. Many people, black and white, came to her funeral, and I heard only portions of their shared stories. I was not the only one whose life had been touched and changed by her.

Ora Mae's physical gift to me was naming me heir of her small estate—a small house and its modest furnishings. Estelle had promised that she would take care of Ora Mae. What no one knew at the time was that Ora Mae was Estelle's heir. Her not so modest estate passed on to me as well.

"Daddy, I know you would do anything for me. Did mother love me as much as you do?" Caroline asked, interrupting my reflections.

"Of course she did. Why do you ask?"

"Ora Mae said that a mother would do anything to protect her child," Caroline said. "Is it true?"

"Of course it is," I said, staring into the face of my beloved daughter. I would gladly take on any pain or shame to protect her.

Immediately the faces of Laurel and Miss Winnie flashed before me. A chill and an uncertainty traveled up and down my spine, as did Ora Mae's words. A mother would do anything to protect her child. A mother would do anything to protect her child.

I might not ever know the truth behind the mystery of Miss Winnie, Laurel, and Wayne. Ora Mae's willows had played a significant role in both her redemption and, unexpectedly, in my own. Whatever the unsetting truth might be, their story and their truth belonged neither to Ora Mae nor to me.

Only Caroline's persistent questions called me back to her. "Is it time to go, Daddy?"

"Yes, darling. Time to go," I answered.

We went to join Maggie's family and Corrine for a barbeque and the last summer dance.

THE END

www.ingramcontent.com/pod-product-compliance
Lightning Source LLC
Chambersburg PA
CBHW061522050726
47503CB00015B/2613